THE WILD THYME FARM MURDER

An absolutely gripping crime thriller

JUDI DAYKIN

DS Sara Hirst Book 6

Joffe Books, London
www.joffebooks.com

First published in Great Britain in 2024

Cover art by Dee Dee Book Covers

ISBN: 978-1-83526-421-8

I know a bank where the wild thyme blows,
Where oxlips and the nodding violet grows,
Quite over-canopied with luscious woodbine,
With sweet musk-roses and with eglantine.

William Shakespeare, *A Midsummer Night's Dream*

AUTHOR'S NOTE

I have been delighted to call Norfolk my home for the last forty years. As with all regions, we have our own way of doing and saying things. The accent is lyrical and open, just like the countryside and skies. If you would like to pronounce some of the real place names in this book like a local, the following may help:

Happisburgh = Haze-bruh
Wymondham = Wind-am
Belaugh = Bee-la'
Hoveton = Hov-tun
Norwich hides its 'w'.

For the benefit of my readers who might not know:

NIMBY = Not In My Back Yard.

PROLOGUE

The accelerant stank as it splashed up the barn doors. Paint was peeling away from them, exposing centuries-old brittle timber. The Norfolk bricks that made up the walls were pitted and friable. The thatched roof was grey with age, and there were bald patches where it was falling into decay. It would all burn quite easily. A pile of old clothes, dead twigs and dry leaves lay on the ground at the base of the doors. The remnants of the liquid were poured over them to give the fire a good start.

A trembling hand struck a match. It wavered in the slight breeze. Protecting the tiny flame, the figure bent down to drop it on to the pile. For a moment, it seemed as if it would go out, then it found the accelerant and blossomed into life. Heat pushed outwards as the blue-and-red flames licked at the wooden door, making the paint bubble and blister. A bloom of fire raced across the door frame, burrowing into the rotten joints and emerging with new energy.

The fire starter stepped back to admire their handiwork. Red light flickered demonically in widened eyes as they watched in satisfaction. It was going up nicely. A sense of power swelled from stomach to chest.

The flames took hold in the thatch and roared angrily as the old reeds danced with red angels. Panic rose. It had only been a few minutes and the fire was already fiercer than expected. Vomit rose and was fought down. Shaking fingers stabbed 999 on a mobile phone. A few words gave the address, and the call was cut off before the operator could ask for personal details.

With a muffled curse, the fire starter realised that the red-and-black moped was too close to the fire. Sweaty hands grabbed the handlebars and turned the key, forcing its whiney engine into unaccustomed extreme revs as it pulled away. It masked the sound — a human voice shouting for help, rising to a scream, coughing and choking as the thatch blazed into the night.

CHAPTER 1

It was officially the hottest summer on record. Despite the air conditioning going full tilt, the office of the Serious Crimes Unit at Norfolk Constabulary's Wymondham HQ was unbearably close and airless. Detective Sergeant Sara Hirst contemplated opening a window, knowing it was pointless. It would only let in more hot air. She could see that the plants around the edge of the car park were all either dead or dying, just like in her unmanageable garden. It had been weeks since there'd been any rain. It wasn't just Monday that was making the team lethargic. Mercifully, they weren't busy.

Pulling her plaited dreads tighter in their chic ponytail to keep them off the back of her neck, Sara looked at the incident board, where DCI Hayley Hudson was idly turning a pen in her sunburned hand. Hudson had admitted to forgetting to rub lotion there when she'd walked at the coast over the weekend.

Sara knew better. It could feel much fresher on the coast, especially on the cliffs or beaches, but she wasn't fooled by the deceptive lifting of the stifling heat. The sun was still strong. Sara might be half Jamaican, but it didn't mean her skin wouldn't burn, despite some of her colleagues' suspect jokes. There were three bottles of suntan lotion of varying strengths in her handbag under the desk.

'Let's try again,' sighed Hudson. She tapped at the map fastened to the incident board. It was covered in sticky notes. 'Can anyone see a pattern?'

'Sounds like a question on one of those TV quiz shows.' DC Mike Bowen stretched languidly in his chair and yawned. His rotund food-baby stomach made his shirt buttons strain. Sitting behind him at her desk, their civilian admin Aggie tutted quietly. He swung his chair round and smiled at her. 'All right, missus?'

'There are a couple more incidents just in,' said DC Ian Noble. 'I'd like to try something different.'

Gripping a piece of paper with a printed spreadsheet and a packet of coloured sticky dots, he walked to the board. His uncoordinated arms and legs frequently made Sara think of the cartoon character Inspector Gadget. Noble seemed less bothered by the heat than the rest, as if his height some-how made him cooler, though Sara was sure that hot air was supposed to travel upwards. He began to remove the bits of paper.

'It's too confusing like that,' said DI Edwards. 'Make some sense of it, eh?'

The DI lounged in a spare chair in the main office, arms spread out along the desk behind him. Sara had worked with Edwards for three years now. In that time, she'd watched him grow more distinguished-looking, his hair becoming pep-pered with grey, and fine lines gathering around his mouth and eyes. He was more contented these days than when Sara had first joined the team. He even had a whacky-looking lady friend with magenta hair who was an art professor at the Norwich University of the Arts.

With Bowen and Aggie getting married in February and Noble having a steady girlfriend, it felt to Sara that she was the only one who still had a suspect love life. It wasn't sup-posed to be so difficult. With a little pushing from Aggie, Sara had begun to date DC Dante Adebayo from the drugs team. Everyone thought they were the perfect couple, but it was turning out to be more of a burden than a pleasure.

'How can we tell if these are deliberate or natural?' asked Sara. 'Everything is so dry that it only takes a random piece of broken bottle to start something.'

Serious crime didn't always mean murder, of course. Norfolk was a quiet place most of the time in that regard. Vice and drugs were dealt with by two separate teams, while SCU got to mop up anything that didn't fit those particular specialities. There had been no major incidents since Christmas, so here they were, trying to make sense of a series of wildfires.

'Agreed,' said Hudson. 'Or just people being stupid. Like this new one from yesterday.'

She looked down at a wodge of printed reports in her hands. Flipping over several sheets, she held one up. 'Family having a picnic on the dunes at Holkham Beach. Decided to use one of those disposable barbecue things, despite the signs saying not to. *Woosh!* Half the dune's on fire in ten minutes.'

'Bet that put a damper on their Sunday afternoon,' murmured Bowen.

Hudson frowned at him. 'Not much fun for the fire boys either.'

The fire service was stretched to the limit. The hot weather was causing problems for others, too. Paramedics were carrying buckets of ice in their ambulances to keep people cool. The hospital emergency departments were full of sunburn victims. Tomorrow was 1 August, and the farmers around Sara's home village of Happisburgh were already harvesting grain that wouldn't normally be ready for weeks. The heaths and commons were covered with swathes of straw-like vegetation, which could ignite with a casually dropped match.

Wildfires were flaring all over England, terrifying farmers, homeowners and local businesses equally. Every evening television news reports were full of horrified families who watched as their homes burned to ash. The pictures reminded Sara more of Californian or Australian disasters, with the bands of fire marching across the landscape faster than the planes dropping water could cope with. Here, the fire brigade did their best.

'People just don't think, do they?' Sara asked rhetorically. 'These things are only done by others, not by them.'

'Weather forecast?' Edwards looked at Aggie.

'Getting hotter, I'm afraid,' sighed the administrator. She raised her voice slightly to speak over the whirring noise from her tiny handheld fan. Her homely, well-fed figure made her extra hot in this weather, though her supply of shape-shifting home-baked goodies never wavered. 'I got in touch with the Met Office. It looks like they'll declare a heatwave Tuesday through Friday. Second one this year.'

The team groaned at the prospect. Edwards tried to sound positive. 'Keeps things quieter for us.'

'That's it,' said Noble. He stepped back from the map. 'I made it more obvious and did a grid. I've used the fire service reports. The yellow dots are definitely natural or spontaneous. Like Sara's broken glass.'

He glanced at her, and Sara smiled in return. Once nervous and overawed, he was growing into his job as well as his lanky figure. He was now their technology expert, able to manipulate CCTV footage or understand mobile phone data faster than the rest of them.

'Orange dots are people-related.' He pointed to the dot at Holkham Beach. 'Unintentional but traceable to a particular source, like our family and their barbecue. The red ones are suspicious in the fire service's view. This area in particular seems badly affected.' Noble indicated an area near Wroxham.

Sara got out of her chair and went to look more closely. She felt Bowen move in behind her to look over her shoulder. She heard Edwards yawn.

'Well?' demanded Hudson. 'What do you all think?'

'It's on my route home,' said Sara. She pointed to the main road east of the patch, which Noble had peppered with dots of all colours. Sweeping her hand to the right, she added, 'The Broads are on this side, so lots of water and heathland. The other side is mostly arable farms and holiday attractions.'

'Such as?'

'Children's adventure park, Junior Farm, Hoveton Hall, craft barns. That sort of stuff.'

Bowen stretched his arm past Sara and pointed. 'Not just farms. There's the fruit-growing place here.' His finger stabbed at the map. 'Acres of glasshouses. They must be having a bad time of it. Then there's the herb place. Growing herbs commercially, as well as a shop and café.'

Sara stepped back, bumping into Bowen as she did so. 'Sorry, Mike. Just wanted to see it from a distance.'

It was making sense now that Noble had tidied up the map. 'These are the main incidents.' He selected several sheets and held them up. 'Looks like one particular farm may have been targeted. Or else they're pretty unlucky.'

'I'll drop in on my way home,' offered Sara. It was the perfect excuse to avoid staying with Dante that night.

'Good idea,' agreed Hudson. She drifted wearily towards her glass office as if she needed to sit down. At the door, she turned and looked back at Sara.

'Can I have a word with you before you go?'

CHAPTER 2

'You wanted a word, Miss Turner?'

'You can call me Claudia,' said the office manager with a sigh. She'd told Eric often enough, but it was too hot to worry about such a small point. It was after four o'clock, and the teams had just returned to the construction company's yard. 'Have a seat, Eric.'

The squat, well-muscled older man sat on the edge of the visitor's chair. A fan thrummed on Claudia's desk, moving the warm air without cooling it. Sweat trickled annoyingly between her shoulder blades, and limp strands of fine blonde hair stuck to her forehead. The fan had been a bad choice, she conceded. She should have insisted on one of those posh air-conditioning things.

The offices and builders' yard of Coles Construction were down a side road on the North Walsham industrial estate. Her office was up a set of wooden stairs on a gantry above the main parts store. The building comprised little more than a metal frame and steel panels, which made it cold in winter and airless in summer. This heatwave was almost unbearable for herself and the two other admin workers who sat in a larger office next to her own.

Eric looked around the office cautiously. Claudia knew the man hated being indoors when he could be outside, and even her small amount of authority troubled him. All he seemed to want was a quiet life getting on with the task at hand. She ventured a smile.

'I just need to chat about how Kyle is getting on.' Claudia indicated a manila folder on her desk. 'You know, like we've done before.'

'Oh!' Eric sounded surprised. He ran a knobbly hand through his silvering hair, then nodded as if he had just remembered. 'Like three months ago.'

'Exactly.'

Sometimes Claudia wondered what had made one of their quietest, albeit most experienced, ground workers offer to help Kyle Atkins on his apprenticeship. When she had broached the idea of bringing an apprentice into each builder's team last year, there had been a few sarcastic comments and scornful faces. Not only had Eric been the first to voice his quiet agreement, he had also volunteered to be his team's mentor. Stepping up like that had made the other teams accept their own youngster. She was grateful for his support. It was a personal pet project for Claudia. Once she'd heard about the apprenticeship scheme, she'd become determined to give some local youngsters a chance, even though it would cause extra work.

'Last time, we put down that Kyle was going to the college to improve his mathematical skills,' she said, glancing down the report from May. 'How did that go?'

'He've improved a bit,' replied Eric. His strong local accent would be impenetrable to an outsider. Claudia adjusted her thinking to accommodate it. 'I'm still checkin' his work.'

'Did he take the test? He should have.'

'I reckon so. Had the day off, anyhow.'

'I'll call the college for the results.' Claudia felt annoyed with Kyle. He had been told to bring the certificate in for her to see.

It had come as a surprise to Eric that so much paperwork would be involved. There was nothing wrong with his skills when it came to reading ground plans or estimating the depth and length of a trench. There was little that Eric didn't know about land drainage, sewage pipes or the composition of the soils in the region, which made him invaluable on any building site. Form-filling was another matter. Claudia accepted from the start that she would have to do it herself.

'Anything else we can add for this quarter?'

'He be mobile now.' Eric sounded almost proud.

'You were picking him up, weren't you?'

The older man smiled. 'He found this scheme. A charity place. They loan him a moped for a year, so he can get to work.'

Claudia scrunched her eyes as she tried to dredge up an old memory. 'I think I've heard of that.'

'They give him lessons, an' a helmet an' everything.'

Claudia tapped at her computer for a minute before bringing up a website called *Scoot! Rural*. 'Is this it?'

Eric squinted at the screen. 'That's it.'

'And he found this himself?' she asked.

Eric nodded but avoided her gaze, making her assume that he'd pointed Kyle in the right direction. She flicked open the tabs on the site. One showed the available options, and another detailed the requirements to qualify for help. She took a minute to read it more carefully.

'That looks like a great idea.' Claudia smiled at Eric. 'Good initiative on his part. I'll put that in. What do you think he should learn next?'

'Thought I'd get him going on the Bobcat.'

The Bobcat was a small, ride-on digger commonly used on building sites. Claudia paused and checked Kyle's file. It had been his birthday in June, so he was seventeen now. 'There might be some health and safety regulations on that. I'll check and let you know. He could train on the other one to start with.'

'The walk-behind? That'll build his muscles.' Eric smiled to himself.

'That all sounds fine, thank you. I'll write this up. I'd be grateful if you could pop back tomorrow after work and sign it off for me.'

'Course,' said Eric. Despite the heat, he walked quickly away.

Claudia watched him go, ensuring her office door was closed before standing up and checking through the window. Happy that no one could see her, she pulled at her blouse where it stuck to her chest and bent forward over the fan. Her simple cotton top and skirt were loose-fitting. They were still too tight on a day like this.

The air swirled between the fabric and her skin for a few blissful moments. It bubbled around her breasts, cooling the rivulets of sweat that ran down them. She had to be careful that no one saw her. Construction was still male-dominated, and there would be days of ribald or salacious comments if one of the men caught her doing this. At thirty-six and undergoing an acrimonious divorce, Claudia was 'available' in the men's eyes.

There was one man she would be happily available for, she mused, wafting the blouse front gently. Jamie Waller was one of their site managers. The same age as Claudia, he had the advantage of a university education to keep him on the promotion ladder. He also had a cheerful grin and happy disposition that she would like to feel the benefit of one day. She hadn't adapted very well to being single again.

Feeling refreshed, she sat down. The *Scoot! Rural* website was impressively detailed. Perhaps she could dazzle Jamie with her knowledge of the scheme. It might also be something the other apprentices could take advantage of.

One thing was soon clear to her. Although the hire fee included insurance, which was expensive for youngsters like Kyle, the charity provided these mopeds at a subsidised rate. They weren't free. The apprentices weren't paid much on the government scheme that had brought them here, and even though Coles Construction added a small amount each month for them, Claudia doubted Kyle could afford the machine's hire and running.

So, who was helping him? She was pretty sure it would be Eric Beatty.

CHAPTER 3

'What a time to ask,' grumbled Sara to Dante as they clattered down the stairs from the offices. His car was in the garage for repairs, and she was giving him a lift home. 'It's far too hot to worry about anything important like that.'

'Has she spoken to personnel about it?' asked Dante.

As the front glass doors swished open, he held out his hand for her to exit the building first. An old-fashioned gesture that was typical of him but made her feminist mind bridle.

Sara was tall. Dante was even taller. His arm muscles rippled under the short sleeves of his sharply cut, expensive pink shirt. The colour suited him, though few other officers would have worn it for fear of smart-arse comments from their colleagues. No one would dare say these things to Dante in case he let rip with his sarcastic tongue or his large fists. Sara couldn't deny that the man was handsome, or that they looked like the perfect couple. A wave of super-heated air hit them as they stepped out into the car park.

'Not yet.' Sara shrugged. 'Says it's up to me. It feels just the same as before.'

'In what way?'

'When I first inherited Dad's cottage, I didn't know if I should sell it or move in.' She growled in frustration. Her brain was slowly turning to mush in the heat. 'I don't know what to do about this either.'

'You don't have to do anything at the moment, do you?'

They reached her new car. When Sara had moved to Norfolk, she had brought her natty Fiat 500 with her. It wasn't the best choice, she realised, once she had moved into her late father's cottage in the coastal village of Happisburgh. Her journey to work on rough rural roads and through bad weather had battered the life out of it. Six months ago, she had upgraded to a new Volvo hybrid SUV. Its black bodywork gleamed in the sun. When they opened the doors, heat rushed out. She started the air conditioning and waited in the car park for about thirty seconds. When they climbed inside, it was already pleasantly cool.

'Ah,' murmured Dante, 'the Chelsea Tractor wins again.'

'It hardly counts as one of those,' said Sara. If she wasn't so worn out, she would have felt offended. 'Sometimes I need it to get in from home when the weather is foul.'

'I know.' He stretched over to hold her hand. She curled her fingers over the hot gear stick and put the car into gear with a shrug.

They had officially been a couple for several months. Long enough for them to get used to each other's habits. For the life of her, Sara couldn't decide why it was that she felt so uncomfortable in the relationship. Dante was an astute copper with a sharp mind. Was that the problem? Unlike her previous boyfriend in Norwich, Dante understood what the job entailed.

'Have you spoken to anyone else about it?' Dante asked.

Sara shook her head. 'I don't want to offend the boss. He's always been good to me. If he thought I was trying to move on, it might upset him.'

'You think he might feel you were trying to replace him?'

Damn right, thought Sara. *It's hard to fool this fella, so why doesn't he get it? Why doesn't he sense my reluctance?*

'There isn't room for two inspectors in the department. The odds are that I'd have to move department or even forces.' She edged out of the car park and on to the main road.

'Leave Norfolk?' Dante sounded surprised. 'What about your home?'

Sara didn't answer. It wasn't just the cottage that was home to her. These days it was Norfolk itself. The rural life she was learning to enjoy was a far cry from her former home in Tower Hamlets. Her work in the SCU could be just as exciting as her time with the Metropolitan force, though it would be ridiculous to claim that there was anything like the same workload or pressure. She could feel Dante watching her.

'The next set of inspector's exams are in November,' she said. 'I don't have to submit an application for a few weeks yet.'

'Detective Inspector Hirst,' murmured Dante. His tone had a hint of jealousy. 'Has quite a ring to it. Unlike Detective Constable Adebayo. That needs an upgrade.'

Sara grimaced. 'She only said I should consider it. That's all I'm going to do for now.'

She turned up the bypass rather than heading for the city. A few months ago, Dante had moved to a house on a new-build estate near the Norfolk Showground. The place was neat and clean, like Dante's mind. It was also soulless and bland, which Sara took as a warning.

'What are you working on?' he asked casually.

Sara had rarely spoken to Chris, her former boyfriend, about work. He'd resented that, among other things. It seemed she didn't have much luck where men were concerned. She explained about the wildfires as the SUV swung off the bypass and over a roundabout. A few hundred yards later, she turned into the new estate.

'God, all these places look the same, don't they?' She blushed. 'Sorry. I don't mean that.'

'It's what I can afford,' Dante grumbled. 'We're not all as lucky as you. Your cottage is old and very pretty. A bit like you.'

'Hey!' Sara flung her hand sideways and slapped him on the arm. 'Cheek of it.'

Dante laughed. 'You're definitely the prettier of the two.'

'Less of the old.' Sara slowed to a crawl. 'This one?'

She pulled up outside a semi-detached house in the corner of the cul-de-sac.

'You staying tonight?' asked Dante hopefully.

'Sorry, not tonight.'

His eyes narrowed as he hurriedly tried to mask his frown. It had been at least two weeks since they had shared a bed. Sara used the heat as an excuse, unwilling to admit she didn't enjoy their sex life much and simply preferred her own company.

'I'm going to call at a farm near Wroxham,' she said as he climbed out. 'I want to interview the farmer.'

As she drove off, she glanced in the rear-view mirror. Dante was watching her leave. His mouth was bent down in an angry curve as he turned haughtily away.

CHAPTER 4

Rachel, the café manager at Wild Thyme Herb Farm, drove out of the small gravel car park as Jean walked across the courtyard to lock up. They exchanged a brief wave. The café was a brick-and-timber building with a patio outside holding a dozen sets of tables and chairs with large sunshades. A stickler for order, Jean walked around them all, replacing the chairs moved by the customers until there were four around each table. She let down the shades as she went, although the plastic clips were hard on her arthritic fingers.

'Don't want them blowing about in the wind,' she muttered. 'Mind you, a breath of wind would be welcome.'

Jean entered the café, locking the front door behind her, and surveyed the place. It was hot in here. No wonder the customers had preferred to sit outside today. At least the curve of mature beech trees around the yard provided some shade. She nodded approvingly at the pristine cleanliness of the seating area. It was just as immaculate behind the counter. Cakes for tomorrow sat in the glass-doored fridge. The butter pats, milk and other food items were all correctly stored. Under the counter, every piece of crockery was clean and stacked. A zipped bag lay in the till drawer waiting for Jean to take it back to the office for counting. Sometimes the day's takings in the café made the difference between profit and loss.

'Thank you, Rachel,' said Jean. 'I can always rely on you.'

Beyond the wall, the kitchen would be just as immaculate. Jean knew she could also trust Mavis, who cooked the delicious food they offered and ran the kitchen with a benign rod of iron, to leave it perfect. She heard the chink of mugs being dumped on to a worktop. With luck, it would be Darren. She had a question for him. Jean went through the swing door into the white-and-steel kitchen. The back door was open and her daughter, Faye, stood at the work surface. She didn't look up as Jean came in.

'Using up the coffee?' asked Jean. Faye started as if she hadn't heard the door opening. 'Do me a mug, will you?'

Faye looked at the jug in her hand as if she wondered what it was doing there. She shook it, making the contents slop up the glass sides. 'I guess there's enough.'

Jean struggled to bite back a sarcastic comment. The damn jug was nearly full. Why did Faye make even the tiniest thing such a performance? It was just a cup of coffee, for goodness' sake. Jean brought a bottle of milk to the table. Her daughter placed a third mug next to her own and filled all three.

'This for Darren?' asked Jean. Faye nodded, reaching for the sugar bowl. 'Where is he?'

'In the shop, taking off the till,' replied Faye.

Spooning sugar into a mug, she stirred it slowly. Her face was covered in a film of sweat. Her short, mousy hair spiked up from her scalp and was covered in dust, as were her jeans and T-shirt. Faye was tall and thick-set, but her hormones hadn't gifted her a bosom to match her height. She was flat-chested and square-shouldered, making her look mannish half the time.

If only she made a bit more of herself, thought Jean. *Faye is really pretty when she chooses to show it.*

'Perhaps we shouldn't be having hot drinks in this weather,' said Jean conversationally.

'Need the caffeine.'

'I could get us some of those energy drinks. You like those, don't you?'

'Not really.'

Recently, Jean had often felt frustrated trying to hold a simple conversation with her daughter, which she sometimes found hard to hide. Faye avoided her mother's eyes. She had been slowly growing more antagonistic for months, and Jean didn't understand why her daughter had become so difficult. The nursery was a family business, and someone had to be in charge. Jean knew she said no to Faye more often than her daughter appreciated, but there was little spare money. Didn't Faye understand that?

'What are you going to do now?' asked Jean.

Faye glanced out of the window. 'Cool enough. I'll start watering.'

'Shall I take this to Darren?' Jean pointed to the sugared mug. Faye nodded and loped off.

Leaving the kitchen open, Jean carried the two mugs of coffee to the large shed at the edge of the ornamental growing beds and display tables, which served as their shop. It was after five, their official closing time. A glance across the yard told her that Darren had already shut the main gate and put up the closed sign. Painted in jaunty shades of green and lilac, the shed was large enough for a counter, with a packing area, a few tables and shelves of gardening accessories. At one end, her son-in-law, Darren, was running off the till report for the day. He had already counted the cash into piles and money bags and was now thumbing through a sheaf of card machine receipts.

'Here you go,' said Jean. She placed the mug of coffee on the counter.

Darren looked up with a smile. He was handsome in a youthful way, not looking his age of thirty-seven. He was seven years older than Faye, though the difference didn't bother them. The attention-grabbing things about Darren were his piercings and tattoos. Multiple rings and studs adorned his nose, ears and eyebrows. When he spoke, Jean could see another one through his tongue. The tattoos were less easy to spot. Most of them were on his back and torso, apart from a complicated dragon which wove its way down one arm, and a 'wyvern' (apparently) down the other. They were only visible today when the heat made him wear a sleeveless T-shirt. He ran his hand through his spiky blonde hair before reaching for the mug.

'Thanks, Mum.' He waved the receipts. 'Good day, I think.'

'It felt busy,' she agreed. They needed these summer days when locals and tourists flocked out for small treats like potted herbs or tea and scones. 'How are you getting on with the old barn?'

'Okay.' Darren stuffed the money and paperwork into the zip-lock bag and handed it to Jean. 'Once I've finished the clear-out, the extra space should be useful.'

'It might help to extend our season, with luck.' Jean sipped her coffee before speaking cautiously. 'Darren, can I ask you something?'

'Sure.' His smile became fixed. 'Personal, you mean?'

She nodded. 'Look, I know it's none of my business. I realise that all three of us living together can sometimes be difficult.'

'We have plenty of privacy,' said Darren guardedly. 'You made sure of that.'

'I just wondered . . .' Jean paused and checked outside. No sign of Faye. 'Well, if everything was all right between you two.'

Darren's face became inscrutable. When Faye married Darren, it seemed sensible for the three of them to share the large farmhouse that went with the herb farm.

'Everything's fine,' Darren assured her. 'Why do you ask?'

'Oh, no reason,' sighed Jean. It was too delicate a subject to broach without causing ripples in their tight-knit world. Maybe she was just getting old and oversensitive. Her stomach grumbled a warning that her head would soon be spinning. 'Was that Kevin Howard I saw in here earlier?'

'Yeah.' Darren sounded relieved at the change of subject. 'He's worried about all these wildfires. Wanted to get a few local businesses together for a chat. See if there was anything we could do for each other.'

'Don't see how,' said Jean. She drained her coffee mug. 'Have you got a float for tomorrow?'

Darren nodded. 'Where did Faye go?'

'To start the watering. The basil polytunnel, I imagine. We've an order due out tomorrow, so they need to be in tip-top condition.'

'I'll go down and help,' said Darren as he drained his mug. Jean held her hand out for it.

'I've got to go back to the café kitchen anyway.'

They parted near the kitchen door. Darren walked briskly through the public part of the herb nursery towards a tall hedge. A wooden gate set into the thick greenery led to the back of the farm, where half a dozen thirty- by nine-ty-foot polytunnels housed the growing areas for the various herbs they prepared for shops, garden centres and supermarkets. It was the heart of their business.

Jean stacked the dishwasher before collecting the café takings bag. Clutching it, she locked the kitchen door before heading for the farmhouse and her office.

'Just like Kevin Howard to be trying to organise something,' she muttered as she settled down to do her daily books with a handful of biscuits. Cooking their evening meal would have to wait half an hour. 'Always was a bit of a busybody.'

CHAPTER 5

Sara had noted the farm address and the name of its owner. According to the satnav, it was only a few miles from the main road she took home.

The school summer break made this the height of the holiday season, and there was a queue of cars on both sides of Wroxham's ancient narrow road bridge. As she inched along, Sara could see there was also a queue of Broads cruisers waiting for the pilot to take them underneath the bridge on the River Bure. Even with the current low water level, there would only be a few inches of headroom for inexperienced holidaymakers in their hired boats.

Finally escaping Hoveton on the far side of the river, she turned off the main road into a tangle of minor roads. There was a wide swathe of farming land here, with tiny villages dotted among the fields. Some were little more than hamlets and had names like Belaugh Green or Crowgate Street. The place she was searching for was called Belaugh Manor Farm. The route took her past Hoveton Hall and a complex of craft barns before turning by the entrance to Wild Thyme Herb Farm, one of the businesses Mike Bowen had mentioned.

The farm stood down a short dirt track about half a mile past Wild Thyme. Her SUV left a cloud of dust behind her as she bounced along the rock-hard surface. When she pulled up, aggressive barking exploded from inside the old-looking farmhouse. Gathering her warrant card and the fire officer's reports, she hardly had time to step out of the car before the front door swung open and a pair of snarling dogs hurtled out. A large man in his late sixties loomed out after them, taking a few steps towards her.

'Lads! Lads! Good boys, come here,' he shouted.

To Sara's relief, the dogs largely obeyed. One skidded to a halt a few feet away from her, barking furiously. The other ran past, snarling, turned a circular trajectory and raced back to the man. Sara's heart was beating furiously. The man didn't move any closer. He stood with his arms folded and his head cocked to one side, eyeing her up defensively. She opened her warrant card and held it up.

'I'm Detective Sergeant Hirst,' she called loudly. 'I'm here about the wildfires.'

The effect was amazing. The man suddenly relaxed, not a reaction Sara often got when she produced her ID. He reached into his pocket and fished something out.

'Come on, my good boys,' he crooned to the dogs. His tone changed the dogs' attitude, who rushed to sit at his feet. 'You look after your dad, don't you?' He handed out dog treats to the expectant pair. 'Don't you mind them. They won't hurt you if I don't tell them to.'

Sara wasn't sure about that, but she nodded anyway. 'Mr Willmott?'

'Yes, that's me.' He ran his hands down the front of his already grubby T-shirt before holding one out. Sara shook it firmly, safe in the knowledge that she had hand sanitiser in the car somewhere.

She offered her warrant card again. The man squinted at it. 'Need my glasses. Never mind. Come in.'

He went inside with the dogs close at his heels. It was gloomy in the entrance hall, and there was a musty, damp smell. The walls were panelled in wood, and, apart from the doorway, the only light came from a window halfway up the stairs. Old, cracked tiling covered the floor, littered with the detritus of a working farm — dirty, worn-out boots; wellingtons with holes in them; torn waxed jackets; well-used dog blankets and leads. A dust-covered grandfather clock ticked slowly in an alcove. A couple of tatty armchairs sagged by a broken hall stand covered in piles of farming magazines and unopened envelopes.

Mr Willmott walked down the side of the staircase to an open door. The dogs trotted ahead of him, their claws clicking on the old tiles. Sara followed, trying to ignore the smell of unwashed bodies, human and canine.

The kitchen was filled with evening light. A long row of mullioned windows took up most of the outside wall, letting in the mellow sunshine. The back door stood ajar. Hens clucked as they strutted and scraped in the dusty yard. One even came inside to check out their visitor. Its scrawny neck was short on feathers. The few on its head stuck up, half-formed, making it look like a punk rocker.

'Can I get you a cup of tea?' the farmer asked. 'Sit down, won't you?'

Sara made herself comfortable on one of the rickety pine kitchen chairs. 'No tea, thanks. We've been asked to look into the wildfires in the county.'

'So I should think,' said Willmott, settling in the opposite chair. 'It's getting out of hand.'

'How?'

'Three times they've done it to me,' he replied. 'All in the last few weeks.'

'The fire service came out?'

'Of course. Can't let that spread, and it soon does.'

'What did they say about it?'

'Said they'd report it.' Willmott shrugged. 'Isn't that why you're here?'

'Yes, it is.' Sara watched in horrified fascination as one of the dogs went over to the exploring chicken and licked it. The chicken made an aggressive squawking noise and tried to head-butt the dog, making the canine pull away sharply. It had the attitude to go with the hairstyle.

23

'Stop it!' snapped Willmott. The dog backed off. Sara could have sworn the chicken smirked.

'Do you have a lot of animals, Mr Willmott?'

'Nope. Arable land, this.' He followed her gaze as the chicken strutted past. 'Just the chucks. I rescue them.'

'Rescue?'

'From the rehoming place,' he said, waving vaguely behind him. 'When they don't lay so well, they get sent off to be turned into curries and that.' Sara wasn't sure she wanted to know. As far as she was concerned, chicken breasts came in plastic wrapping from the supermarket. 'This woman in Hoveton takes a few in and finds homes for them.'

'They're pets?'

'Still give me eggs. Just not as many as the commercial people like.' Willmott cleared his throat as if embarrassed at being sentimental about chickens.

Sara looked round the kitchen. There were stacks of dirty crockery on the draining board. A half-empty bread bag stood near a chopping board. The dogs' dishes looked as if they needed a good clean. 'You live here alone, Mr Willmott?'

'Since my wife left me,' he nodded. 'My son helps me work the land. He lives in Hoveton with his girlfriend and kids.'

'There's no one here with you at night?'

Willmott whistled softly to the dog, who went over to him. He fondled its head affectionately. 'Just me, the chucks, Reggie and Ronnie here.'

'I'm afraid I haven't had time to plot the fires fully,' said Sara. 'There seem to have been quite a few in this area.'

'That there has. Kevin Howard is calling a meeting about it. For the local business community.'

'Kevin Howard?'

'Owns the glasshouses and food processing place. Up towards Marlham.'

Bowen had mentioned something about that. Sara knew she should have been paying more attention. The heat wasn't really any excuse. 'Can you give me the details of that?'

'Best ask him yourself,' replied Willmott. 'I'm not sure.'

Sara had every intention of doing so in the morning. 'What did the fire service say to you about the ones on your property?'

'They reckoned the first one was just an accident. Didn't agree. I think that was the start of it.'

Sara checked the fire reports she'd brought along. 'They've put it over to us as suspicious. Possibly in the light of the subsequent incidents.'

Mr Willmott nodded slowly. 'That was just a bit of old scrubland. I expect they didn't think it was worth anything 'cos it ain't. Took out part of the hedge, mind.'

'Then two more?'

'Different nights, at different places.'

'The reports say the fires were set deliberately. Fire officers found evidence of accelerants at the seat of each fire.'

'That's right. I lost at least three acres of good wheat crop, ready to harvest, before they could sort it out.'

'Valuable to you, then?'

'Margins is tight on anything these days,' confirmed Willmott. 'It was the old cow sheds that were the worst. That was the last time.'

'Buildings? Not hedgerows or crops?'

'I'd let them go,' admitted Willmott. 'The sheds, I mean. Got tumbled down in the winter. Thought I might be able to sell them for a house conversion or something, but they're not really big enough. So I'd just left them.'

'Are they near to the house?'

'No. On the other side of the farm, towards Belaugh Common.'

'How did you know they were on fire, then?'

'My lad called me. Said the fire people had rung him. Someone had reported it. We met them there. It was too late, of course. They'd burned down by then.'

'What sort of time was this?'

'About one in the morning.'

'The others?'

'All about the same time.'

'Mr Willmott,' said Sara. 'Do you have any idea why anyone might be targeting you?'

'Perhaps,' said the farmer with a sneer. 'Been sniffing around my boy again after all these years. Trying to cause more trouble for us.'

CHAPTER 6

It turned out that Thomas Willmott firmly believed that the fires on his farm were being set by his former wife, despite them having been divorced for several years.

'She's bin trying to talk to our Jake for weeks now,' the farmer almost growled. 'Said it was time they spoke again. He told her where to go.'

'Jake?'

'My boy. Our son. He stuck by me when she waltzed off.'

'Do you have any contact details for her?' asked Sara.

'Be damned if I do.' Willmott paused to consider the situation. 'Would it help? Best you ask Jake, then.'

Sara took the son's details from Willmott and headed home. It would have to be followed up. It was still a hot evening when she got home, and she didn't object when her neighbour, Gilly Barker, joined her in the garden bearing a nicely chilled bottle of white wine. The age gap between the two women hadn't stopped them from becoming firm friends. They sat watching Tilly chasing butterflies in the twilight. The cat pounced through the dry, weed-infested undergrowth and vanished. Sara snorted with laughter.

'Could be days before she gets out of there. I tell her she's off into the jungle.'

'Your garden needs some help,' said Gilly tentatively.

'It does indeed,' agreed Sara.

'I know—' Gilly held up a hand to stall the reply — 'you don't have time. But there is someone I could introduce you to. He's been working on my daughter's garden at her new house. You'd like him.'

Sara looked at the wilderness and the tumbledown shed with its drunken roof. She had expended a lot of energy on the inside of her cottage after she had moved in. Perhaps it was time to start on the outside. 'Some help would be very welcome.'

'I'll see if he's available.' Gilly left the name and number of the gardener on a scrap of paper on the kitchen table as she left.

* * *

Sara slept soundly, disturbed only by the chittering of Tilly as she sat on the bedroom window ledge in the early morning, excitedly watching the small birds in the creeper outside. An update text to DCI Hudson over her morning coffee brought the reply Sara had hoped for.

Speak to Kevin Howard. I'll send Bowen out to meet you. Two more fires overnight in your area.

Sara hadn't got on with Mike Bowen when she had first moved to the team. Three years working alongside him had taught her to trust his instincts as much as her own. He'd also been learning more interpersonal skills, courtesy of the office romance that had blossomed between himself and Aggie, their admin. They'd married in February and honeymooned on a cruise in the Caribbean. A trip they'd so clearly enjoyed that Sara wondered how long it would be before they both decided on early retirement to take up travelling instead.

Sara was pleased to see Bowen leaning on his car when she drove into the staff car park at Howards UK, though she didn't show it. He grinned at her obvious surprise at the size of the place. Ranks of huge commercial glasshouses stretched in all directions. An old barn had been converted into an office block; the reception was clearly marked by the entrance. To one side of the large and full car park stood a tall, new-looking steel-framed building. A refrigerated truck stood beside a large open door, the gap protected from the heat by long, thick, clear rubber strips. A man came out with a pallet mover stacked with boxes. A wisp of vapour puffed up into the air as the strips dropped back into place.

'I brought the two new ones,' said Bowen, waving some printed pages.

'How do they fit?' Sara glanced at the reports.

One was in a piece of woodland near a public car park at Wroxham Broad. It had been spotted by a yacht club member and dealt with in minutes. The waste bin in the car park had melted with the heat, but there was no other damage. The other report was more troubling.

Bowen had been fiddling with his mobile and showed Sara a detailed map of the area on the screen. She was impressed. Bowen didn't usually take much of an interest in this kind of technology. It must have shown, as he looked a bit red-faced.

'Ian showed me how to do it,' he admitted. Noble was obviously managing to encourage Bowen into the twenty-first century, after all.

'This borders Belaugh Manor Farm, doesn't it?'

'Between their border and the herb farm along the road.'

'We should go and look when we've finished here.' Sara told Bowen about her visit to Thomas Willmott. 'We'll have to trace this ex-wife, unlikely as it seems.'

Bowen agreed. 'Let's see what Mr Care for the Community has to say for himself first.'

The young woman behind the desk smiled politely when they entered the reception. Kevin Howard didn't take long to appear from the first floor.

'My office is up here,' he said. 'Do come up.'

Howard was much younger than Sara had been expecting, especially given the size of the business on display. No more than mid-thirties, he was well-toned and tall. His dark hair was fashionably cut and swept back. With his pale-coloured chinos and short-sleeved checked shirt, he looked the epitome of a modern farmer who didn't often get his hands dirty. More business owner than a man of the soil. He led them into his smart, airy office, gesturing to two comfortable visitor chairs.

'How can I help you? Or perhaps you'd like to give me the details after Sally has brought up the drinks?'

Sara could wait a few moments rather than have their conversation interrupted. She bought time. 'This is a big enterprise. Have you been here long?'

It was only meant as a friendly opening, but Kevin Howard replied by launching into a speech that he obviously made regularly.

'The business was started by my grandfather in the 1930s.' He drew a deep breath. 'We were just a normal farm back then. The food drive between the wars encouraged Stephen Howard to invest in the first glasshouses.'

The receptionist carried in a tray with a teapot, cafetière, crockery and a plate of hand-made biscuits, which she handed round with an elegant bustle. Kevin gave an enthusiastic account of the Howard family and their business legacy until Sara had had enough of the lecture.

'Mr Howard,' she interrupted. Who knew how long the story would go on for? 'I really need to ask you about the local wildfires.'

That made him pause for breath. He leaned back in his executive chair and gave Sara a speculative look.

'I understand from Mr Willmott of Belaugh Manor Farm that you're calling a meeting of local businesses about it.'

Kevin Howard pursed his lips for a moment as if trying to decide what to say. 'Yes, I am. Trying to get as many people to attend as I can.'

'When is this?' asked Bowen through a mouthful of biscuit crumbs. Sara frowned at him.

'Thursday evening,' said Howard. 'At our house.'

'What do you hope to do at this meeting?' Sara deliberately injected an officious tone into her voice.

'I just thought we could pool any information,' replied Howard. His eyes narrowed. 'See if we could help each other out somehow. Fire patrols, maybe.'

'Help putting out small fires, you mean? That might be dangerous.'

'Just trying to spot them and call the fire brigade.'

'Or trying to see who might be starting them?'

Howard shifted uncomfortably. 'I doubt that would be possible.'

'But if you did?' Sara pressed on. 'If you saw someone?'

'Er, call the police?'

'Do you feel we haven't given the matter enough attention?' asked Bowen. 'After all, here we are making enquiries into them.'

'I didn't know you were coming, did I?' Howard was beginning to bluster. 'No one has been interested up to now. I'm glad you're here, as a matter of fact.'

'Oh? Why is that?'

'Well, I, erm . . .' Howard was obviously improvising, and inspiration arrived. 'Would you be able to send along a representative? Someone official? It would be good for the locals to see that you were investigating.'

'I'm sure someone could be found,' said Sara smoothly. In truth, she wasn't at all sure that anyone would be sent along. She'd probably have to do it herself.

'Good. That's great.' Howard's face brightened. 'After all, it's not like everything even gets reported.'

'What do you mean?' Sara asked sharply.

Howard stood up and went to his office window. He beckoned the detectives over to look out with him. There was a good view of the working yard from the first floor. Howard pointed to the various buildings, starting with the new steel-framed block. 'That's the food processing plant. We process and pack all kinds of fresh food by season. Not just our own.'

He pointed to the ranks of glasshouses. 'We grow a variety of soft fruits and salad crops in there. Can you see the older ones?'

Bowen caught on faster than Sara. 'The two smaller ones to the left?'

'They were built before the Second World War,' said Howard proudly. 'They're wooden framed, so they can't be used anymore because of food regulations, but my mother loves them. She uses them to grow food for our family and staff.'

The buildings were lower than the modern versions. A mid-century family home stood between the old glasshouses and the yard, a well-tended garden to one side. Mrs Howard was obviously green-fingered. Sara shifted impatiently.

'Why are you showing us this?'

Howard stabbed a finger at the glass. 'See at the back of the old glasshouses? Where that little bit of meadow is? Mum keeps that for wildflowers. Two weeks ago, it began to burn. In the middle of the night. Started in the hedge along the back lane.'

'Why wasn't this reported?'

'We didn't want to bother anyone unnecessarily,' said Howard. 'It may not look it, but this business is worth millions. We have a good CCTV system covering the yard, factory and glasshouses. There are also two security guards at night. They watch the system and do patrols. They spotted the fire and had it out before we were awake in the house.'

'That was lucky,' said Bowen.

'It was. I could put in a report now, if it would help.'

Sara looked at him. 'I've made a note, Mr Howard. I think we'd better speak to these security guards, don't you?'

CHAPTER 7

Claudia had gone to the office earlier than usual to finish some paperwork before it became too hot to think. By half past nine, she had printed out various documents, including the apprentices' reports and some health and safety notices for their newest project. It gave her an excuse to get out of the office and visit Jamie Waller. A trip out and a chat might cheer up her day.

'I'm going to take these papers to the West Ruston site,' she said to her two assistants. They looked relieved. Once she had gone, they wouldn't have to keep up the pretence of trying to work.

It was a good twenty-minute drive from the North Walsham industrial estate to the building site in West Ruston. The small village was nestled in the hinterland of the farming community between the Broads and the coast. Once, the place would have had a post office, shop, school and pub. The first two had long since been turned into houses. Three years ago, the pub had failed, leaving the school as the last facility.

Despite a modest amount of nimbyism from the locals, the area's housing association had acquired the pub, with its extensive car park and gardens. They were converting it into sheltered pensioners' flats while a new terrace of five family houses was to be built in the gardens. Social housing like this was given priority in the area, where second-home owners raised house prices out of the reach of many locals. They would be a welcome boost to the local community, no matter what the not-in-my-back-yarders said. Coles Construction often worked on these projects with the association and had begun work on this one the previous week.

Claudia wound her way through the lanes until she passed the school and found the old pub. She wasn't often required to visit a site. Even so, she kept a reflective jacket and hard hat on the back seat of her car. They might not make her attractive, but she put them on before heading to the site office. It made her feel more official.

The pub building had a ground and first floor, with three doors facing into the car park. All of them stood open, and inside, Claudia could see what remained of the bar. The windows were mullioned, though whether they were original or fake 1950s ones, she couldn't tell. The thatched roof had once been beautifully done with a stepped and sculpted ridge. Replacing the ageing reed would be a highly specialised job.

The car park was full of vans and workers' transport. Parked carefully under a tree on a patch of dry grass was a moped with a *Scoot! Rural* sticker on the fuel tank. Claudia assumed it belonged to Kyle Atkins. He was assigned here alongside Eric Beatty, who was leading the groundworks team. She paused to check out its shiny red body and black trim. Give the lad his due; he kept the thing clean. Shame it was showing signs of a hard life. A helmet was clipped to a rail behind the seat.

'How trusting,' she said to herself.

There was the sound of a crash from inside the pub. A rapidly expanding cloud of dust shot out of a first-floor window. She held her breath briefly, then heard the men's laughter. Everything was fine. As she headed to the gate in the wire fence around the garden building site, lumps of old bricks rattled down the large plastic chute from the first-floor pub window into the skip in the car park below.

There was plenty of activity in the gardens too. A digger engine was chugging; a strimmer was hacking at dense undergrowth; a pneumatic pick rattled at an old concrete pad. The men worked in various states of undress, sweaty and hot. Some wore little more than their steel-toecap boots, a pair of shorts and hi-vis vest, the outfits incongruously topped off with hard hats.

The site office was in a modular cabin behind the gate. A double chemical toilet unit leaned at an off-putting angle at the far end. The site manager, Jamie Waller, was standing by the cabin door, trying to hear someone on his mobile.

'Signal is shite here.' He grinned as Claudia approached and poked at the mobile to end the fruitless call. 'Waste of time.'

Claudia searched her mind for good news. 'The temporary landline should be put in by the end of the week.'

'Yeah, that was them I was trying to speak to.' Jamie waggled the phone. 'Can you check when you get back to the office?'

'Of course.' She handed over a file with various forms in it. 'This lot needs displaying. Have you had any inspections yet?'

'Not so far. I'll get them up this morning. Did you just fancy a run out then?'

They both knew she could have left the papers for him to collect at the office. Claudia blushed. 'I thought they should be with you as soon as possible.'

'Very efficient.' Jamie grinned. It made his cheeks dimple attractively.

Claudia fished around for something else to keep her there. 'I could quickly check your first-aid kit while I'm here.'

'And there was me hoping you'd visited for the sake of my riveting company.' Jamie laughed. 'With us both being young, free and single.'

Claudia smiled at the cliché, then covertly sized him up. Jamie was not much taller than herself, with brown hair and the ubiquitous suntan all outdoor workers acquired. His muscles looked toned, and he wore jeans with a tight T-shirt which showed off his figure. He radiated an air of friendly efficiency. Some people might call him handsome. Claudia certainly thought so.

With an apologetic shrug, she turned to watch the men at their tasks. The clearance was moving rapidly. A large pile of debris, mostly wood, was growing at the far end of the garden.

'You're not going to burn that, are you?' she asked, suddenly worried.

'God, no,' said Jamie hastily. 'There's a couple of skips coming tomorrow. We'll get it chopped down and loaded out then.'

'Good,' said Claudia. 'It's just, with all these fires at the moment—'

'Don't worry,' Jamie interrupted. 'I'm aware. The first-aid kit is fully stocked, by the way. Is there anything else I can do for you? Cup of tea, perhaps?'

Ice cream would have been more welcome. Claudia shook her head. 'If you have a minute, I'd like to chat about Kyle Atkins.'

'Of course.' Jamie led Claudia inside the cabin.

It was divided into two unequal halves. The bigger side contained a rest area for the site staff, with tables, chairs and drinks-making facilities. Piles of dirty mugs already filled the sink in the kitchen area. The queasy smell of old food in jammed rubbish bins hung in the heat. Jamie's office occupied the other third. Despite all the windows being open and the door propped wide, the room was far too hot for comfort.

'Is Kyle in trouble?' asked Jamie reluctantly. 'He seems to be doing well, and Eric is happy with his work.'

'No trouble at all,' Claudia assured him. 'I'm just doing his apprenticeship report. I wanted to add your opinion as his site manager.'

Jamie paused thoughtfully. 'Hard working. Learning steadily. Sometimes his timekeeping leaves a little to be desired.'

'Oh? Eric didn't mention that.'

'Aren't we all a bit like that to begin with?' asked Jamie with a shrug. 'When we're making the jump between being at school and being a worker. I know it took me time to get used to the discipline.'

'I guess so,' she agreed. 'I won't mention that. Anything else.'

Jamie looked past Claudia into the kitchen as if he was checking the room was empty. He lowered his voice. 'I think I can trust you.'

It was flattering. Claudia hoped they were going to share a secret and nodded.

'I don't want this to go any further,' he said. 'I like the lad.'

'All right.'

'I've already had a go at him about this,' said Jamie quietly. 'But on the last couple of occasions when Kyle has been late, his breath smelled strongly of alcohol.'

CHAPTER 8

Jean couldn't decide what it was that drew her attention to the man and the woman as they got out of their separate cars — perhaps it was the way they drove up. It was mid-morning, and the nursery wasn't busy yet, although a few customers' cars were parked on the gravel near the display area and café. She had deliberately arranged the parking area in front of the farmhouse so she could keep a watchful eye on her business from the kitchen window. The family vehicles stood separately between the house and the old barn. From the way the pair stood talking to each other and looking at their surroundings, it was clear they were not shopping.

Sighing, she dried her hands and headed out the back door to speak to them. She was too tired for this today and already thirsty again, less than half an hour since her last cup of tea. Her bloods were fine when she'd checked them in her private bathroom. The millimole count was 7.5, exactly where the doctor liked it to be after her breakfast.

'How can I help you?' she asked.

The tall, graceful woman opened her warrant card and held it forward for inspection. 'Detective Sergeant Sara Hirst.'

Jean nodded her acknowledgement. 'Jean Simpson. I'm the owner here.'

The second officer joined them, card half open in his hand. 'DC Bowen.'

The man smiled at Jean. She didn't smile in return. In fact, she was tempted to tut at his appearance. Clearly older than the woman, not to mention lower in rank, the contrast in their turnout was quite marked. She was smartly dressed, her multi-plaited hair in a smart ponytail. His shirt flapped at the back of his trousers, and his tie was pulled loose at the neck. In Jean's opinion, it might be hot again today, but that was no excuse for slovenliness. It must have shown on her face. The DS glanced at her companion and frowned.

'Tuck yourself in, Mike,' she whispered. The man patted at his behind, then shoved his shirt away with an apologetic grin. The woman turned back to Jean. 'We're here about the fires in the area.'

'Really?'

'Is there somewhere we can talk?' asked DS Hirst.

Jean nodded. 'It's pleasant outside the café.'

They followed her to the patio. Only one other table was occupied — an elderly couple sat in a shady corner, buttering their scones. DS Hirst picked a table on the opposite side.

'You're aware that there was a fire adjacent to your property last night?' she asked.

Jean shuddered. 'Yes. We didn't realise at first. We'd already gone to bed.'

'We?'

Jean pointed to the farmhouse behind its ornamental railings. 'My daughter, her husband and I all live on the premises.'

'Nice place,' said DC Bowen. 'Just the nursery?'

'That's enough for us.' Jean felt herself becoming cross with the man. It was none of his business. She must need a snack or a glass of orange juice to counter her tiredness. 'What do you want to know about the fire?'

'When were you first aware of it?' asked DS Hirst.

'I was the last one to bed. It's so hot that I was still reading when Jake Willmott came hammering at the back door.'

The name caused a flash of recognition to cross the woman's face. 'I've spoken to Thomas Willmott.'

'Jake is his son,' explained Jean. 'Works on the farm with his dad. There have been a few fires on their land recently, so Jake has taken to driving around the lanes checking. Last night it was on Bell Lane, between the back of our place and their fields.'

'He came straight here?'

'Rang the fire brigade first.' Jean shuddered. 'Thank goodness. It had taken hold. Luckily, they got here in time. We might have lost our polytunnels if they hadn't.'

The memory of last night was still vivid to Jean. The fire growing, the anxious wait for the fire engine, the stink of the burning crop. Helplessly watching the flames billowing along their fencing. It could have spelled disaster for them as a small business, and she hadn't been able to sleep when they'd finally got back to bed in the early hours.

'Could you show us where it happened?' asked Hirst.

With a nod, Jean led them out of the café courtyard.

'This looks nice,' said the DS conversationally. 'I've never been to a herb farm before.'

'This is our display area. The tables around the edge have herbs for sale on them.' Jean waved at the colourful shed. A chalkboard on an A-frame stood outside with a list of dates and times. 'Till and wrapping station is in there. Darren, my son-in-law, does regular talks about how to grow different herbs. Very popular.'

'You don't use that building?' asked the DC. He pointed to a rundown red-brick barn behind an old fence. As they passed the double wooden doors, there was a crash inside.

'Not at the moment,' replied Jean. 'Darren is looking into how we might use it best. Seems a shame to waste the space. That will be him in there now.'

Darren appeared in the barn doorway. He rubbed at his arms and shook his head to get rid of a cloud of dust. He looked up at Jean and raised his hand in acknowledgement, face piercings glinting in the sunshine. Jean didn't allow the detectives to stop, leading them firmly towards the hedge gate.

'Not open to the public?' asked Hirst, looking at the sign screwed into the gate. 'No other security?'

'We've not needed any,' said Jean defensively.

She ushered the pair through and closed the gate with a slam. The polytunnels ran in either direction beside a wide path. It had once been gravelled. Now the grass grew through, much to Jean's annoyance. She would have preferred it to be tidier, but they had agreed last year that this area was her daughter's domain. It was pointless raising the issue with Faye again. They would only argue about it. Jean had insisted on keeping control of the paperwork and, therefore, the business in general. She pointed inside the tunnels as she led her visitors along the path.

'This is the commercial side,' she said. Inside each tunnel were ranks of growing tables, each set at the best height for a worker to look after the potted plants that stood in rows on them. 'We do living herbs for supermarkets. Basil, mint, coriander, parsley, thyme. All very popular.'

'Different sizes?' asked Hirst. She stopped to look inside one of the tunnels.

'Sequence growing,' said Jean. There was no reason to feel annoyed with the woman because she didn't know about their business. All the same, she wished Hirst would hurry up. 'Orders go out over time; you can't have them all ready at once.'

A bright-green logistics truck was ready to leave in the small yard at the back of the property. The driver was trying to sign the paperwork as quickly as he could. Faye flicked over the pages on her clipboard in confusion. Unable to bear it being wrong again, Jean marched over to her daughter, holding out her hand.

'Let me, Faye,' she snapped.

Faye looked up at her mother in embarrassment. 'It's all right, I—'

'Just give it to me.' Jean snatched the clipboard from Faye.

'I can sort it, Mum. Leave it alone,' Faye hissed.

'Give me a minute,' Jean said to the driver.

Jean could feel her daughter's resentful gaze on her back as she turned through the paperwork she'd carefully prepared the previous day. Running her finger down the column, Jean counted the items ticked off. This upmarket food chain was a regular client; they couldn't afford to annoy them. The idea made Jean feel a heat that had nothing to do with the temperature. Faye had no idea how close to the edge the business always seemed to be.

'Twenty trays of basil, fifteen of broadleaf parsley and ten of coriander?' she asked the driver. 'No mint?'

'That's right,' he agreed. Jean signed the despatch note and handed the man his copy. 'Thanks a lot. We'll get the gate.'

The driver swung into his cab and edged the lorry into the narrow lane beyond the corrugated metal fence. It was a tight turn. Jean waited until he had manoeuvred his vehicle, then pulled one half of the high gate shut, grunting at the weight. When she turned to speak to the detectives, Faye was still standing in exactly the same spot. Jean had to fight her impatience at the angry tears in Faye's eyes. She handed the clipboard back.

'Can you take that to the office for me?'

Faye nodded. Pulling the board close to her chest, she kept her eyes on the floor as she passed the two visitors. With a pout of annoyance, Jean realised that her daughter didn't even want to know who they were.

'It's this way,' said Jean. She led them out of the gate on to the lane.

It was only just wide enough to allow the delivery truck to pass. Several large trees stood on the verge, shading the old tarmac. A ribbon of dust and small stones ran along the centre of the lane, where the small amount of traffic had pushed it. The verges should have been full of wildflowers now, yet this year the plants were desiccated and straw-like. She marched on about thirty yards before stopping.

'It started over there.' She pointed to a field full of ripe barley. 'Willmott's land. Under that tree, they reckon. Took out several acres of the crop in there.'

The two detectives looked carefully around the burn site. Hirst traced a wide black mark across the narrow lane.

'It jumped across to your property here?'

'That's right. Luckily, the fence was treated last year, and we have a couple of old containers behind that bit for storage. Not so easy to burn. Did a fair amount of damage, though.' Jean pointed to the charred fencing and an area of wet mud. It stank of burning. 'Fire engine was there.'

'And the first you knew about it was when Jake Willmott came to find you?'

'Yes. Darren and I came straight over here. It was frightening, but the firemen soon had it under control.'

'Not your daughter?' asked Hirst.

Jean felt the woman was watching her carefully. She schooled her face into as near a blank as she could. The truth was that when Jake had hammered on their door, Faye had been missing. So had her moped. Something she wasn't going to admit to these people. 'No, I asked her to stay in the house.'

CHAPTER 9

Like most detectives, Sara was used to reading people. She felt annoyed at her confusion over the mixed messages that Jean Simpson was giving out. Mrs Simpson was polite to them, and her tone was professional. On the other hand, she didn't answer all their questions, and there was an edge to her behaviour that made Sara uncomfortable. Perhaps that was because the owner of the nursery had clearly taken against DC Bowen's state of dress and chipper attitude. The fire could have been a disaster for their small business, but the woman had hidden her feelings about the incident very well. How she'd reacted to her daughter over a simple piece of paperwork had been more telling. She had nearly reduced the younger woman to tears. They said a polite goodbye in the car park, and Jean Simpson marched off.

Sara turned to Bowen with a shrug. He waited until he saw that Mrs Simpson had gone inside, then he frowned in return as she asked, 'What did you make of that?'

'Hardly the happy family,' said Bowen. 'Doesn't mean anything, I guess. They're only accidental victims here, aren't they?'

'Why would she ask her daughter to stay in the house?'

'That was odd, wasn't it? You'd think the woman would have rushed there with the rest.'

'That's what I'd do. Their business was in danger.' Sara scanned the car park. It was filling up with customers.

Bowen nodded. 'It's a pity we can't talk to those security guards at Howards until tonight.'

'I don't think we need to wake them up just yet. It can wait until teatime when they come back on duty. Let's speak to Jake Willmott while we're here. I've got his contact details somewhere.'

'Give them to me and I'll call him.'

Sara zapped open her car and reached in for her purse. 'While you're doing that, do you know what I'm going to do?'

'What?'

'I'm going to buy a few plants for my garden. Won't be long.'

Sara walked casually around the display tables, selecting half a dozen pots of herbs. Her route naturally took her past the old barn. It looked dilapidated and out of place among the neat display tables and plant beds. It reminded Sara of her tumbledown garden shed, only much bigger. Another crash preceded a puff of dust billowing out as she made her selection. A teenager with a welcoming smile took her money in the colourful shed.

'Bet I forget the bloody things,' she murmured as she dumped the brown paper carrier bag in the back of her car. Bowen was grinning when he joined her.

'Doing up your garden now?'

Sara slammed the car door. 'Looks like it. Well?'

'Jake Willmott is happy to talk to us and is off home for lunch. Said we'd meet him there.'

* * *

Jake Willmott's house was on the edge of Hoveton village. It was a semi-detached, red-brick 1950s rural council house. Or so the tablet inset on the wall said. It was in the middle of a street of perhaps twenty similar houses. A dusty, ancient

Nissan SUV stood ticking over on the gravel drive. Jake had only just arrived.

A stressed-looking woman with streaked blonde hair answered the door. She glanced at their cards without much interest.

'I'm Maddy. Jake told me you were coming,' she said. Pulling open the door, she waved down the hallway to the back of the house. 'He's in the kitchen.'

She walked in front of them and, without pausing, carried on to the rear garden. Sara could hear the sound of splashing and children's voices outside. The woman shouted at one of the children as a squeal erupted.

Jake Willmott was standing in front of a kitchen work-top buttering bread. He was tall and ash blonde. A long fringe fell in front of his eyes, which he kept swiping out of the way. He glanced round at the detectives. 'Making a sandwich. Sit down, why don't you? I won't be long.'

'I spoke to your father yesterday,' began Sara.

Willmott nodded. 'He told me.'

'Was that why you checked the farm boundaries last night?'

'No. I've been doing it for about a week now. Go round before I go to bed, in case they've been here again. Can't be a coincidence, can it?'

'You may have been singled out,' agreed Sara. 'The question is, do you have any idea why?'

'Nope.' Willmott sat at the table with them and bit into his sandwich.

'No one that you've fallen out with recently?'

'Not recently, no.' He swallowed. 'We get on well enough with our neighbours.'

Sara knew that in the local farming community, neigh-bourliness was necessary. Farm boundaries butted against each other, or against housing estates and the gardens of village homes. Disputes were inevitable and needed to be kept to a minimum.

'Like the herb farm?'

'Yeah, Mrs Simpson is all right,' nodded Willmott. He took another large bite from his sandwich.

'You found the fire last night?' asked Bowen, keen not to be left out of the conversation.

'Yup.' The last of the sandwich vanished, and Willmott stood up to make another. 'I rang the fire brigade, then went round to warn Mrs Simpson.'

'Was it well established?'

'Yeah, it was moving along the verge and into the wheat. I couldn't tackle it on my own.'

'Did you see anyone near the fire?' asked Sara.

Willmott paused and gazed blankly as he reran the evening in his mind. 'It was already going across the lane to the nursery. I knew I had to hurry. Didn't want to drive through it, so I had to turn round.'

'And you hadn't passed anyone to reach it?'

'Nah, it was late. Almost midnight. I've been leaving it as late as I can manage.'

Sara knew he would have to be up at dawn if they were harvesting. 'So, you didn't see anyone on the way round to the nursery?'

'No.' Willmott pushed down on the bread to trap a slice of cheese. Then he said thoughtfully, 'There were some lights, like bike lights, going up the lane on the other side.'

'Was it a motorbike?' asked Bowen.

'Couldn't really hear for the noise of the fire,' replied Willmott. 'Wasn't going that fast. So it could have been a push bike.'

'When you got to Wild Thyme, who was there?' Sara asked.

'Mrs Simpson came down first.' Willmott smiled briefly. 'She was in her nightie, bless her. Then that son-in-law of hers.'

'And you all went to the site of the fire?'

'To wait for the fire engine at their back gate.'

'Mr Willmott,' began Sara, 'your father seemed convinced that these fires are being deliberately started as revenge. By his former wife — your mother, I assume.'

'Mum?' Willmott snorted. 'Hardly likely.'

'Why not?' asked Bowen.

'They split up years ago. She married again after that and moved to Devon. Five years ago.'

'Your father said she's been trying to contact you recently.' Sara watched the young man closely as he blushed under his field tan.

'Could have.'

'Have you actually spoken to her?'

'No, I haven't,' Willmott answered vehemently. 'And I won't, neither. She can ring all she likes. Shouldn't have left me and Dad like that.'

'She found your phone number?'

'It's not a secret. Rang the house a couple of times. Maddy took a message, but I didn't call her back. Then she wrote me a letter.'

'Did you keep it?' Bowen asked. 'Do you have an address for her?'

Willmott looked at Bowen and then nodded slowly. 'Do you think she might have started these fires, then?'

Sara stayed still as Bowen shrugged. It was a coincidence, and none of them liked those.

Willmott nodded at Bowen as if he was satisfied. 'I'll get it for you when I've finished this.'

CHAPTER 10

Claudia should have gone straight back to the office. Instead, she drove to the next village where the signal was better and rang an old friend. Amanda was a teacher at the local high school in Hoveton and had been for the last ten years. If anyone could remember any gossip about Kyle Atkins, it would be her. Amanda adored gossip.

The pair met in the café at Hoveton Hall Gardens. Claudia treated them both to cool drinks and then led her friend to a table in the shade. Their colourful floral summer dresses glowed in the dappled sunlight. Above them, the leaves rustled gently in the slight breeze.

'I know I shouldn't be asking this,' began Claudia. 'And really, I'm just being nosey.'

'Something about my work?' asked Amanda. She smiled conspiratorially. 'You know I'm not supposed to talk about individuals.'

'I know.' Claudia tipped her posh lemonade over the ice cubes in her glass. It fizzed and crackled for a moment. 'You remember you helped me to set up the apprenticeship thing at work?'

'Of course.' Amanda frowned. 'They aren't pulling out, are they? It's hard to get places where the youngsters actually learn something like your lot do. Most people treat them as cheap labour.'

'No, nothing like that. In fact, it's going well so far.'

'Then what?'

'One of our placements is Kyle Atkins. Did you teach him?'

'Yeah, I remember him. His younger brother is still with us.'

'What did you make of Kyle?'

'School didn't suit him,' said Amanda thoughtfully. 'His circumstances were a bit difficult. Although he was bright enough, he wasn't academic like you have to be these days.'

Claudia pulled the apprentice report out of her bag and offered it to Amanda. 'It doesn't seem to be holding him back as such. I'm not showing you this.'

Amanda sipped her drink as she read the report. After a few minutes, she returned it to Claudia. 'Apart from not bringing you his maths results, it seems fine.'

'I agree. He is being mentored by one of the more senior workers. A man called Eric Beatty. Have you heard of him?'

'Can't say I have. Why?'

'I didn't expect it of Eric. He was the first to come forward to support the scheme. Then he proposed Kyle to work with him.'

'Is that a problem?'

'They seem to get on really well. It's just that I wondered why Eric was so keen to get involved. Then it struck me that they might be related or family friends.'

Amanda chewed her lip thoughtfully. 'Is there a rule about relatives getting you a placement?'

'I don't think so. What circumstances?'

'Hmm?' Amanda turned her glass around, wiping away the water droplets from the ice.

'You said his circumstances were a bit difficult. Can you tell me?'

'Why don't you just ask him?'

'Like I said, it's none of my business, really. It's just that there's a potential problem which I haven't put in the report. If I knew more about Kyle, I could find a way to put it to him.'

'What problem?' Amanda sounded curious.

'His site manager thinks he's drinking,' said Claudia. 'Enough for it to still be on his breath when he gets into work in the morning.'

'Which could be dangerous on a building site. Lots of seventeen-year-olds drink, don't they? Be fair, we did.'

Claudia smiled. 'I know. It seemed a bit of a game, didn't it?'

'Like a rite of passage,' nodded Amanda. 'You're worried he might hurt someone?'

'Or himself. He gets to the sites on a moped. What if he had an accident that way?'

'He'd get breathalysed, wouldn't he? You have his home address and next of kin on the paperwork, right?'

'Yes.'

'Try driving round there sometime. Officially it's in Belaugh. It's really remote. Three little cottages at the end of a side road. Pretty lonely, I'd say.'

Claudia returned the report to its file and looked at the other details. 'Kyle put his mum as next of kin.'

'Ah, well, he wouldn't have any choice.'

Claudia let her glass plonk onto the table. 'Why not?'

'That's the difficult circumstances. His father died when Kyle was ten. An accident on a farm. When he came to us, he was attending Nelson's Journey for bereavement counselling.'

'And his brother?'

'Ryan? He's still with us. He's only thirteen, so he would have been six when the accident happened.'

'Their poor mum. Managing two young boys like that when she'd lost her husband.'

'I know.'

Claudia had struggled to cope when she had lost both her parents in quick succession. Her lazy husband had refused to help. Everything had fallen to her as an only child, from emptying their council house to settling their debts. She knew about bereavement and felt a pang of sympathy for Mrs Atkins. 'Do you think Kyle felt he should take on responsibilities at home?'

'The pressure to be the man of the house?' suggested Amanda. 'Looking out for his mother and little brother? Could be.'

'What's the brother like?'

'Ryan?' Amanda paused thoughtfully. 'I only have him two periods a week, so I don't see him much. Quiet sort. Doesn't seem to have many friends, though. Look, unless Kyle is turning up incapable, I don't think I'd be too worried about his drinking. That could just be bravado. If this Eric chap is being protective, get him to have a quiet word.'

'I'd better get back to work.' Claudia finished her drink with a few hurried gulps. 'I'm supposed to be attending a meeting this afternoon. Thank you for telling me all that. I won't let on.'

'Right you are, 007.' Amanda smiled and gave her friend a hug.

They walked back to the car park together. Amanda drove off in a flurry of dust while Claudia opened the file again. She punched the postcode into her satnav. The place was surprisingly close. The lane ran towards a bend in the River Bure, ending in a patch of bright green on the screen.

'It might as well be a houseboat,' she said to herself. 'Let's go and have a look.'

CHAPTER 11

Jake Willmott handed over the letter. 'She hasn't spoken to Dad or me for years.'

'Why would that be?' asked Sara quietly.

Willmott began to look mulish. 'Family stuff.'

'Why is she trying to contact you now, do you think? Is it in the letter?'

'I've no idea,' snapped Willmott. 'I haven't read the damn thing.'

Someone had read the letter; at least, the envelope had been torn open. Sara turned it over to examine it.

'Who opened it?' she asked.

'Girlfriend,' replied Jake shortly.

The address was correct, and it had been sent to 'Jake and Maddy'. There was no postmark. 'May I?'

'Sure. I don't care.'

'Do you know if she's visited locally?' asked Bowen.

Willmott shrugged. 'If she did, she didn't come here. At least, not as far as I know.'

'Thank you for your help,' said Sara cautiously. They had clearly hit a raw nerve. She gave Willmott one of her cards. 'In case you think of anything else that might help us. And if you see any more fires, perhaps you could call me?'

She didn't feel very confident that he would bother. The conversation had turned sour when his mother was brought up. Whatever had happened during his parents' break-up, Jake held a deep grudge.

Bowen returned to the office separately, zooming his car away in a shower of grit and dust. Sara drove more slowly, listening to her phone messages as she went. She had barely got out of Wroxham when Dante called.

'Having a good morning?'

'It's been interesting,' she replied. 'How about you?'

'Routine. I've drawn the short straw tomorrow, obs outside a suspect's house all day.'

'Bad luck.' Sara couldn't stop a snort of laughter escaping.

'Oh, very funny,' said Dante with mock offence. 'Just because your case is more interesting than watching paint dry. What have you found?'

'It must be something in the air around Wroxham,' she replied. 'Two families who don't get on. One a victim of these arson attacks, the other a neighbour.'

'Do they know each other?'

'Only in the way of two businesses working side by side.'

'Will you be round tonight?' Before Sara could refuse, he carried on. 'One of my neighbours in the close is having a barbecue, and we're invited.' When Sara didn't reply immediately, he added in a cross tone, 'It's not compulsory.'

'It's not that,' she said with relief. 'I've got to take a statement on my way home.'

'See you later, then,' he said. He sounded irritated.

'Yeah. I'm on my way into the office. Perhaps a quick coffee in the canteen?'

Besides, I'd rather be out at the coast, thought Sara. *At least there's a breeze. And I don't fancy cremated sausage.*

Sara knew she couldn't keep avoiding the man or how she felt. If there was no spark, it was time she told him so. Unlike some of his colleagues, she wasn't afraid of his sharp tongue. Whatever the reason, she shouldn't be leading him on like this. But she couldn't forget that he had helped to save her life the previous Christmas; she owed him a debt of gratitude. Despite the air conditioning, Sara felt unable to form her thoughts, and she gunned her car down the bypass in exasperation.

* * *

The team were all present when she got back. A more detailed map of the area around Belaugh and Hoveton had been pinned up with its own rash of dots. The office was hot, and the team lounged languidly. The heatwave was overpowering the air conditioning. Aggie had managed to rustle up some ice cubes for a jug of squash. With Bowen to keep her on track, Sara filled them in on her interviews.

'Two not very happy families,' she concluded.

'I'd like you to get hold of his mother in Devon,' said DCI Hudson. Sara nodded. 'Get a bit of background and see if she ever came up here. What does this letter say?'

'It asks how he and the family are.' Sara spread the two pages on her desk and speed-read the contents again. 'She seems to know all about the grandchildren. Offers them a free holiday in Devon. Ah, this is the interesting bit: her second husband has been diagnosed with cancer. She doesn't say what sort. Says it's made her think of rebuilding bridges, and that she could come up to stay with Michelle. Who's Michelle?'

'Ask about that as well,' said Hudson. 'Anything else?'

'It might have been hand-delivered.' Sara held up the envelope. 'There's no postmark.'

'Arrange for a local officer to call for a statement once we've established contact.'

'Yes, ma'am,' Sara said. 'No problem.'

'Noble?' asked Hudson, pointing to the new map.

'I've updated the grid with new fire reports,' said DC Noble. 'It's getting worse out there. I'm following the fire service's internal website.'

'You got permission for that?' Hudson sounded surprised.

'Yes, ma'am,' Noble assured her. 'Wouldn't do it without. Most of what's going on today seems to be spontaneous.'

'Let us know if anything else happens. What about this herb place?'

'The fire was definitely aimed at Willmott's fields again,' said Sara. 'I think the wind direction made it spring across to Wild Thyme. They don't seem to have been the target.'

'And you felt that this family was also dysfunctional?' Hudson frowned. 'What makes you say that?'

'The daughter and the mother don't get on,' said Sara carefully. 'There's obviously some dispute there, which must be difficult when they run a business together.'

'We're not sure that it matters . . .' said Bowen. He glanced at Sara for her agreement, and she nodded. 'But it seems odd to us that the daughter wasn't on hand when the business was threatened like that.'

'The fire officer's report is clear that accelerants were used in the field,' said Noble. 'I booked a visit by forensics like you said, ma'am.'

'Good. Have you added the fire at the Howards glass-houses to the map?'

'Yes, ma'am. And I put it on the database.'

'What about these security guards?' Hudson looked at Bowen.

'I've arranged to speak to them on my way home tonight,' said Sara. 'When they go on shift.'

'Good. When is this vigilante meeting that Kevin Howard is arranging?'

The description wasn't unfair, but then who could blame them? It was easy to see how it might help. After all, it was Jake Willmott that had found the fire next to Wild Thyme.

Sara checked her notes. 'Just a gathering of local businesses that might be affected. To arrange some self-help.'

'So long as it doesn't turn into amateur detective hour and a lynch mob.'

'It's on Thursday evening. Half past seven at his house.'

'Can you cover that on your way home too? We can call it an official presence, and I don't think you should go alone.'

Hudson looked pointedly at DI Edwards.

He shrugged. 'All right. I'll do it.'

CHAPTER 12

The hot day passed slowly once the two detectives had left the herb farm. Jean sorted out the paperwork which Faye had dumped on the kitchen table, then went through the post. Neither her daughter nor her son-in-law appeared at lunchtime. She spent the afternoon in her office, processing the online orders, which she took out to Darren in the old barn just before closing time.

'You're making good progress,' she said, looking around the various piles that Darren had created.

'I think we could start with a barn sale.' He waved at a group of old farm items. 'Some people might use them as garden decoration, and the old table sets from the café have the potential for re-use.'

'You think people would come?'

'They might, and it could raise some funds.' Darren glanced over the small pile of orders. 'We can advertise it online. Then just open the place with someone in here for safety's sake.'

'And the rest?' Jean pointed to the dead boxes and old pallets closest to the barn doors.

'Get a skip in,' said Darren. 'Wouldn't take long to clear it. Then we can see its true potential. I don't think it would take much to tart it up. I'd be able to do most of it. Then we'd have space for all sorts of things, like Santa at Christmas or music evenings. We could even hire it out for events.'

Jean grimaced. 'I love your enthusiasm, but one step at a time. Think of the costs of setting up these things. The insurance alone would be a fortune.'

'Isn't it insured?'

Jean almost hated herself for putting a damper on his ideas. 'Only as an agricultural building. Not as a public space. It might be expensive to change that.'

Darren's face turned grim. 'Are things really that bad?'

'Yes, they are. As usual,' said Faye. Jean swung round at the unexpected voice. Her daughter stood in the doorway, arms folded and a look of disgust on her face. 'This place doesn't make any money. Or so she always tells us.'

Jean felt the heat rising in her cheeks. She wondered how long Faye had been listening. 'We've talked about this. Your father left us in a bit of a financial pickle.'

'Dad's fault again. He's been dead for three years. After all this hard work, why haven't we got back into profit?'

Because he borrowed a lot of money to expand the place, thought Jean. *Because he was a great plantsman but crap at business. But I can't tell you that. You adored him.*

'We're getting there,' was all Jean could find to say.

'Then where is the money? Keep it to yourself, do you?'

'How dare you!' said Jean angrily. 'I work as hard as both of you.'

'Then why can't Darren and me have our own place?' Faye demanded with a sneer. 'You promised when we got married. Living in the farmhouse together was only temporary.'

'We can't afford it, not yet,' huffed Jean, as her brain worked overtime trying to justify her failure to keep her promise. 'Besides, sharing the farmhouse works well, doesn't it?'

'Oh sure, for you,' snapped Faye.

Darren walked towards his wife, arms held out for a hug. She deliberately sidestepped him and strode towards her mother. The anger on her face made Jean take a step backwards. Darren swung round and grabbed Faye's arm.

Faye turned on him and peeled his hand away. 'She said we could have our own place. Or if we worked on the place for a few years, she would retire, get a bungalow and move out. Leave us in peace. That's what she promised.'

'I don't mind,' began Darren.

'Well, I do,' snarled Faye as she turned back to face her mother. 'And I've had enough. You're nearly seventy, Mother. When will you retire?'

When Jean didn't reply, Faye rushed on, 'You don't trust us to run this business. You can't allow Darren to have an idea to improve the place without putting the brakes on it. You don't think I'm capable, do you?'

'That's not true.' Jean shook her head vehemently.

'Then why do you keep putting me down in front of people? Like the driver this morning.'

'I don't mean to. I just don't want to lose the supermarket orders. They keep us going.'

'I know,' snapped Faye. 'I'm not stupid. And who were those damned people you were showing round this morning?'

'A couple of police detectives.' Jean's heart was in her mouth. She had never seen her daughter so incandescent.

'What?' gasped Darren. 'Why?'

'They came about the fire last night.' Jean began to stammer. 'That's all . . . Just . . . about Willmott's . . .'

'Bloody great,' shouted Faye. 'It's not enough that you embarrass me in front of one of our regular customers, you also have to put me down in front of two police officers. How wonderful. You made me look like an idiot.'

Anger came to Jean's rescue. 'If you behave like a fool, you get treated like one.'

Darren gasped. Faye sneered.

'Oh, that's right,' she said, sarcasm dripping from every word. 'You've always had me down as the village idiot, haven't you?'

'How can you say such a thing?'

'I always knew.' Tears began to run down Faye's cheeks. 'Only Dad believed in me. Told me once that he was making a new will, and you wouldn't be in it.'

'What? He never said that.' Jean was becoming indignant. 'He would never have done that to me.'

'He told me he didn't trust you to leave the place to me.' Faye stepped closer. Her face inches away from Jean's blinking eyes, she dropped the volume of her voice and hissed, 'Because you didn't actually like me. Your own daughter. Your only child.'

'How can you say that?' Jean clenched her hands open and shut, resisting the temptation to slap her daughter's face. Faye and her father had been so close that Jean had often felt excluded by them. How could a mother admit that she was jealous of her own daughter?

'Said he thought you would disinherit me,' Faye went on, 'because you didn't think I was capable of running the place.'

'Then why didn't he?' demanded Jean, aware that her voice was almost as loud as Faye's.

'Because he died a week later.' Faye was openly crying. 'Was he right? Did you ever love me?'

'Of course I do,' blustered Jean. Faye shook her head in disbelief. 'I have from the moment you were born.'

'Have you left me anything? After all, that's the only way we ever communicate, you and me, right? Over the money.'

Jean blushed as she thought of her current will, leaving a controlling share of Wild Thyme to Darren, even if he divorced Faye.

'You've cut me out of the will, haven't you?' Faye read the answer she expected on her mother's face. 'No matter how hard I try, no matter what I do, nothing about me is ever good enough for you, is it?'

Jean stepped back defensively. 'Well, if that's what you think of me, can you blame me?'

'Enough!' said Darren loudly. 'Stop this.'

Faye turned her back on Jean. 'Are you taking her side?'

'No, of course not.' Darren held out his arms to Faye. 'Come here. It's you I love.'

She half ran, half stumbled into his arms, and he pulled her close against him. Jean felt a pang of envy. She couldn't remember a time when Malcolm had told her that he loved her like that. It just hadn't been his way. Darren watched her over Faye's shoulder as she sobbed into his chest.

'Have you cut Faye out?' he asked quietly.

'That's my business,' said Jean, her lips pursed flatly with anger.

'Well, let me tell you that if you've left the place to me, I would simply gift it back where it belongs. To my wife.' He turned away, pulling the distraught Faye with him. 'Come on, sweetheart. Let's go.'

CHAPTER 13

Sara spoke over the phone to Jake Willmott's mother in Devon. Mrs Lawson, as she was now called, had been shocked to hear about the trouble at Belaugh Manor Farm.

'I did try to contact my son,' she confirmed. 'Jake was a teenager when we split up, and he took it badly. His reaction was extreme. He blamed me for everything, which was rather unfair. We haven't spoken since.'

Although she knew the answer from the letter, Sara asked why she'd tried to speak to Jake now.

'My husband has bowel cancer,' Mrs Lawson explained. 'Luckily, they caught it early, and his prognosis is good. The shock made me think about healing old wounds with Jake, even if Thomas couldn't forgive me.'

'Have you been up to Norfolk?'

'I did come up for a few days. Jake wouldn't take my phone calls, so I tried a face-to-face meeting. I have a friend up there who found his address.'

'It didn't work?'

'Unfortunately, no.' Mrs Lawson sounded sad. 'I went to the house, and his girlfriend answered the door. When she refused to let me in, I wrote him a letter, which I dropped off.'

'And when was this?'

'Back in May.'

'Have you been up to Norfolk since?'

'Good Lord, no,' said Mrs Lawson. 'I have to run the farm while my husband is ill.'

'Can I ask where you stayed?' asked Sara.

'With my friend, Michelle. You want to check the dates with her? Of course you do.' Mrs Lawson gave Sara the address. 'Good luck with your search.'

As they wound up for the evening, Sara recounted her conversation to the rest of the team. 'I'll follow up with this Michelle.'

'Also on your way home?' laughed DI Edwards.

'Actually, it's not far from Belaugh Manor Farm, so yes.'

'Mrs Lawson doesn't sound a likely candidate for vindictive fire starting,' said DCI Hudson. 'I wouldn't make it a priority.'

As Sara left the office, she avoided looking through the plate glass windows at the drugs team in case Dante was still at work. Their coffee in the canteen hadn't gone well. Dante was obviously hurt by her refusal to stay at his place, and the conversation had been tense. She was grateful to get away quickly.

* * *

A single car and a motorbike stood in the car park at Howards UK when Sara arrived. The factory, office building and greenhouses were all locked up. Two security guards emerged from a small door at the side of the factory. They had clearly been waiting for her.

Both men were middle-aged and dressed in uniform navy-blue trousers with blue polo shirts. The shorter one was tubby and going bald, while the taller one was grey-haired and thin. Neither seemed very fit. Sara wondered what they would do if some real villains turned up. Run a mile, probably.

'Come in,' invited the shorter one. It was a small office with a desk and an area for making drinks or eating food. A small bank of screens showed images from security cameras.

'We keep an eye on all the buildings from here,' said the tall guard after introducing himself as Derek and his colleague as Shorty. He tapped on a screen, which blinked briefly. 'Front doors, at the back, and on the other bits of land the company owns.'

'Is that how you saw the fire?' she asked.

'We didn't spot it until it had caught,' explained Shorty.

Sara wondered if they did much apart from sitting here all night. Maybe they took turns napping in the easy chairs near the kitchen area. 'Don't you patrol regularly?'

'Of course.' Shorty sounded offended.

'We go round at different times,' said Derek with a smile. 'So there isn't a routine, like.'

'On foot? Together?' Sara turned to talk to him.

'Usually,' said Shorty shortly.

'And on this night?'

'It had been quiet, as usual.' Derek extracted an A4 notebook from the desk drawer. He opened it, turning the pages, until he found the place he wanted. He ran his finger down the handwritten list. 'Monday the twenty-fourth of July. We walked round at nine o'clock, then again at half past ten.'

'After that?' Derek handed the book to Sara, and she looked at the carefully written log. The next entry was timed at 1.15 a.m. He leaned over her shoulder to point at the entry. 'We did that when we got back, so we spotted it about a quarter to twelve.'

'What did you do?'

'We grabbed a couple of fire extinguishers.' Derek began to speak faster with the excitement of recounting the only real drama they'd had in years. 'Bunged them in the back of my car and drove round there. Quicker in the car than running, though it's not that far.'

Sara couldn't imagine either of the pair running more than a few yards. 'Did you pass anyone as you drove?'

'Nope, buuuut . . .' Derek paused for dramatic effect. 'We did hear a moped, didn't we? Drove off when they heard us coming, I reckon.'

'Did you?' asked Sara. Knowing it was a long shot, she asked, 'Did you see it? Get the number plate?'

'It was dark,' said Shorty. Derek looked rather deflated.

'Could you show me the scene?'

Sara suppressed a smile as Derek perked up again. 'We can walk over there, if you don't mind.'

'I'll stay and keep an eye on the screens,' said Shorty, slumping into the office chair and adjusting the desk fan on to his face.

Derek led Sara between two glasshouses. The path should have been grassy, but the heatwave had parched the ground, and now it was as tough as concrete. She could hear something hissing inside one of the houses. When she glanced around, Derek pointed through the glass.

'Watering system,' he said. 'Comes on when it cools down.'

They crossed the open grassy area that Kevin Howard had described as his mother's wildflower meadow. At the moment, it was mostly growing hay. The untidy hedge was at least twelve feet high, with an old wooden five-bar gate half hidden by greenery in the middle. Derek lifted the gate open with some difficulty. Sara followed him out into the narrow lane beyond.

'Is this used much?' she asked as Derek halted about five yards along the lane.

'Not really. Locals sometimes use it as a cut-through.' He pointed to an area of badly charred hedging. 'This was it.'

'Lucky you spotted it as soon as you did,' said Sara. The fire had destroyed about fifteen yards of the hedge. It looked like it had run along at ground level, though some damage stretched to the top of the bushes.

'There isn't much to see normally,' said Derek. 'We could see it was a fire because it was dark. The colour and the movement were unusual.'

'And the moped.'

'I'd pulled up there.' Derek pointed at a passing place further down the lane. 'We'd jumped out to grab the extinguishers when I heard the engine start.'

'You're sure it started then? It wasn't someone who came down the lane from the other direction and had to turn round?'

'Yeah, pretty sure. He was pulling on his helmet when we spotted him.'

'What made you think it was a moped?'

'I recognised the sound. Farty little things,' said Derek dismissively. 'It drove off that way, towards Hoveton. Really straining, it was. Like the rider was afraid we might catch up with him.'

'You think it was a man?'

'We could see him a bit in the light of the fire. Tall, big shoulders. Jeans and a dirty T-shirt.'

'Girls can dress like that too,' suggested Sara. 'Would you recognise them again?'

'Like in an identity parade? Like on the telly?' Derek sounded keen.

'We tend to do it on a computer now.'

Derek looked disappointed. 'I think we'd be wasting your time. I don't think we got a good enough look at him.'

CHAPTER 14

Despite having the window of her bedroom wide open, Claudia was restless. She was naked under a single sheet, and a fan hummed as it moved the air. It was still too warm for comfort. After staring at the ceiling for a considerable time, she rolled over and picked up her phone: 1.20 a.m. She began to scroll. When the phone pinged up a local news alert on her feed, she clicked idly on the message.

Breaking News. Locals report a fire breaking out at the old Hog in Armour public house in West Ruston. Fire crews are racing to attend. More to follow.

Claudia nearly dropped the mobile in surprise. Fumbling in her haste, she selected *Jamie Waller* from her saved contacts. Swinging out of bed, she was already hunting for her stuff when he answered.

'I'm so sorry if I woke you,' she said. 'Have you seen the news?'

'I'm already here,' he said. Claudia could hear chaos behind him. 'How did you find out?'

'I couldn't sleep, and then I got an alert on my phone,' said Claudia. 'What's going on?'

'It's our West Ruston site.' Jamie was shouting now. 'Someone set that wood pile on fire, and it's caught the old pub. It's madness. Fire engines everywhere.'

'I'm on my way.' Claudia dragged on some practical clothes, strapped on her trainers and grabbed her handbag as she dashed through the kitchen.

There was no traffic between her house in North Walsham and the village of West Ruston. The red glow in the night sky grew larger as she drove round the winding back road that was the most direct route to the old pub. The road through the village was shut off by a police cordon. She dumped her car on the verge and walked towards it carrying her hi-vis jacket and hard hat.

One officer was trying to calm a small crowd of villagers, who stood in their pyjamas and dressing gowns, bombarding him with questions. Claudia remembered there was a small estate of houses next to the pub. These poor souls must have been evacuated for safety, and they were none too pleased about the situation. A second officer spotted Claudia and headed over to intercept her at the tape.

'You can't go in there, Miss,' the woman said. 'Far too dangerous.'

'I work for the builders,' explained Claudia. 'The site manager called me.'

It wasn't quite true, but it did the job. The officer hesitated. There was a shout behind the woman. Jamie Waller strode over to join them, waving as he approached. 'It's okay. Claudia is with the company.'

As he put his hand on the tape to lift it, the officer placed her own firmly over it. 'It's very dangerous, sir. Only emergency services should be up there.'

'We won't get in their way,' he promised. 'I just need someone else from the company here with me — for legal reasons.'

The officer considered this before letting go of Jamie's hand. 'All right. Stay over there by the hedge, and don't interfere. Stand where I can see you.'

'Sure,' agreed Jamie. Claudia ducked under the tape, and they walked a few yards towards the fire.

'What legal reasons?' hissed Claudia, grateful he was playing along.

'Don't know,' said Jamie with a grin. 'I'm sure you can find one. Insurance?'

They reached the hedge the officer had pointed to and stopped. From here, Claudia could see a bank of fire engines. Hoses trained water at the roof of the old pub and along the derelict garden. The noise was deafening — the roar of the fire as it leaped from place to place and into the sky, the shouting of the fire crew as they fought the blaze, the drubbing of the fire engines as they pumped water, a sudden crash as something inside the pub collapsed. Behind them came the sound of another fire engine racing to join the fight, followed by a lorry carrying a mobile incident unit. They screamed up the road, forcing the evacuated families on to the narrow pavement, where they shouted or screamed in fear. Claudia could see that there were several children in the group. The officer ripped down the tape to let the engine through, and it accelerated past Jamie and Claudia.

'I don't fancy the chances of the portaloos, do you?' asked Jamie. He sounded amused at that thought.

'Is there nowhere these folks can go?' asked Claudia, watching the families pushing forward as soon as the tape was put back. 'Why is no one organising that?'

'Who knows?' Jamie pointed to the new arrivals. 'Their job?'

Claudia ignored him. 'A village hall or something? I'm going to ask.' She strode over to the officer controlling the tape.

'Not my village,' said the woman. 'I'm afraid I don't know.'

'I do,' called a man from the back of the crowd. 'Yes, we have a village hall. It's on the other side of that lot.'

'Along the road?' asked Claudia. The man pushed forward to speak to her.

'Up near the school.' He pointed past the blazing pub.

'Is there another way round? Apart from this direct road?'

'You could go on a circular route through the lanes,' he said. 'Too far to walk. Especially for the little ones.'

'What about your cars?'

The man scowled angrily at the police officers. 'They turfed us out before we could move them.'

'Okay,' said Claudia in her calmest voice. 'Do you know how we could get in and use it?'

'Elizabeth. She's the nearest. She'll know what's happening. Her house is on the other side of the pub.'

'Let me have her number,' said Claudia. She punched it into her mobile and waited as it rang.

'Hello? What is it?' asked a breathless voice.

Claudia explained what was happening on this side of the blaze and asked if the village hall could be opened. 'My company will pay for it if you wish.'

'Oh, I should have thought of that myself,' said Elizabeth. 'Can you get people up there? The road is shut off on this side as well.'

'There are a few cars here. We could ferry people round. It's got to be better than standing on the roadside.'

'I agree. I'll go and put the urn on.'

And make a cup of tea, thought Claudia with a smile. *The English answer to everything.*

The local man seemed happy to take charge of the families. She let him organise them into the available vehicles. By now, more cars had arrived, some with relatives of the affected families in them. In short order, a convoy was setting off to circumnavigate the village.

Another crash and roar from the pub made Claudia and Jamie turn back to the fire. His face flickered red and yellow as it reflected the flames. In a devilish way, it made him look even more handsome. She knew her own would look just as demonic, but was it attractive to him? With a huge bang, something exploded. Claudia jumped in shock.

'There goes the gas in the portacabin,' said Jamie. 'I did warn the fireman in charge. Perhaps we should go to the village hall as well.'

'If we can find it,' said Claudia, and they headed to her car.

CHAPTER 15

Sara lay on her bed with the windows open to combat the night-time heat. She barely managed to doze. Even Tilly had abandoned her, lying stretched out on Sara's old dressing gown crumpled in a corner. The ringing of her mobile on the bedside cabinet sounded shrill in the velvety-dark, airless room. With a sigh, Sara picked it up.

'DC Noble? Are you on call or something?' They all had each other's contact details, but she was aware that none of them needed to be available tonight. Her alarm clock blinked red in the gloom, telling her it was well after one in the morning.

'I'm sorry if I woke you,' said Noble. 'I thought you might like to know about this. West Ruston isn't far from you, is it?'

'Other side of the Marlham Road.' Sara pulled herself up and glanced at the lounging cat. Tilly frowned at the disturbance. 'What's up?'

'I was checking on the fire service website again.'

'At home? In your own time?' Sara didn't tell him he needed to get a life, not when she needed one herself.

'I know,' mumbled Noble. 'Girlfriend's in Ibiza with her mates. Hen party. I'm on my own.'

'Well?'

'Do you remember there being a pub in West Ruston? The Hog in Armour?'

'Vaguely.' Sara sometimes used the road as a cut-through to North Walsham.

'It's burning. Big shout. Engines going from all over the county. What if it's been set deliberately?'

'It's a long way from Belaugh if it has been. Can the service tell yet?'

'Don't know. North Walsham nick is out there shutting the area down. Just wondered if you wanted to go and check it out.'

'Better than lying here staring at the ceiling,' she agreed. 'Want to join me?' He cheerfully agreed. In a matter of moments, Sara was dressed and in her car.

The night sky was cloudless, barely lit by a sliver of moon and twinkling with an astronomer's delight of stars. As she drove to the Marlham Road, Sara could see an orange glow in the sky across the fields. When she reached the West Ruston turning, it was flickering brightly. As she got to the outskirts, the Edwardian village hall shone from behind its hedge. Lights blazed from its windows, and the car park looked unusually full. Not far beyond the village school, Sara reached a police cordon.

'They've had to evacuate all the homes around the old pub,' said the officer she showed her warrant card to. 'Taken people down to the hall until we see how it goes.'

Leaving a message for Noble, she returned to the hall, pulling up on the gravel area next to the football pitch. The hall doors were propped open, and the accessibility ramp had been laid out, ready if required. There was a queue for the toilets just inside the front door. Sara skirted the waiting women, working her way inside the warm room.

An elderly, thin-looking woman was supervising the setting up of a tea bar. She looked well over eighty but was clearly in charge. Behind her, in a kitchen area, Sara could hear urns being filled and crockery being prepared. People were unfolding tables and unstacking chairs as others guided the less able to somewhere they could sit.

Sara introduced herself, and the woman shook her hand. 'Elizabeth Thompson. I'm chair of the village hall committee. It seemed the best place to bring people while things were difficult.'

'Clever idea of yours,' said Sara, shaking the bony fingers carefully.

'Oh, it wasn't mine. Credit where it's due. It was that lady over there.' Elizabeth pointed to a thirty-something woman who stood talking earnestly to a suntanned man of similar age. 'They're from the building company working on the pub.'

The woman was called Claudia Turner. Sara flashed her warrant card. 'You work for Coles Construction, is that right?'

The woman nodded. Her face seemed very pale. 'I've never been that close to such a large fire before.'

'I'm Jamie Waller, the site manager,' said the man beside her. Claudia seemed shaken by what she'd seen, while Jamie looked rather more excited than frightened.

'Can you tell me about what state the site was in?'

'It's early days,' said Jamie. 'This is only our second week, so we were still clearing the rubbish out of the old garden and the fittings from the pub.'

'How long would you allow for the whole project?'

'Six months, maybe seven.'

'How do you think the fire might have started? Old cabling or something?'

'I'd be surprised.' Jamie sounded thoughtful. 'There's no power in there. It was cut off for safety reasons. I think it's probably kids mucking about.'

'Really? Why?'

Through the village hall windows, car headlights announced another arrival. A moment later, the queue for the ladies' toilet parted to let DC Noble in. He paused to scan the room until he spotted Sara.

'Just in time,' said Sara as he joined them. 'Jamie, why do you say it was kids? How did you know to come out to the site?'

Jamie stood close to Claudia. He could barely take his eyes off his colleague. The woman looked at him gratefully, distracting him.

'I got a phone call. There are ten other housing association properties next to the pub. One of the tenants agreed to keep an eye on things at night.'

'And this person rang you?'

'Said it woke him up when it started. Sounded like an explosion. It was already blazing when he got outside to check. He called 999 and then me.'

Sara felt her stomach sink. The setup sounded so amateur. 'You don't have a professional security patrol?'

'Officially, yes. They drive by a couple of times in the night. I often find someone local is more likely to spot something, to be honest. Naturally, when we started on the site, they were interested to see what was happening, so I chatted with them. Keeping in with the neighbours is part of my job. They call it "considerate construction".'

'These security men, is their route always the same?'

'I think it may be.'

'Someone could work out when they had been and were next due back?' asked Sara. Jamie nodded. She indicated DC Noble. 'Give their details to the officer here, would you?'

'They're in the site office,' said Jamie. He suddenly looked tired. 'I expect that will have burned down too.'

'I'll have them at the main office,' said Claudia quietly. 'I can give them to you in the morning.'

'Fine. Jamie, do you have any suggestions on how a fire could start?'

'There was a large pile of dead wood in the garden area, where we'd cleared the old trees and shrubs.'

'And some old panelling and fixtures from inside the pub,' added Claudia.

Sara rolled her eyes at Noble. 'A bonfire, in other words.'

'Yes, you could see it that way,' said Jamie defensively. 'I had a couple of skips coming in the morning to load it all into. It's so quiet out here. I never thought someone would deliberately start a fire.'

'Why do you think it was deliberate? What made you say it was kids?' she asked again.

'There's a footpath between the pub and the houses,' said Jamie. Sara waited for him to explain the tangential comment. 'It leads to the old common and the other side of the village. Our tenant said he heard someone out there when he went to bed.'

'Is it possible to see into the site from this path? To see this wood pile?'

'Yeah, I guess you can,' he said. 'And there was the moped.'

'A moped?' asked Sara quickly.

'When he called me,' explained Jamie. 'The tenant said he'd heard one driving away along the footpath just after the explosion.'

CHAPTER 16

Wednesday promised to be even hotter than the previous day. It didn't help Jean with her warring emotions. She preferred the autumn and spring, when the weather was neither one extreme nor the other. This hot weather drained her and did nothing to improve her temper. It tended to send her blood sugars crazy too, partly because she didn't eat well when she was hot. It had been nearly a year since the doctor warned her to consider working less and looking after herself more before prescribing a tablet regime. Jean felt revealing her diabetes diagnosis to Faye and Darren would put even more pressure on the couple as they all struggled to keep the business afloat. Now, she regretted deciding to keep it to herself.

Faye and Darren had left the house last night with a small holdall. Jean assumed it contained a few clothes. They certainly hadn't slept in the farmhouse. As she opened the front gate this morning, their car was in the passing place a few yards down the road. They'd turned up for work, at least. Uncertain of what to say to either of them, Jean continued her unlocking routine, giving Rachel her café float and setting up the till in the gaudily painted sales shed. Darren appeared in the doorway as she noisily dropped the last coins into the till drawer.

'I'll carry on in the barn this morning,' he said, his voice careful and devoid of emotion. 'Faye is going to be in the polytunnels. We'd both appreciate being left alone.'

Jean pushed angrily past Darren to stomp across the gravel to the farmhouse. Downing a large glass of orange juice, she worked in the office for an hour, mulling over their row from the previous evening as if she hadn't spent most of the night worrying about it. A new spreadsheet winked on her screen. Jean had been trying to find out if she could afford that bungalow. Unable to bear it any longer, she went to the kitchen behind the café and prepared three lots of coffee as an excuse to track the pair down. She needed to clear the air with them. The local radio station news was blaring above the rattling of Mavis preparing fresh bakery items.

Another devastating fire hit a rural village during the night. A building site belonging to the Georgian Housing Association was discovered to be alight just before 1 a.m. by a local resident. Police and fire crews from around the county were in attendance. It took several hours to control the incident, and the old Hog in Armour public house has been largely destroyed. Our reporter spoke to the CEO of the housing association.

'Would you like some flapjack with those?' asked Mavis. 'Freshly baked.'

Jean turned to find a tray for the drinks. 'No, thanks. Sounds like that fire was deliberate too.'

'Why would anyone want to destroy an old building like that?' asked Faye from the doorway. Jean hadn't noticed her coming across the busy yard. 'Especially when they were converting it to provide affordable housing for local people.'

She had addressed the comment to Mavis, who looked up from spreading egg wash on a batch of sausage rolls. 'Sounds like a bad business.'

Faye pushed past her mother and took a couple of mugs down from the staff cupboard.

'I've already made these for you,' said Jean. She pointed to the three mugs on the worktop. Faye looked stonily at her. For a moment, Jean wondered if her daughter would ignore her and pour fresh drinks. She pointed to the end mug. 'That one's for you. That's for Darren.'

Faye grabbed the mugs without a word and marched back outside. Jean could feel the inquisitive gaze of the cook on the back of her neck. Her cheeks flamed with embarrassment.

'Kids, eh?' said Mavis sympathetically. Jean grabbed the final mug and strode after Faye to the barn where Darren was working.

'Did you have to embarrass me in front of the staff?' she demanded. She swayed angrily, coffee slopping onto the baked earth floor.

Faye turned slowly to look at her mother. She sipped her coffee before answering. 'Did you have to embarrass me in front of two police detectives? Or in front of that driver yesterday? Or all the other times? Now you know how it feels.'

Jean gasped. 'All what other times?'

'Please don't argue again,' said Darren. He reached for his jacket and pulled an envelope from an inside pocket. 'Are you sure about this? Only if you want to.'

Faye nodded.

Darren held the envelope out to Jean. 'This is for you.'

Jean balanced her mug on a pile of rubbish, slopping hot coffee on her legs. She didn't feel the hot dampness as she stared at the white paper, grubby with finger marks. 'What's this?'

'We've had enough,' said Faye, watching her mother intently. 'We're resigning.'

'You can't just resign,' barked Jean with frustration. 'You're partners in the business.'

'Unofficially,' said Darren quietly. 'You never actually did the legal paperwork, did you?'

Jean spluttered a denial. But they all knew this was true.

'We would've had to sign it,' Darren went on, 'and we've never done that.'

'Where is all this coming from? If it's just about the paperwork, we can sort that out.'

'We talked all night, and we've made our minds up,' said Faye. Her eyes flashed with anger. 'Darren will finish sorting out the barn. I'll make sure the polytunnels are in good shape. Then you'll have to get some paid staff in.'

'Haven't I always looked out for you?' demanded Jean. 'Taken care of you?'

'Taken advantage of us, more like,' replied Faye. 'We'll work out our four weeks' notice. Even though we're not obliged to do so. After that, we'll be leaving.'

Jean took two deep breaths to calm herself. 'Look, this is ridiculous. You don't need to do this. I've been looking at the figures all night. We can make some changes.'

'Such as?' asked Darren.

'The business really doesn't make much money. You can come and see for yourselves. I might be able to find enough each month to rent a small place locally for you to live in for now.'

'For now? And how long would that last?' asked Faye. Her voice was hard and cold. 'Listen to yourself, Mother. Everything is always just "for now". Until it's convenient for you to change something, and that time never arrives, does it?'

'It will,' said Jean urgently. 'I promise it will. I've been bashing figures most of the night. If we can get some extra income from using this barn, and extend the season like Darren suggested, then there might be enough to pay a mortgage for you.'

'For us?' asked Darren sadly. 'Why not for you? A bungalow would be easier for you to manage in the future. We could do things with the farmhouse you won't even consider.'

'Such as? I'm willing to try anything you suggest.' Jean knew it sounded as if she were begging. Her heart hammered in her chest. It was hard to accept that she was reliant on these two when she'd been independent all her life.

'Bed and breakfast rooms,' said Faye. 'We've talked about it before.'

Jean opened her mouth and then slammed it shut again. She couldn't bear the thought of strangers in her home. She felt defeated. 'I just don't feel comfortable with it.'

'You need to face up to things,' snapped Faye. 'Something has to be done or the place will go under.'

'What do you think I've been trying to do?'

'I'm going back to the tunnels,' said Faye with a shrug. 'There's still loads to do.'

As she walked past, Jean grabbed her arm. 'Faye, you know I love you, don't you? I'd do anything to help you.'

Faye's lip curled in derision. 'Too little, too late.'

Jean watched her daughter's retreating back with horror.

CHAPTER 17

They had left the village hall in the small hours. Sara had emailed DCI Hudson and Aggie, telling them they would be late. Sara and Noble reached the car park at the Wymondham HQ at the same time the next morning, and they trudged up the stairs to the SCU office together.

'Gosh!' said Aggie. 'You do look tired.'

'Thanks,' said Sara sarcastically. She dropped her bag on her desk. Aggie looked apologetic and tapped on the lid of a cake tin in recompense, which made Sara smile. 'You're right. I think we both are.'

DI Edwards was absent, and Bowen was on the phone. DCI Hudson was almost submerged behind piles of paperwork on her desk. She looked up when Sara knocked on the open glass door.

'You got my message?'

'Yes, thank you,' said Hudson. The DCI stretched and yawned. Rubbing her face tiredly, she pushed the paperwork to one side. 'If they give me any more bloody financial stuff to go over, I think I'll go mad. Shall we do some proper police work?'

They gathered around the incident board. Aggie had stuck up pictures of the fire at West Ruston, which she'd found on the local news website. Noble explained why they had gone out in the middle of the night. Hudson looked at him with one eyebrow raised quizzically.

'I know,' said Noble. 'I should get a life.'

'Your dedication has potentially brought us a new lead,' said Hudson. 'Well done. Tell us about it.' Sara and Noble filled in the team about their overnight adventure.

'We definitely need to speak to this neighbour who reported the fire,' said Hudson. 'DI Edwards is already at the site with the fire chief and a forensic team. Noble, let him know about this neighbour and tell him to have a word.'

Noble nodded and began to type a text on his mobile. DCI Hudson grabbed a pen and started an action list on the board. Despite her protestations, the DCI usually loved organising other people and doing paperwork. Today she seemed overwhelmed and grumpy about it.

'You think it has to be deliberate?' asked Sara.

'I'd be surprised if it isn't,' replied Hudson. 'What do you think?'

'I think it's possible,' agreed Sara. 'But it's a long way from Belaugh Manor Farm, and the Willmott family have no connection with the site as far as we know.'

'Double-check that,' said Hudson sharply. 'Call Mrs Lawson in Devon or Mr Willmott senior. Get the contact details for this friend that Mrs Lawson stayed with on her visit too. You should have done that the first time.'

Sara felt offended. 'I did, ma'am. I just haven't had time to follow it up.'

'Then find time. Aggie, find out who this woman is. Check out Mrs Lawson's alibi.'

Sara schooled her face into stony stillness at the criticism. There was no call for Hudson to speak to her like that, not after the DCI had said it wasn't a priority. Giving Sara's action to Aggie to follow up felt like a deliberate insult. Sara clenched her jaw in annoyance as Hudson turned away to scan the maps on the board. Her boss wasn't going to back down now.

'Erm, it's about ten miles from Belaugh to West Ruston,' offered Aggie quietly. She glanced at Sara and pulled a sympathetic face.

'No great distance at all, in fact,' said Hudson, her tone still critical. She stabbed at the larger-scale map. 'This village isn't far from North Walsham, is it?'

Sara leaned back in her chair and folded her arms mutinously. The woman was pushing her buttons, given how little sleep she'd had, and Sara wasn't going to give her any further reason to have a go at her.

'Three or four miles,' said Bowen carefully.

'We get a fair amount of trouble there, don't we?' demanded Hudson. She turned to glare at the DC.

'Sometimes.' He shrugged. 'Petty crime, mostly. A bit of low-grade drugs stuff now and then.'

'So, what about local troublemakers? Youngsters with ASBOs, or druggies. Get a list of those, and let's knock on a few doors. See if any of the little buggers have been playing bonfires.'

DC Bowen frowned in frustration. Sara reckoned he felt the same as her. It would be a waste of time. Things were rarely that random. 'Yes, ma'am.'

'We also need to arrange a bunch of interviews,' snapped Hudson. 'Hirst, get some uniformed officers to interview all the people who live around the site.'

'Ma'am.'

'Clearly, this isn't just about Willmott's farm.' Hudson turned back to the whiteboard. 'The unreported incident at Howards UK. Where does that fit?'

'The Howards attack would be between fire two and three at Willmott's,' said Noble. 'The fire that caught Wild Thyme was attack number four on their land.'

'There may be other fires that people haven't reported,' mused Hudson. 'Ask around when you are at that meeting tomorrow night.'

Sara scribbled a note in her book.

'We also need to interview everyone working on or visiting the site,' continued Hudson. 'Make sure no one has a grudge or gripe. My gut tells me this is all part of the same thing.'

'Might this moped the neighbour heard be the same one the security guards saw?' asked Noble.

'It could belong to anyone,' said Bowen guardedly. 'It might not have anything to do with it.'

'It can't be a coincidence.' Hudson rolled her eyes in exasperation.

'We can hardly search for every registered moped in the area, right?'

'They don't have a long range or a high speed,' said Noble. Bowen shot him a furious look. He hated having to deal with vehicle searches. 'We could limit the search to a given radius.'

'Make it a fifteen-mile radius of Belaugh,' said Hudson. 'What about traffic cameras?'

'Nothing on the back roads,' said Bowen grumpily. 'Only some of the main roads.'

'Aggie, you get a list of registered mopeds. Bowen, you get on to traffic and see if they've got anything on the given nights, especially last night.' She turned to Sara. 'You two write up your reports, then we must arrange the interviews with the builder's staff. That can't be palmed off on to local officers.'

Hudson threw her whiteboard marker down on the desk in front of her. She strode back to her office, pulling the door closed with a bang. They watched as she sat in her chair with a bump and pulled a pile of files in front of her.

'What was that all about?' breathed Aggie.

'God only knows,' muttered Sara. They scattered back to their desks, and Sara logged on to her computer. She focused on her report about the previous night for the next twenty minutes, the only distraction the sound of the cake tin lid being levered off. Her stomach grumbled as her mobile rang.

'Yes, boss?'

'Glad to hear you're in,' said DI Edwards.

'How's it going at West Ruston?'

'Definitely a deliberate fire. Accelerant's been splashed around the garden and against one of the front doors. Can you do me a favour?'

'Sure,' replied Sara.

'Run a list of locally registered mopeds with the prefix AP19 for me.' Edwards sounded exasperated. 'I know it's only the front end of the number, but the neighbour swears it was on the moped he spotted driving away.'

CHAPTER 18

Claudia had gone home to shower and change before heading into the office without trying to get any sleep. The company owner was standing in the yard with the men who should have been working at West Ruston. Claudia's two office staff and the warehouse team stood behind them, listening. Mr Cole lost no time advising everyone of the fires and telling them the site was closed for forensic investigations.

'Make yourselves useful tidying up the yard,' he said. 'You'll either be reallocated for tomorrow or preparing to clear the West Ruston site for demolition if that's what the client decides.'

With a sinking feeling, Claudia realised she was in for a long day. The boss called her into his office.

'The site could be shut down for days,' grumbled Mr Cole.

'I expect the authorities will want to interview everyone,' she suggested.

Mr Cole grumbled even more. 'You'd better dig out our insurance stuff. No doubt the housing association will try to pin the blame on us. Keep the men here today, and I'll see where they'd best go tomorrow.'

'Where's Jamie?' asked Claudia.

'Thought he'd gone home for a sleep,' said Mr Cole. 'Have you had any rest?'

'Not yet.'

'Don't stay too long, then. Get off once you've got that paperwork out.'

Claudia ignored him and, through a mixture of caffeine and sugar, was still at her desk when Jamie climbed up to her office well after lunchtime. He had a guest with him.

'DI Edwards,' said the man, holding out a warrant card. 'Norfolk Constabulary, Serious Crimes Unit.'

'DI Edwards has been out at the site working with the fire investigators and forensic team,' explained Jamie with a yawn. There were dark circles under his eyes.

'Haven't you been home either?' asked Claudia, trying not to imitate him. She resisted an urge to reach for his hand and comfort him. Jamie shook his head.

DI Edwards eyed the pair. 'You were both at the fire last night, I believe?'

They filled him in on what they had heard and seen.

'I've spoken to your volunteer watchman and neighbour,' he said when they'd finished. 'As you say, he's adamant he saw a moped leaving the scene.'

'Were there any other witnesses?' asked Claudia.

'Not so far. Most people were in bed when it started.'

'What I don't understand,' began Jamie, 'is how anyone would know the wood pile was there.'

'You seem convinced it started there,' said Edwards. 'Could the building have been the main target?'

'I suppose so. Why was any of it a target?'

'Was there opposition to the new houses?'

'Some,' said Claudia. 'There's always a bit of nimbyism on any social housing project. It didn't amount to much. A few letters to the papers. One or two loud voices at a village hall open meeting I attended.'

'The project is small and reusing a brownfield site,' added Jamie. 'I think it would have been approved regardless because it fits the council's current planning objectives.

Would have been a different matter if it had been holiday homes.'

'Do you have a record of who was objecting?'

'I don't,' said Claudia. 'The parish council or village hall committee might, as they organised it.'

'Okay. I'll get the team to talk with them. We also need to interview all the workers from the site.'

'I don't think any of my team would have started a fire,' objected Jamie angrily. 'It would jeopardise their jobs for a start.'

'I'm not saying they would,' said Edwards calmly. 'However, they may have seen or heard something. Anything, no matter how small, can be helpful. They'll need to tell us where they were last night as well. Can you provide me with a list of staff and visitors?'

'I can do the staff. Visitors, Jamie?' Claudia shot a quick frown at Jamie, who settled back in his chair with a grimace. The urge to comfort him was being replaced by a sense of annoyance.

'My logbook has gone up in the portacabin,' he mumbled. 'Along with all my paperwork.'

'You've only been there a few days,' said Claudia. 'You should be able to remember most of them.'

'I suppose so.'

Claudia smiled brightly. 'I think Jamie and I are just tired.'

'No problem,' said Edwards. He took out his mobile. 'Why don't I arrange for a team to come over tomorrow morning to start taking statements? Perhaps you can ensure the men will be here until we've had the chance to speak to each of them?'

'I'll have a word with Mr Cole,' Claudia assured him.

When she had shown the DI out to the yard, Claudia heard Jamie clomping down the metal stairs from the offices. She rounded on him.

'What was that all about?' she asked. She was annoyed, although she kept the volume low. 'Why don't you want to be helpful? This will be enough of a headache without you being difficult.'

Jamie blushed under his suntan. He had a mulish look that spoiled his handsome face. 'I didn't like the suggestion that one of our workers might be responsible.'

'Most of your team have been with us for years. None of them has ever been a problem, have they?'

Jamie shook his head and hissed, 'Only Kyle.'

'Kyle? Eric keeps a good eye on him, doesn't he?'

'Eric's great with him,' said Jamie. He glanced over his shoulder and scanned the yard behind Claudia. Then he grabbed her arm.

'Come and look at this.' He was pinching the flesh with his fingers.

'Let go,' she muttered and batted at his hand.

'Sorry.'

Jamie waited until the DI's car had vanished down the estate road. Then he pulled his mobile out of his pocket and waved it at her. 'After you'd gone last night, I searched on the profile of likely arsonists.'

'For God's sake, Jamie. Leave that stuff to the police and the fire investigators.'

'More likely to be male,' persisted Jamie. 'Usually between ten and twenty-five, peaking as late teenagers. Also, likely to be local and connected to the sites.'

'Which makes you suspect poor Kyle?' asked Claudia in astonishment. 'That could apply to loads of kids in the area.'

'You know that one of the tenants heard a moped driving off?' Claudia nodded. Jamie pressed on. 'I overheard the partial plate number: AP19. He didn't get the rest. Kyle's moped has that.'

'So? There could be dozens of the things starting with that.'

'Go and look at Kyle's moped!' snapped Jamie.

Claudia glanced at the parking area. Kyle's moped was two spaces away from her own vehicle. Kyle was on the far side of the yard, leaning casually against a pile of pallets, having a sneaky break. Eric Beatty stood nearby, chatting to the warehouse manager. The youngster was taller than both the older men. He looked healthy and well-built. Like most of the outdoor staff, he had a deep suntan. His dark hair was cut with a fashionable floppy fringe.

On the pretence of going to her own car, Claudia walked slowly past the red-and-black moped. She was tired and had to scan her memory of seeing it the day before. There was a big gouge out of the paint that she couldn't remember seeing before. The wing mirror on the left side was bent and broken. The number plate began AP19.

CHAPTER 19

Sara was grateful for the light coastal breeze that played around her garden that evening. It was still hot and promised to be another night of little sleep. She took her plate of salad outside and settled on the old plastic garden furniture to eat it. The salad was an attempt to counteract the endless supply of cakes in the office. Dante had been out of the office all day. There were several missed calls from him, which Sara had failed to return. After washing up, she thought about walking on the beach until a visitor knocking at her front door distracted her. She wasn't surprised to find Gilly standing there.

'I thought you'd be in,' said Gilly, pointing at Sara's car. 'I always keep my promises and wanted you to meet Adie Dickinson, the gardener I was telling you about.'

Gilly pulled forward a suntanned man in his late twenties. He was taller than Sara, which was unusual given her own height. His blonde hair fell in dreadlocks around his shoulders and was pulled back from his face by a multi-coloured headband. He wore a sleeveless hemp T-shirt revealing arms that rippled with muscles. Thigh muscles bulged from worn and torn jeans. He held out his hand. When Sara shook it, his grip was firm without being overpowering. He was the most handsome man she had seen in years.

'Shall we come through to look at the work?' asked Gilly. She grinned smugly as she pushed past Sara and into the cottage. 'This way, Adie.'

'Is that okay?' asked Adie in posh tones, making Sara wonder at his family background. 'I don't want to intrude.'

'Yes, of course.'

Adie slipped gently past her to follow Gilly, who was already in the kitchen. Sara shut the front door with a snap and followed them into the garden. Adie was as toned from behind as he was from the front.

* * *

It might have been the previous night's adventures, but Sara was deeply asleep when her mobile rang at half past one. Groping for it on the bedside cabinet, she was unsurprised to see it was DC Noble again.

'Are you sitting up all night again?' she asked grumpily as she rolled back onto her bed.

'Yes, but this one is massive,' said Noble excitedly. 'It's that herb farm where you and Bowen went. An old barn in the middle of the place.'

'Jesus,' said Sara. 'Poor buggers. If it's the one I'm thinking of, their house is next to it.'

'Any chance of it being an accident?'

'Very little. The barn is in the middle of the yard. Unless things around it have also gone up, it's been targeted.'

'Should I ring the rest of the team?'

'I'll go. You can come too, and ring the boss as well.' She meant DI Edwards.

Tilly wound around Sara's legs as she pulled on her clothes. In self-defence, she took the cat downstairs and gave her some extra food. While the cat snacked, Sara escaped and set off for Wild Thyme.

It took her nearly half an hour to get there. Despite producing her warrant card, Sara couldn't drive inside the cordoned-off minor road that led past the herb farm. She swung on to the verge and continued on foot until a shout behind her pulled her up.

'You were quick,' she said as DC Noble jogged up beside her.

'Did my best.' He rubbed his face with both hands.

'You been to bed at all?'

'Nope.'

'Oh, to be young again,' murmured Sara. Noble laughed at her.

They crossed another minor road, flashing their warrant cards at the duty officer. The lane leading to Wild Thyme was jammed with fire engines. Hoses ran along the hedge and from engine to engine. Another truck, with 'Major Incident Office' on the side, blocked access. The side door was open and lights blazed outwards. Sara climbed up the metal staircase and went inside.

'Sign yourselves in,' instructed an officer when he had inspected their credentials. 'Be vigilant and wear these if you're going in the yard.' He handed them hi-vis vests. 'The man in charge is Area Manager Russ Lowe. Report to him first.'

Generators had been hauled into the car park. Poles with banks of LED lamps attached were lighting the place brighter than daytime. Russ Lowe was easy to spot. He stood near a small red fire service van talking to three other firefighters in various layers of protective garb. If he was surprised to find two police detectives appearing in the middle of the incident, he didn't say so.

'You want a quick precis?' he asked. He wrote something on a clipboard and threw it in the back of the van. 'We've been here about an hour. Responded to a 999 call from the resident of the farmhouse. The place was well alight by the time the first two tenders arrived. They upgraded it to a major incident.'

He pointed to the barn. They were at least thirty yards away from it, but Sara could feel the heat pouring off the walls. Several ground-level hoses were directing a steady, strong rush of water at the old brick walls, making them steam in the hot night air. Small pockets of flames still burned among the thatch on the roof. Firefighters aimed water jets from hydraulic ladders at the thatch. As an area of flame was doused, they continued to pour water on to the same patch until it fell inside the barn with a wet thump.

'It would be thatch, wouldn't it?' said Lowe in exasperation. 'Looks like the building wasn't well maintained. The walls have been doused, but we've lost anything wooden. Windows, doors, floors. Just the roof to put out now.'

'At least you managed to stop it from getting next door.' Sara waved at the farmhouse. 'Where are the family?'

Lowe checked his clipboard again. 'There was a Mrs Simpson. She was the one who called us. Says she's the only person here.'

Sara glanced at Noble. 'I thought her daughter and son-in-law lived here too?'

'Not here tonight, at any rate. Mrs Simpson offered to open the café in case the lads needed any refreshments. She should be over there now.'

'You let her do that?' asked Sara.

'Have you met Mrs Simpson?' asked Lowe with a smile. 'Hard lady to say no to. Besides, my risk assessment was that it was an acceptable distance away. The lads are going over for tea in small shifts. They'll be keeping an eye out, trust me.'

What was it about making cups of tea on the edge of chaos, Sara wondered? Like some knee-jerk reaction, every English person reached for the kettle in times of crisis. A handful of fire officers stood in the courtyard sipping at mugs and talking. Sara led Noble past them into the brightly lit café. The owner of Wild Thyme was filling a large teapot from an urn.

'Mrs Simpson?'

The woman spun round. 'Oh, I wasn't expecting you. Would you like some tea?'

'No, thanks. I'd like to talk to you, though. When did you notice the fire?'

Mrs Simpson came out from behind the counter and slumped into a seat by a pine table. 'God! This is such a mess.'

'At least they got here in time to save your house,' said Sara, sitting opposite her. She hadn't asked how old the woman was when they'd visited the other day. It hadn't seemed relevant. Whatever her actual age, Mrs Simpson seemed to have aged ten years since they last saw her. 'Are you up to talking about it yet?'

Mrs Simpson nodded wearily. 'I'd gone to bed. It's so hot that I haven't been sleeping well, and I was only dozing. Then I heard a noise. When I saw the barn was on fire, I called 999.'

'What time was this?'

She looked up at the clock on the café wall and frowned. 'Maybe two hours ago?'

'Mrs Simpson, where are Faye and her husband?'

'Staying at his parents' place for a few nights,' she replied. Her chin began to wobble as she held back tears.

'Have you rung them?' asked Sara gently. When Mrs Simpson shook her head, Sara continued, 'I think you should. No point in dealing with this all on your own.'

'My mobile is in the house,' said Mrs Simpson vaguely. 'I'm so confused, I can't remember their numbers. I never need to call them.'

'Shall one of us fetch it for you?' asked Sara.

'Please. It's on the kitchen table, I think.'

When Sara got back to Russ Lowe, DI Edwards was there. 'Evening, Sara. Or should I say morning?'

'Is it okay to go into the farmhouse?' Sara asked Lowe when she had greeted her boss. 'Mrs Simpson thinks her mobile is in there, and she needs it.'

'I'll authorise that,' said Lowe.

Before Sara could move, a fire officer in full breathing apparatus hurried up to them. He ripped the helmet off so they could hear him. 'Is anyone missing? Staff? Family?'

'Not according to the owner,' replied Lowe. 'Why?'

'I've just done a first check inside,' said the man hurriedly. 'It's difficult to be sure with such poor visibility, but I think we have a problem. Should we keep going, or is there likely to be something inside that might look like a person?'

Footsteps crunched on the gravel of the car park. Sara heard her boss say, 'You should be sitting down, Mrs Simpson.'

Her face pale and drawn, Mrs Simpson approached the fireman. 'What do you mean?'

'Is anything stored in the barn that could look human-shaped?' asked the fireman. 'Life-sized figures for display purposes, maybe?'

'No,' said Mrs Simpson quietly. 'Just old farm equipment. Some tables from the café.'

'I'm afraid you'd better go in and double-check,' said Lowe to the officer, who nodded and began to pull his breathing helmet into place.

Mrs Simpson's face crumpled. 'You think there might be someone in there? Caught in the fire?'

CHAPTER 20

Jean hadn't liked the tall detective with the modern braids during their previous meeting. She felt that the woman hadn't believed her for some reason, which put Jean's back up. By seven o'clock on Thursday morning, she had revised her opinion. DS Sara Hirst had taken control of Jean's well-being and looked after her throughout the night. She had brought Jean's mobile from the kitchen, and when neither Faye nor Darren answered, DS Hirst promised to stay with her until they turned up for work.

'Is there no one else you can go to stay with?' the sergeant asked. 'A relative or friend? You might not be allowed back in the house for a while, and you've been up all night.'

Jean surveyed the remaining fire engines in the early morning light. The barn smouldered and steamed. Firemen were pulling down the remaining thatch from the front of the roof and soaking it with their hoses.

'Later today?' Jean asked.

'There will have to be various investigations,' replied the DS. 'Fire officers to begin with, then maybe our forensic people. Did you manage to reach your daughter? Why don't you try again?'

Faye's mobile went to voicemail, as it had been all night. 'I'd better let Rachel and the other staff know.'

Wearily, Jean rang the three people she had been expecting that day, telling them to stay at home and assuring them they would be paid anyway. Hirst yawned. Everyone had been up all night, realised Jean, although, with her diabetes running wild already, she would cope far less well than they could. At least they were young and fit. Slumped at a courtyard table, Jean stared at the pastry in front of her, unable to raise the energy to lift it. The stink of burning wood and damp thatch hung in the air. It was so acrid it made her cough. Jean felt her head droop on to her chest, and she dozed for a few minutes. With a rasping gulp of air, she shook herself awake again. Hirst sat beside her, watching carefully. Jean looked at the chaos in the yard. It was out of focus, and she realised she was crying again. Scrabbling in her cardigan pocket, she found a tissue and angrily blew her nose.

'What time is it?'

'Half past seven,' replied Hirst. 'Here comes the boss.'

The man was in his mid-fifties. He also looked tired. Fire Officer Lowe walked next to him.

'I'm happy for you to return to your house soon,' said Lowe. 'I'm afraid the area will smell of burning for days. We'll also be here all day doing our investigations, which could be intrusive.'

'I understand,' said Jean. 'I have nowhere else to go.'

'We don't know what's in the barn yet,' said Edwards. Jean could feel him watching her for a reaction. 'There may have to be extensive forensic investigations, and you won't be able to open the nursery again for some time. It won't be easy for you.'

'Are you saying that there is a dead person in the barn?'

'I'm afraid it looks that way, Mrs Simpson.'

'That's awful. What a terrible way to die, being trapped in there.' Jean couldn't stop the sobs. She felt Hirst slip an arm around her shoulder and leaned against the woman, grateful for her strength. 'Oh, and what will it mean for us? Who will want to come here now?'

'Mrs Simpson, I have to ask you a few questions,' said Edwards. 'Can you manage that?'

'I suppose so.' Jean tried to straighten up.

'Do you have any idea who might have been in the barn?'

'None at all.' Jean sucked in a noisy breath to calm herself. 'There's only me, my daughter and her husband here at night. But they're away for a few days.'

'Is the building locked at night?'

'It has been for years.'

'You were hoping to use it again, weren't you?' asked Hirst. 'When we visited you the other day, that's what you said.'

'Darren has been clearing it out recently. To see what we might do with it.'

'Could he have left it unlocked?'

'It's possible. Do you think someone might have wandered in there? Or broken in?'

'What made you think of that?' Hirst frowned.

Jean shifted uneasily on her chair. 'There was a tramp hanging around a few days ago near the back gate. I sent him off as quick as. Then Mavis, our cook, saw him later near the front gate.'

'Did you move him on again?'

'I didn't see him that time,' replied Jean. 'I would have told him to leave if I had. Instead, Mavis gave him a sandwich and a piece of cake. I wish she hadn't. Charity only encourages them to come back.'

'Do you have CCTV?' asked Edwards. 'Would it cover the barn?'

'No, we don't,' muttered Jean. 'Never needed it and couldn't afford it.'

'That really is a shame,' said the inspector. Jean was sure he might have said more, but a white van with a large aerial pulled up outside the gate with a spray of dust from the dry road.

'Oh God,' Edwards groaned. 'The news people are on to it. Hirst, go and sort them out, will you?'

'Statement, sir?'

'Later. I'll speak to the big boss first. They prefer to do that sort of thing. And get some uniform backup to keep them at bay.'

'Who is it?' asked Jean as the DS marched away to prevent the people climbing out of the van from getting into the car park. She was talking rapidly on her mobile.

'Looks like ITV. It could still be local.' Edwards turned his attention back to Jean. She had been hoping the distraction would move him on.

'Mrs Simpson,' he said quietly, 'I'm going to have to be blunt. Can you think of anyone who might want to harm you? Or who might have a grudge against you or the business?'

It was the question she had been dreading. Before she could answer, her mobile vibrated, making it dance on the wooden tabletop. She grabbed it.

'Mum? Why have you been calling me so often?' Thank goodness, it was Faye. 'And is Darren with you? He's been missing all night, and I can't get him on his mobile.'

CHAPTER 21

Kyle had not been happy at Claudia checking out his bike, and an argument had begun to break out. Realising they were tired, Claudia had sent Jamie and Kyle home and went home shortly afterwards herself. Despite the heat, she slept for over twelve hours, and this morning felt better than anticipated. Expecting the police to need somewhere private to interview people, Claudia moved her laptop into the front office, leaving her room for their use. She caught one of the other office staff rolling their eyes heavenwards as she settled to work on the spare desk.

'We'll have to put up with it for today,' she said blithely. She dropped a notepad on to her assistant's desk. 'You can start by reallocating these people in the schedule. Leave Jamie at West Ruston.'

The interview team arrived at 9 a.m. exactly. Claudia was surprised to hear one of the officers introduce herself as DCI Hudson.

'I wasn't expecting anyone with such a high rank,' she said as they followed her upstairs.

'I wouldn't normally be this hands-on. But there you go,' said DCI Hudson in a grumpy tone. 'This is DC Mike Bowen.'

The man grinned cheekily at Claudia. He carried a buff folder and a laptop, which he set up on one side of her desk. Claudia handed them a list.

'This is every man who worked on the site,' she explained. 'Not everyone was there the day before the fire, but they all had access at some point. They're all waiting for you, except Jamie Waller, who's at the site with your investigators. Let me know who you want first, and I'll bring them up.'

'Fine,' snapped the DCI. She scanned the list. 'May as well start with the team leaders. Let's get on with this.'

Claudia found a small group of workmen clustered at the bottom of the metal office stairs. She asked the nearest team leader to go up, then told the rest to hang around. 'The sooner we get it done, the sooner we can all get out to the other sites.'

The detectives seemed to give each man no more than a few minutes. Claudia watched them through the partition windows when she thought no one was looking. After about an hour, DC Bowen came out to see her.

'Do you think you could organise some water?'

'Sure. Tea or coffee as well?'

'No, thanks, just the water. Cold as you like.'

She nodded to her assistant, who went off to the kitchen area in the warehouse downstairs. Bowen stood idly waiting for the drinks. Claudia leaned forward conspiratorially.

'I hope you don't mind my asking, why is there a DCI in my office? I thought having an inspector here yesterday was high-ranking enough.'

Bowen grinned and replied in a whisper, 'Had no choice. The rest of the team is at Wild Thyme Herb Farm. That left her and me.'

'Wild Thyme? I sometimes went there; they have a nice café.'

'Yeah, it's popular, I believe.'

The final team leader, Eric Beatty, clomped up the metal stairs, and Bowen led him in for his interview. When the assistant returned with the drinks, Claudia took the tray and knocked on the door. Slipping quietly in, she placed the tray on a small filing cabinet and overheard the bored voice of the DCI asking a question that she was clearly reading from a list in front of her.

Back at her laptop, Claudia typed 'Wild Thyme Herb Farm news' into her search engine. In a few seconds, she had a list of outlets showing everything from photos to live interviews outside the place.

'Looks like we're not the only ones to be targeted.' She beckoned her two assistants over. 'See?'

'Oooh!' said one. 'It says they've found a body inside.'

'Poor soul,' said the other assistant. 'What a dreadful way to die.'

'Thank goodness that didn't happen at our site. It's bad enough as it is.' Claudia shivered, and then felt guilty that she hadn't sounded more concerned. 'I mean, you're right, of course. Horrible thing to happen.'

The morning wore on, with a string of workmen coming and going to make their statements. Claudia's stomach was beginning to rumble for her lunchtime sandwich when DC Bowen followed the latest one out.

'I think there's only one more to go,' he said. 'A youngster by the name of Kyle Atkins? He's seventeen, yeah?'

'Yes, that's right.'

'If he's happy to give a voluntary statement, he'll need someone with him. An appropriate adult, as it were.'

'I can do it if he's agreeable.'

'Let's ask him, then.'

Claudia followed DC Bowen downstairs. It took a moment to spot Kyle. He was on the far side of the yard, lounging behind the pile of pallets, just as he had been yesterday. Eric Beatty hovered nearby as Bowen explained the situation.

'Are you happy to give a statement like the others?'

Kyle shrugged. 'I've got nothing to hide.'

'Never said you had, son,' said Bowen.

'I can come in with you if you like,' offered Claudia. Eric Beatty stepped up behind Kyle.

'I'll do it,' he said firmly.

Bowen looked between the two grown-ups, then back at Kyle. 'Strictly speaking, both these people represent your employers. We could do it later with your parents, if you prefer.'

'Only got my mum,' said Kyle. 'She'll be working.'

'No other family you trust?'

Kyle looked at Eric casually. Eric frowned in return. 'I'd like Eric, then. He's my uncle.'

Claudia blinked in surprise. 'You never told me that.'

Eric looked at the floor, avoiding her gaze. 'Thought you might object, and I wanted him to have the apprenticeship. It was the best way I could help him.'

Suddenly things made a lot of sense to Claudia. There was no point in going over it now; there was too much else to worry about. 'No rule against it, as far as I know.'

'Let's get this over with, then,' said Bowen breezily. 'Shouldn't take long. Up you go.'

As Eric and Kyle walked up to the office, Bowen beckoned to Claudia and pointed across the yard. 'I noticed that moped when we came in. Who does that belong to?'

Claudia paused. It was obvious even from here that the moped had been damaged, and she could hardly lie to protect the lad. 'It's Kyle's.'

CHAPTER 22

It was as if there was a truce between them. Or at least neither her daughter nor Jean referred to their previous arguments once Faye had roared up the lane in a taxi twenty minutes after their conversation. Another television crew and the local BBC radio news van had arrived. The lane outside the herb nursery was becoming crowded. The uniformed officer at the gate let Faye inside.

'I can't reach him,' she said as she stumbled across the car park. 'I've tried and tried.'

'I've tried too,' Jean assured her daughter. 'It's not the first time, is it? He could turn up any time.'

'Meaning what?' snarled Faye.

Jean was too tired to deal with her daughter's nonsense. 'The last time you had a big row, he vanished for days, didn't he?'

Faye gasped with indignation. 'Who says we've had a big row?'

'Oh, grow up, Faye. He's gone off on a bender, like last time.'

Faye's shoulders slumped and she stood swaying, looking bewildered at the mess in the car park and the burned-out barn.

'Who could have done such a thing?' she muttered.

'Vandals?' suggested Jean quietly. 'Have we offended someone? Whoever is attacking Willmott's place? God knows.'

'We could all have been burned to death in our beds,' began Faye, then she stuttered before slumping down into a chair. 'What if we had been caught in the house?'

'Well, we weren't,' snapped Jean. 'It's bad enough as it is. They say they've found someone in there.'

'Oh God!' wailed Faye. 'What if it's Darren?'

'They don't know if it's male or female yet.' Jean sat down heavily next to her daughter. 'Why would he be here anyway?'

'Why isn't he answering my calls?' demanded Faye.

Jean gave up. Faye could find catastrophe in a burned sausage roll. She'd always been that way. Jean would often encourage her to try new things, but if they didn't go to plan immediately she'd go to pieces. Only her father had been able to calm her down when she got upset. It was another thing Jean had felt excluded about.

'You should speak to that detective.' Jean pointed to DS Hirst. 'I told her what you said, and she's put out a call for Darren as missing. She asked if you had a recent photo of him.'

Faye looked around the people in the yard. 'That one? The police aren't usually very helpful.'

Hirst was heading towards them. By the time she reached them, the request for an image hovering on her lips, Faye was scrolling rapidly on her phone. The DS glanced at Jean as Faye held up her phone.

'Like this?'

'Perfect. If you could send me a copy.' They exchanged mobile numbers and Faye despatched the image. There was a moment of suspense, followed by a ping. 'Got it. Thanks. I'll get on to that. Although strictly speaking, as he's an adult, we wouldn't normally look for him yet. Are you sure he hasn't just slept at a mate's place?'

'I *tried* his best friend,' said Faye. She flashed her mother a look. 'He says they haven't met up for weeks. We're usually here all the time.' She ducked her head to hide the blush spreading across her cheeks.

'You didn't sleep here last night?' asked the detective. 'It's your busiest time of year, isn't it?'

'We've been staying at Darren's parents for a few nights,' said Faye without looking up. 'Hadn't seen them in a while.'

Jean felt Hirst examining her by the prickle of tension in her neck.

'Faye, I'm sorry to ask this.' Hirst sat opposite Faye. 'Is there any chance your husband could have returned here last night?'

'I still have his keys, the ones for here,' said Faye tearfully. 'He couldn't have got in, and his car is missing.'

'No,' snapped Jean, as the DS took Darren's car registration number from Faye. 'I would have heard him if he'd come here.'

'How?'

'We shut the front gate at night. It creaks when it opens. Or the car, I would have heard that too.'

'What about any other vehicles he could use?' asked DS Hirst. 'Your car is here, Mrs Simpson?'

Jean nodded.

'Faye? Can you drive?'

'Only my moped. Not a car. It was here, though.'

Hirst swivelled in her seat and looked around the yard. 'Where?'

'Behind that fireman's van,' said Jean.

'Wasn't it by the barn before?'

Damn the woman for being so observant, thought Jean. 'So was my car. I had to move them both when I realised the fire was bad.'

'That was very brave, Mrs Simpson.' The detective actually sounded disapproving. 'Did you try to tackle the fire at all?'

'No,' said Jean angrily. 'It was too hot after I'd moved the car. I had to wait for the fire engines.'

'That's odd, because there's an empty fire extinguisher in front of the barn. As if someone was trying to put out the initial fire. Thank you, Mrs Simpson. I'll leave you both in peace.'

Jean sighed with relief. This would just be the start of the questioning, she felt sure. Faye was blowing her nose. There was a shout, followed by more damp thatch sliding to the floor with a crash and a slither, making them both look at the barn. Dust puffed into the shimmering morning heat.

'I don't think we will be able to salvage it, do you?' Jean asked her daughter. Faye looked at her in shock.

'That could be my Darren in there, and all you can think about is the damn barn?'

'Don't be silly, Faye.' Jean was out of patience. 'Don't get hysterical.'

Before Faye could snap back an answer, there was confusion in the lane as three vehicles arrived together. One was yet another television crew. A uniformed officer waved it out of the way, while a second officer opened the gate and let in a white van marked 'Forensic Team' followed by a smart private car.

A dapper-looking man wearing a suit and bow tie despite the heat had joined the group comprised of all the detectives and Russ Lowe. Jean walked as quickly as she could to join them. Her legs were heavy with tiredness.

'I think it's safe now,' Lowe said to the inspector. 'We're just double-checking what's left of the thatch. As a precaution, I'll leave one crew on site. My investigation team are already building their picture of events.'

'Mrs Simpson,' acknowledged Edwards as Jean joined them.

'You can go back into your home,' said Hirst with a smile. 'I suspect you might need some sleep.'

Jean nodded. 'I'll take Faye with me.'

'If you hear from Darren, you will let us know, won't you? Faye has my number.'

'Of course.'

'Right,' said Edwards, 'I think it's time we all had some sleep. Hirst, you and Noble can get off home.' He waved forward the dapper man. 'Mrs Simpson, this is Dr Stephen Taylor. He's our forensic pathologist and will be directing the forensic team.'

The doctor shook Jean's hand. 'We'll be here for some time, I'm afraid. You should get some rest.'

Jean was becoming vague with tiredness. 'Thank you.'

She told Faye to come inside, and her daughter reluctantly followed her into the farmhouse. It was only a few minutes before Jean had stripped off her grimy clothes. She knew she stank of burning but was too tired to contemplate getting a shower. As she fell on to the bed, her final thought was that she'd have to deal with it later. Her eyes closed in seconds.

CHAPTER 23

Sara was grateful to have snatched a few hours of sleep before returning to the Wymondham office in the afternoon. It was still incredibly hot, and she could feel the sweat gathering on her face and back as they began the team catch-up.

'Right,' said DCI Hudson, standing at the whiteboard with her marker pen. 'I'm sure we have lots of news to share. Let's start with Wild Thyme.'

'You got my message that I sent these two home for some rest?' asked DI Edwards. He flipped a hand at Sara and DC Noble.

'Yes, thanks,' replied Hudson. 'Did you get any yourself?'

Edwards raised an eyebrow in surprise. 'Yes, thank you, ma'am. A few hours. I rang Dr Taylor for an update on the way in.'

'And?'

'They've got the body to the mortuary and will do a post-mortem tomorrow.'

'Did he give us anything?'

'Although it's badly burned, Taylor says it's a white male. He can't give an age or full cause of death until he's done the PM. From the body's position in the barn, his hypothesis is that they were trapped by the fire and tried to get out of the back through a door or window.'

'Overcome by the smoke?' asked Hudson.

'Maybe,' agreed Edwards. 'Forensics and a fire investigation officer are going over the place. They'll be able to report their first findings tomorrow.'

'Let's work on the assumption that it was started deliberately until we know otherwise,' said Hudson. Everyone nodded in agreement.

'The layout of the farm would indicate that,' said Sara. She took an enlarged photo to the whiteboard and pinned it up. 'This is a satellite view of the place. The building is in the middle of the nursery, between the farmhouse and the display area.'

She pointed out the café, the farmhouse, the sales displays and the old barn.

'It's cut off from the public in a token way by these old wooden fences,' she said. 'The main gate to the car park would have been shut. It's only a five-bar wooden one. Hardly a distraction to anyone able-bodied enough to climb over it.'

'Easily accessible, then?' asked Hudson.

'Very,' nodded Sara. 'Mrs Simpson said the barn was locked up. I'm not sure that's true. Her son-in-law was clearing it out, intending to bring it back into use. He might have left the door unlocked.'

'This is the missing bloke?'

'Yes.' Sara tapped the picture of Darren on the board. 'His wife is Mrs Simpson's daughter. The business is a family affair. No word from him all day, it seems. His car is missing as well. I've got an active misper and car search out.'

'What about staff?'

'A teenager or two in the holidays,' said Sara, checking her notebook. 'Two regulars in the café. A waitress-cum-manager called Rachel, and a cook called Mavis.'

'Let's get their details and arrange interviews.' Hudson nodded to Aggie. 'One for you.'

'Yes, ma'am.' Aggie jotted a note. 'I followed up on where Mrs Lawson stayed when she visited from Devon.'

'Turn up anything useful?' asked Hudson.

Aggie looked at DC Bowen, and they both grinned.

'Might be,' she said. 'She stayed with Michelle Atkins, who has two sons. One is at the local high school. He's called Ryan Atkins, aged thirteen.'

'And his big brother is Kyle Atkins,' interrupted Bowen triumphantly. 'He works as an apprentice for Coles Construction.'

'The youngster we interviewed this morning?' Hudson smiled. 'So, there is a connection with the Willmott family at the West Ruston fire.'

'*And*,' Bowen carried on excitedly, 'Kyle has a moped. It has the right start to the number plate. Did you see how damaged it was this morning?'

'Okay, okay.' Hudson held up her hands to placate Bowen. 'That's good work, both of you. However, the lad gave us an alibi for the night of the building site fire. Have we had a chance to verify that?'

'Not yet.'

Hudson began to scratch orders on the board. 'First thing tomorrow, Noble, get on to following up the alibi.'

'Faye Rushworth at Wild Thyme also has a moped,' said Sara. She flicked back through her pocketbook. 'The number plate for that also has the same opening letters.'

'Is it damaged?' demanded Hudson.

'I didn't look that closely,' admitted Sara. 'It looked dirty the other day when we first visited.'

'Aggie, did you get a list of likely vehicles?'

Aggie waved a sheet of paper. 'Using your criteria, twenty-seven small motorbikes or mopeds are registered within a fifteen-mile radius. Quite a few belong to a rural transport scheme called *Scoot! Rural*. The one used by Kyle Atkins is hired from them.'

'We may need to speak with them,' suggested Sara.

'Add that to your list,' said Hudson. 'Not a priority. Sara, take Bowen and start with the nursery. Interview those café ladies to get an idea of how the place runs. We also need official statements from Mrs Simpson and her daughter, and give that moped a quick look over. Aggie, you can run the background checks on Wild Thyme. The usual stuff. Bank statements, social media, local newspapers. We can't do much about our victim until we have the PM.'

'What about the workers at the West Ruston fire?' asked Sara. 'Anything of interest?'

'Nothing obvious,' admitted Bowen. 'Most of them could give us alibis and seemed content to work for Coles. Skilled builders can move around a lot to keep their wages up.'

'The majority seem to have been with the company for years,' agreed Hudson. 'Although that's not the same as being happy to be there, I suppose. Bowen has been putting the statements from the laptop on to the main system. I'll have another look through them tomorrow morning.'

'I've sent uniform round to speak to the objectors to the development,' put in Aggie. 'The people living nearby as well. Their statements are getting added regularly. I'll give those a look, shall I?'

'Good idea,' agreed Hudson.

'These have to be connected, don't they?' asked DC Noble. He was gazing at the map on the board. 'Surely we only have one fire starter in the area.'

'Keep an open mind, DC Noble,' said Hudson briskly. 'I guess we can call it a day and regroup tomorrow afternoon.'

'Speak for yourself,' snapped Edwards. 'Some of us have a vigilante meeting to go to. The one being organised by Kevin Howard.'

'Ah yes, that should be interesting.' Hudson suppressed a frown.

'Fancy going instead of me?'

'Nope. You and DS Hirst are more than capable of handling it. And you two can go to the post-mortem as well.'

Sara groaned inwardly. It felt like DCI Hudson had it in for her at the moment.

CHAPTER 24

Mr Cole had asked Claudia to attend the meeting at Howards that evening. 'After all, we're victims too.'

Jamie Waller had agreed to go with her as it was his site that had been attacked, and Claudia felt excited when he picked her up in his car. It was almost like a date.

Claudia wasn't sure what to expect or who might turn up, and it was busier than she'd imagined. The staff car park was full of all sorts of vehicles. The meeting was being held in the large conservatory of the house where Kevin Howard and his mother lived. There must have been at least twenty people there when they arrived, and Kevin kept disappearing to bring in more chairs as the numbers grew. Claudia sat at the back, with Jamie next to her. As Kevin called the meeting to order, she did a quick head count. Thirty-two interested parties, including the detective that Claudia had met at West Ruston village hall. The middle-aged man who sat with her was introduced as DI Edwards.

'As you are all aware,' began Kevin Howard, 'there has been a spate of fires in the area, which seem to have been deliberately started. I asked you here to discuss if there was anything we could do collectively about what was happening. However, some of you may not be aware that this has now gone beyond minor property or crop damage. DI Edwards, could you update us?'

The man stood up and turned to face the meeting. 'Last night, about midnight, a fire started in an unused barn at Wild Thyme Herb Farm.'

Claudia could see heads turning to whisper or nod, depending on how up to date the person was compared to their neighbour. The murmuring grew as DI Edwards continued.

'Unfortunately, someone was in the building at the time.' He paused to look over the audience. 'They didn't escape.'

The murmur exploded with shocked voices. A man in the middle of the group shouted, 'Are you saying they died?'

'I'm afraid I am,' said Edwards.

'Is it murder?' demanded a woman.

'We're treating it as a suspicious death.' Edwards waited for the conversation to ease before holding up a hand to quell the group. 'Under the circumstances, we are reviewing all the local fire reports to see what we can learn.'

'Not before time,' called a man's voice.

An older man dressed in dirty jeans and a grubby polo shirt stood up. 'You can't really say that, John. They bin to see me days ago. That young lady there.' He subsided into his chair after giving the previous speaker a hard stare.

The detective that Claudia remembered stood up. She seemed uneasy speaking in front of a hostile crowd and cleared her throat before beginning.

'I'm DS Sara Hirst. Thank you for that, Mr Willmott. We have included your issues in our enquiries, as you rightly say. I've also interviewed staff here at Howards about an incident that wasn't, in fact, ever reported to us. So if any of you have had any suspicious incidents on your properties that you haven't reported, I'd like to speak to you at the end of the meeting.'

'What's happening at the herb farm, then?' asked another man. Although Claudia could only see him from behind, his rigid back and folded arms suggested that he wasn't very happy. He sat in the middle of the second row.

'We have a forensic team at the scene,' replied DI Edwards. 'We would appreciate it if you could stay away from the place for a few days.'

'Although, I'm sure Mrs Simpson would appreciate some support from her friends and neighbours,' suggested Hirst. 'It's a difficult time.'

'We'd also like any information on the whereabouts of Darren Rushworth,' continued Edwards. 'Many of you will know him; we need to trace him urgently.'

The room exploded. Some people stood up. Others began to shout. Claudia looked at Jamie, who merely shrugged.

'You mean Jean's son-in-law is missing?' shouted the first angry man, apparently called John. He was on his feet and trying to push along the row. Deciding people weren't getting out of his way fast enough, he pulled aside the one empty chair in the row in front and rushed towards the detectives, yelling, 'Why are you trying to find him? Are you trying to pin the fire on him? Wouldn't put it past you!'

'John' reached DI Edwards. He had almost got chest to chest with the detective when Hirst stepped behind him. She grabbed the man's arm, spinning him away from the group. Loudly protesting, she marched him several paces away before pushing him into an armchair. The shouting from the shocked crowd increased.

'That's police brutality, that is!' he shouted, although he remained where the detective had put him, Claudia noticed. She couldn't help wondering if Hirst was tempted to offer him some actual brutality, but this wasn't a TV show, and the detective kept her temper in check.

'All right,' shouted Edwards, 'let's all sit down again.'

He had an air of authority and remained standing so that calm radiated from him. As the meeting finally came back to order, Claudia watched Hirst allow the grumpy man to push his way back to his seat in the audience. His neck was bright red, whether through embarrassment or adrenaline, Claudia didn't want to guess.

'Thank you, Mr Howard,' said Edwards. 'Could we move on to the main reason for the meeting?'

Kevin Howard waited until the two detectives were seated before speaking. 'I originally invited you all here to consider how we could help the police in their enquiries and protect ourselves. Does anyone have any suggestions on how we might do that?'

Thomas Willmott put up his hand. When Howard nodded at him, he stood up again. 'Some of you know my boy, Jake. Since we started having problems, he've been driving round our boundaries late at night to check them. He found a fire the other night and called out the fire brigade. Perhaps we could do that for each other in turn? Keep an eye on stuff?'

There was a murmur of agreement. Claudia felt Jamie put his hand up. When Kevin nodded, he stood and introduced himself, then explained about the fire at West Ruston.

'Although we're some distance away from what seems to be the centre of the activity here, we think our problems may be connected to yours.'

'We don't know that yet, sir,' said Hirst. She turned to look at the back row. She nodded when she recognised Claudia. 'It's part of an ongoing investigation.'

'Indeed,' Jamie carried on. 'We have a security company who drive past our site regularly.'

'Doesn't seem to have done you much good,' laughed someone. He was shushed by the people sitting near him.

'Perhaps not,' agreed Jamie. 'However, I can tell you that our boss has agreed to pay for additional time with the security company. This will allow them to share in any area checks later at night than you might be able to cover yourselves.'

'That's very kind of Mr Cole,' said Kevin Howard. 'I can also do some later cover with my own security men. Let's get together on that. We could do with some kind of rota.'

'Who's going to organise that?' asked a woman from the middle. Claudia shifted uncomfortably in her chair. When no one else spoke, with a sense of inevitability, she stood up and introduced herself.

'I'd need to check it's acceptable to Mr Cole,' she cautioned, 'but I would be willing to give it a go. I'd need everyone's contact details and areas you could cover.'

Claudia sat down, her heart thumping. She didn't like speaking in public. She thought she could probably manage a rota in her spare time if Mr Cole didn't like it. Jamie patted her arm and whispered, 'Well done.'

Claudia felt a glow of warmth at his appreciation. It was a long time since anyone had given her a compliment.

'I think my mum has organised some refreshments,' said Kevin Howard. 'Let's take a break now, and anyone prepared to help can give their details to Ms Turner.'

'I just want to make one thing very clear,' said Edwards before anyone could move. 'If you see anything suspicious, you dial 999. No matter how upset or worried you are, you should not attempt to detain anyone you see. We will prosecute anyone who does that sort of thing. This is not to become a vigilante movement. This is Norfolk, not the Wild West.'

CHAPTER 25

The next morning, Sara was glad to see there had been no major fires overnight. The temperature had dropped to a more seasonal 32 degrees, which seemed almost acceptable compared to the last few days. The sun was masked by a thin layer of misty cloud, which Sara knew would burn off quickly. She slapped suntan lotion over her face and arms before pulling on a lightweight sleeveless blouse and cotton trousers. She hoisted her plaited dreads as high on the crown of her head as she could with a bright-coloured scrunchie before checking her appearance in the bedroom mirror.

'This has absolutely nothing to do with greeting my new gardener before I leave,' she told herself wryly. 'I just want to look smart for work.'

Sara knew she was lying when she opened the front door to Adie Dickinson. His van was pulled up next to her car as he unloaded the equipment he needed for the day. She could see the muscles in his bare arms bulging under his beautifully tanned skin. Adie was wearing another of those brightly coloured, sleeveless hemp tops. His cargo pants were sawn off above his knee and frayed in lumps, revealing his toned calves. A multicoloured fabric headband pulled his blonde hair away from his face.

So fit I could eat him, she thought, before mentally slapping herself to buck up her ideas. *I don't know the first thing about him.*

They had agreed on a plan of action on his previous visit. Sara knew that Gilly would keep an eye on him during the day. In fact, she was unlikely to keep away. She suspected her older neighbour enjoyed the view as much as she did, although hopefully in a more academic way. Adie thought it would take him about a week to dig out the worst of the overgrowth and tame any shrubs that could be kept.

'I've booked a skip for Wednesday,' he told her as he dropped his tools in the back garden. He eyed Sara with a slightly worried expression. 'You understand that it will look worse before it gets better?'

'I expect so,' she agreed. They shook hands. The touch of his calloused workman's hand sent a tingle up Sara's arm. 'I don't know what time I'll be finished at work. If you could leave the keys with Gilly at the end of the day? And I'll see you again in the morning.'

'Super,' said Adie. His upper-class plummy accent seemed out of place with his laid-back persona. 'Have a good day, yeah?'

Concentrate on your job, Sara told herself sternly.

Aggie had been busy setting up interviews for the morning. The first was with Mrs Atkins. DCI Hudson had decided they needed to know more about Kyle and his family, and Sara was due to meet DC Mike Bowen at the address they had. Just after nine, her satnav faltered at the entrance to the narrow lane as if it didn't recognise it. The single-track road had the feel of a green lane. The narrow verges were parched yellow, and the high, unkempt hedges on either side drooped occasional ropes of wild dog rose to scratch at the sides of her car. At the end of the lane stood a terrace of three tiny cottages. To the front was a small, gravelled turning area containing a couple of vehicles. One was being loaded up with young children for a family outing. The other belonged to Bowen. Sara drew up next to him.

'The one at this end is where the Atkins live,' said Bowen.

'The scruffy one?' The difference was marked. The far-thest cottage on the right looked immaculate. This was where the family were loading up picnic baskets and a buggy. The one in the middle looked as if it had been empty for a while. Curtains were drawn across the windows, although a pile of decorating equipment outside suggested that work might be ongoing. The Atkins' cottage looked unkempt. The tiny front garden was covered in uneven, broken flags. It con-tained a few plant pots overgrown with weeds, which looked as parched as the verges. The front door stood open.

'Hello?' Sara called as she knocked. 'Mrs Atkins? Are you expecting us?'

'You from the police?' called a voice from the back room. 'Best come through.'

'Thank you.' Sara led the way, and Bowen closed the door behind him. The front room was suddenly a lot darker. She followed the light past a set of narrow stairs and into the kitchen at the rear. Here, the sun blazed through a wide window. The back door was open, letting in some fresh air.

'I haven't got much time,' said Kyle's mother. She glanced at their warrant cards without much interest before returning to the washing up in the sink. 'Ryan, budge up and make some room.'

A lanky teenager sullenly gathered up his limbs so Sara and Bowen could sit at the kitchen table with him. His unkempt hair fell over his face as he spooned down cereal with barely a glance at them.

'You gonna be long?' his mother asked. The boy spooned faster, lifting the bowl to his lips to drink off the last of the milk. He took the empty bowl and put it by the sink. He towered over his mother and was clearly going to be very tall when he'd finished growing.

'Going out,' he muttered.

'Where?'

The lad shrugged and headed out through the front room. The door slammed behind him.

'Oh well. I'll just finish this, then we can talk.'

Sara glanced at Bowen. There was an awkward pause as Mrs Atkins finished washing up, and the two detectives waited at the kitchen table. She was quite short, perhaps five foot two or three. Her clothes were clean, if well-worn, and a catering tabard stopped her from getting wet. When she'd finished, she settled at the table with Sara and Bowen as she dried her hands on a tea towel.

'I can't be too long,' she explained. 'I'm due at work at half past ten, and it's a bit of a way to cycle. What can I do for you?'

'We'd like to talk about your son, Kyle, Mrs Atkins,' began Sara.

The woman held up an admonishing finger. 'Not Mrs — *Ms*. A smart lady like you should know the difference. I reverted to my maiden name after my husband died. You can call me Michelle.'

'And changed your boys' surname too?'

'Absolutely,' said Michelle. 'I didn't want them to have any association with their dad's family. Not after what happened.'

'What did happen, Michelle?' asked Sara. 'If you don't mind me being nosey.'

'Copper's job to be nosey, isn't it?' Michelle nodded. 'I see all those things on the television. Love 'em. Detectives like you asking all those awkward questions. Well, you won't find anything difficult about my boys. They're both good lads.'

Sara ignored this last comment. That was what they were here to find out. 'What was your husband's name?'

'Colin. Colin Willmott.'

Sara sucked in a breath. 'Any relation to Thomas Willmott of Belaugh Manor Farm?'

'Of course,' said Michelle. She frowned. 'I don't know why you need to know all this old history. Colin was his son. He's the boys' granddad. Thing is, we don't talk anymore. Haven't for years.'

'May I ask why?'

'Because he caused Colin's death. He killed his own boy.'

CHAPTER 26

When Claudia had reported back to her boss the follow-ing morning, Mr Cole had swiftly agreed to her running the rota for night patrols as part of her workday. She thought he seemed genuinely worried about what was going on. By mid-morning, she'd typed up a spreadsheet of details and emailed it around for confirmation. She also worked up the first week of the suggested rota and circulated that too.

'I'm off to the West Ruston site,' she told her two staff. They already looked wilted in the heat, although it was slightly less oppressive than it had been for several days. 'Got a meeting.'

Driving through the lanes to West Ruston, Claudia cranked up the car's air conditioning and the radio, singing along loudly to an old song she recognised. The fields and verges drifted past as she enjoyed the moment. It was good to feel useful. Her mobile trilled on the radio console, inter-rupting her pleasant thoughts.

The caller was another site manager. Kyle Atkins had been reallocated to the Paston building site but hadn't turned up this morning. Claudia wondered where he'd got to and why. Her annoyance was rapidly replaced by worry that he might be ill.

Jamie Waller was waiting for her in the car park of the burned-out old pub. Torn blue-and-white police tape fluttered in the light breeze. Two workmen were re-erecting the security fence. Claudia could hear someone trying and failing to get a mechanical engine running inside the compound. The portacabin office was a blackened shell, and the two chemical toilets had melted into a strange lump that looked more like a modern art sculpture than something useful.

Mr Cole stood talking to a pair of businessmen in suits under a large horse chestnut tree, its trunk scorched on one side by the fire. Claudia assumed they were from the housing association. Everyone was looking at the site despondently.

'We'll get a surveyor to look at the building,' said one of the businessmen. He pulled at the knot in his tie and unbuttoned his collar. Sweat was trickling down his cheeks, despite the tree's shade. 'I suspect it will have to be demolished.'

'It was once three cottages, you know,' said the other housing man. 'You can see that more clearly now. Perhaps this gives us an opportunity to return to the old layout.'

'Easier to rip it down and start again,' muttered Jamie, leading Claudia along the fence out of earshot. 'At least the fire and forensic people have finished.'

'Did the fire do us any favours?' she asked, peering through the fence at the fire-damaged garden.

'Some.' Jamie pointed at some old apple trees. Claudia could see that they were little more than burned sticks now. 'They could have been a pain during construction. It will be easier to chop them down and plant something new.'

The engine that had been coughing and spluttering suddenly burst into life. From behind the mass of blue plastic a Bobcat mini-digger emerged on narrow caterpillar tracks, being driven by Eric Beatty.

'I thought he was out at Paston?' Claudia turned to look at Jamie.

'I asked Mr Cole to reassign him to me,' said Jamie. 'I need someone to see what equipment is still useable and what needs replacing. Most of it belonged to his team.'

Eric parked the Bobcat by the fence and nodded at Jamie. Claudia waved at him to join them. He looked reluctant as he peeled off his gloves and removed his hard hat.

'Miss Turner.' He acknowledged her with a nod, but kept his eyes on the floor until Jamie spoke.

'What's the score so far?' asked Jamie.

'The small stuff in the container should be okay,' said Eric. A lockable shipping container had been dropped into the garden to store tools. 'Fire didn't get inside that.'

'I'll arrange for them to be individually tested,' said Jamie. He pulled a notepad from the back pocket of his jeans and wrote on it. 'Bigger stuff?'

'The two rotavators are dead,' replied Eric. Jamie scribbled another note. 'This Bobcat will need a clean and service for smoke damage, but it's useable.'

'Any other stuff?'

'Got to check the other trench digger. Can I get on?'

'I've got a question, Eric,' said Claudia as the man began to turn away. 'It's about Kyle.'

Eric glanced at her quickly, then dropped his gaze again. 'Why? What?'

'I thought he had been reallocated to the Paston site for a few days?'

'That's right,' nodded Eric.

'Is it too far for him to go?'

'He seemed happy to do it.' Eric sounded puzzled. 'What's the problem?'

'He hasn't turned up on site today,' said Claudia carefully. She didn't want to upset Eric more than necessary.

He looked up at her confidently. 'Didn't the little bugger ring in? I told him to let Ian know.'

'You know where he is?'

'Gone to *Scoot! Rural* with his moped,' said Eric. 'He fell off it a few days ago and damaged it.'

Claudia nodded. Damage that Kyle had been keen for her not to look too closely at in the works yard. 'Why has he gone there?'

'I rang them up and explained. They said to bring it in so they could assess it. They'll either fix it up or give him another one. It's part of the contract.'

CHAPTER 27

Sara didn't want to rush Michelle. She wanted to hear the full story of the Willmott family rift. On the other hand, Michelle made it obvious that she didn't want to go into details.

'I work in the café at the Junior Farm,' she said, pointing to the logo on her tabard. 'I work in the kitchens. It helps pay the bills.'

'I'd just like to get the background in my head,' said Sara. 'Belaugh Manor Farm has been targeted several times, and we need to look at any possible links.'

'You think it might be one of my boys?' asked Michelle defensively. 'Why would they do that?'

'Your eldest son works at the West Ruston building site that was targeted,' put in Bowen. Michelle flashed him an angry look. Bowen ducked his head down. 'He gave us an alibi for that.'

'Then you'd better believe him, hadn't you?'

'Michelle, we're not accusing Kyle of anything,' said Sara calmly. 'We just want to understand this family connection.'

'I have to go soon.' Michelle looked at the kitchen clock. 'My husband, the boys' father, was Colin Willmott. We were happily married for several years. Lived in one of the farm cottages while Colin worked for his dad. Thomas is famously penny-pinching. Colin's wages were really low. We always struggled.'

'Was he the eldest son?'

'Yes. There'd been a little girl after him, who'd died before she was a year old. Cot death. I'm not sure Sharon ever quite got over that.'

'Sharon?' asked Bowen. 'Mrs Lawson?'

'That's right. My mother-in-law, as she was at the time. Jake came along after that. There was quite an age gap between the two boys. Then there was the accident.'

Michelle stopped, her lip trembling. She brushed away a tear on her cheek.

'On the farm?' asked Sara gently.

'That's right. It would never have happened if Thomas had kept up with the maintenance.'

Sara thought back to the farmhouse with the sink full of dirty pots and the punk chicken wandering about the kitchen. The place was covered with the dust and grime of years of neglect. Thomas Willmott wasn't bothered about the state of the house. The same was likely true of the farm buildings.

'My Colin was on a wooden floor high up in the barn. They stacked bags of animal feed there. Shouldn't have been using it because the supports were all rotten. It collapsed under him, and he fell. He broke his back, and his head was damaged. Died three days later in the hospital.'

Michelle blew her nose. Sara noticed that Bowen's attention had wandered. He was staring out the kitchen window. Sara nudged his ankle with her foot, none too gently.

'That broke up the family?'

'Sharon told Thomas it was his fault. So did I, and there was a huge row. It was a very bitter time. She walked out. I went with her and took my boys with me. Jake was a moody teenager, and he took his father's side. Refused to go with Sharon.'

'And since then?'

'We shared a house in Wroxham to start with,' said Michelle. 'Sharon kept trying to persuade Jake to join us until he refused to see her. Then she met this man, this farmer from Devon.'

'We've spoken to Mrs Lawson,' Bowen put in. 'She said she only kept in touch with you.'

'We talk on the phone sometimes. It's easiest because the boys and me have to move around a lot. When she told me about her husband's cancer, she came up to stay with us for a few days to try and see Jake. That was the only time we'd seen each other for years.'

'Why do you have to keep moving?' asked Sara.

'I've not got much money, and it's difficult on my own. We've been on the housing association's waiting list for years. Somehow, we never seem to get a look in. Renting private is expensive. If my rent gets put up, I have to look for somewhere cheaper.'

'Who do you rent this place from?' asked Sara.

'An agent in Hoveton.'

She looked around the kitchen with its damp walls and battered cupboards. 'Your landlord should take better care of it than this.'

'I don't argue,' said Michelle hurriedly. 'It's cheap, and I have a three-year lease. Gave us a bit of stability. When they throw us out, they'll turn it into a holiday let, like the other two.'

'Do Kyle and Ryan know what happened to their father?' asked Bowen.

'Kyle does,' nodded Michelle. 'He asked me when he turned sixteen, so I told him my side.'

'Did he try to contact his grandfather at all?'

'Not that I know of. Spoke to his grandmother about it at the time.'

'And Ryan?'

'Oh, my baby is still too young to bother with all that,' said Michelle firmly. 'If he wants to know, I'll tell him when he's sixteen, like his brother.'

'Can I also ask about Eric Beatty?' Sara leafed through her notebook. 'Mike, didn't you say he was Kyle's uncle?'

'That's right,' replied Michelle. 'He's married to my sister. They've been good to us when they can.'

'He got Kyle the apprenticeship at Coles Construction, didn't he?' asked Bowen.

'Yes. It was no use Kyle keeping on trying to do exams. He was no good at schoolwork, but he is good with his hands. Eric suggested he try construction. Said there was always work for good people in that industry. Kyle seems happy enough.'

'Is Ryan still around?' asked Bowen. He looked out of the window into the back garden again.

'He'll be long gone,' said Michelle, standing up. 'Birdwatching by the river or down at the Broad. I ought to be going too.'

'Thanks for your time, Ms Atkins.'

Michelle ushered the pair of them out of the front door. Sara heard her lock it as they walked down the path. They had barely reached their cars when the woman reappeared round the end of the cottage, wheeling an old-fashioned lady's bike, her handbag stuffed in the basket on the front. With a nod of acknowledgement, Michelle sat on the bike and, with a slight groan, wobbled off.

Sara and Bowen watched her go. The family from the holiday let had gone out for their day trip, and they were alone. All Sara could hear were occasional birds tweeting and the rustle of wind in the dry grass.

'Do we believe her? That Ryan doesn't know about his father?' asked Bowen. He zapped his car lock, and the noise disturbed the birds, who fell silent with disapproval.

'She may believe it, but I wouldn't put it past Kyle to have told him.' Sara opened her own car.

'Is he mobile, do you think? Ryan? Could he get to these places?'

'Kyle's the one with the moped,' Sara said, weighing the options. 'Would Ryan know where his brother was working at West Ruston?'

'Who knows? Wasn't Ryan wearing an olive-green T-shirt this morning?'

'What?' Sara was startled. 'I didn't notice.'

'Good job I did, then,' smirked Bowen. 'Because I think he sneaked into the back garden and listened to our conversation with his mother. Thought I saw him trying to duck under the kitchen window. If he didn't know before, he does now.'

CHAPTER 28

Despite her daughter's objection, Jean insisted that Faye stay with her at the farmhouse overnight. At some time, when it was still dark, Jean heard her daughter in the kitchen. She was too exhausted to join her, and lay on her duvet, trying to doze. She must have dropped off eventually, as it was nearly eight o'clock when she woke up. Jean showered quickly, pulled on some clean clothes and went downstairs. Faye sat at the kitchen table, her fingers stabbing at her phone. Jean's phone lay on the worktop, blinking as it charged.

'I brought yours down, just in case,' mumbled Faye. Her mobile was on speaker mode. As Jean slipped into the chair next to Faye, she heard it ring then cut to the answering service.

'*You've reached Darren Rushworth,*' the familiar voice intoned cheerfully. '*Sorry I can't take your call right now. Leave me a message and I'll get back to you.*'

The long tone beeped, and Faye cut off her call before it went through.

'How many times have you tried?' Jean asked.

Faye looked up at her with haunted eyes. The skin around them was shrunken and dark grey with tiredness. She dropped the phone on the table with a clatter.

'I don't know,' she said vaguely. 'I've tried everyone I can think of. I've tried using your phone in case it's something I've said or done. Then I just kept ringing him. Just to hear his voice.'

'Did you have an argument? Honestly?'

Faye nodded, her eyes trained on the mobile's screen. 'He wasn't sure about us leaving.'

'You remember the other time you had a major row? He went off with his mate, and they spent several days drinking in Norwich, right? Took his car with him that time as well. Wouldn't talk to you or answer his phone. He's probably done the same this time.' Jean placed her hand over Faye's trembling fingers. 'Leave it for a few minutes, eh?'

Jean needed to eat something. Her diabetes test this morning was showing bad results, and it would leave her too tired to cope. 'Could you manage some breakfast?' When Faye shook her head, Jean squeezed her hand. 'Cuppa, then?'

The sound of vehicles arriving in the yard distracted both of them. Through the kitchen window, Jean could see the investigation teams had returned for the second day. Mercifully, the people in the television vans had lost interest yesterday once the body of the poor soul in the barn had been removed by the private ambulance.

Jean felt too weary to deal with it but knew that she must because she couldn't expect Faye to cope until they knew where Darren was. Straightening her shoulders, Jean walked out to meet them, taking her mobile. She couldn't manage these visitors alone with Faye in this state. She would have to ask her two older employees to come in today. At least they could help look after the forensic team. Perhaps they would also be allowed to clean the café kitchen.

There was no sign of that nice Dr Taylor this morning. When she asked, the forensic team leader permitted her to start in the café. In return, he asked her for something with Darren's DNA on it, and Jean brought them an old toothbrush, which was dropped into an evidence bag.

She didn't dare mention that to Faye. Instead, she persuaded her daughter to go for a shower, promising to keep the phones with her. Mavis and Rachel turned up just after ten and immediately opened the kitchen before beginning the onerous task of deep cleaning every nook and cranny of the café.

The pair had just given the forensic team their mid-morning drinks when Jean saw two more cars pulling into the yard. She was cleaning the patio tables and chairs. The bucket of soapy water turned grimy in minutes as Jean scrubbed at the plastic and metal. Her hands dripped with grey suds as she straightened up with a groan at the stiffness in her back. Her heart began to pound as she watched DS Sara Hirst unfolding her long legs from the high SUV. Jean pursed her lips angrily when she recognised the second car's driver. At least the man had his shirt tucked in properly this time. They paused to consult with the forensic team leader.

'Do you have news of Darren?' Jean demanded when they approached her. She was grateful that Faye had agreed to lie down after her shower. With luck, she had fallen asleep.

'I'm sorry, nothing yet,' said DS Hirst. 'We put out the photo that Faye gave us. How is she this morning?'

'How do you think? Stupid question.' Jean dropped her scrubbing brush into the bucket. The grey water splashed over the side, making a pool on the flagstones. She glanced at it angrily and wiped her wet hands down the leg of her jeans. 'What about this body you've found? Tell me that's not him.'

'Why don't you sit down, Mrs Simpson?' suggested Hirst.

Jean flinched. 'I don't want to sit down. I want to know what's going on.'

'We can't tell you much at the moment,' said the man. Jean's mind flickered, trying to remember his name. Bowen, wasn't it? 'The victim will receive their post-mortem this afternoon. We'll know more after that. And when the forensic team report back to us.'

'Is it murder?' demanded Jean. She dreaded the answer as much as she needed to know it.

'We don't know,' said Hirst carefully.

'So, what are you doing here?' Suddenly Jean felt tired.

'We need a chat with your staff,' said Bowen.

'Really?' She was puzzled. 'They weren't here when the fire happened.'

'Every little helps,' he said cryptically. It didn't amuse Jean in the slightest.

'You're in luck,' she said, waving at the café. 'They're here helping me clean the place.'

'We also need to interview Faye and yourself about the incident,' said Hirst.

'Can't you leave my daughter out of this?'

'I'm sorry, Mrs Simpson, we need your memories and movements to help us piece things together.'

Jean flopped defeatedly on to a wet chair. The water seeped through her trousers and underwear. She no longer cared. Her head dropped into her hands and she shuddered. She'd known this was going to happen. She had just hoped they would give them a few days of breathing space. Obviously not. Well, everything would come out in its own way, no matter how difficult or uncomfortable that would be.

CHAPTER 29

Mavis, the café cook, looked delighted when Sara and Bowen asked the two women for a chat. Rachel, the café manager, appeared far less enthusiastic.

'We weren't here,' she said dismissively. 'Gone home hours before.'

'We're interested in more general stuff,' said Bowen. He offered the cook his best winning smile, which did the trick. 'Such as, what is it like to work here and how do you get on with the family? We can take your official statements later.'

Mavis smoothed her apron and leaned on the stainless-steel central preparation table, ready to gossip. With her floral dress, rosy cheeks and tightly curled grey hair, she looked old enough to retire but clearly still enjoyed her job.

Rachel was about ten years younger. Her well-cut jeans and grey blouse revealed a thin figure. She wore make-up despite the heat and the fact that they were obviously there to do a dirty job. Her pale hair was pulled back into a ponytail. She folded her arms defensively and openly looked Sara up and down with a little sneer on her upper lip.

'What do you want to know?' Mavis encouraged Bowen. 'Tea? Scone?'

Bowen accepted both with alacrity, but Sara declined. His attitude and methods had changed since he'd married Aggie, Sara mused, as she watched the older pair gently flirting. Gone was the dinosaur of her early days on the team. Now Bowen was happy to use his newfound skills if it got a result. Nor did he make the casual sexist or racist remarks he'd once been prone to. His instincts remained the best in the team, in her opinion.

Sara regarded Rachel across the kitchen. The woman was making no attempt to hide her distrust. She tried to break the ice with a smile. 'Is this a good place to work?'

Rachel frowned. 'Yes. I like it.'

'Mrs Simpson treats us very well,' concurred Mavis. She bustled about her domain, bringing drinks and cakes.

'Seasonal work?' asked Bowen.

'Full-time in the summer,' replied Mavis. 'Part-time in the autumn and spring. Nothing at Christmas.'

'Isn't that difficult?'

'I work at the Junior Farm then. They have their Santa Experience in December, so it's busy.'

'Do you know Michelle Atkins?' Sara was curious. Rachel snorted.

'Sure.' Mavis nodded. 'Amazing lady. Bringing up those two boys on her own.'

'Does she worry about them?' Bowen prompted. 'Do they give her any trouble?'

'Of course. What mum doesn't worry?' Mavis nodded sagely. 'They don't give her more cause than the average teenage lad. Unlike some we could mention.'

'Mavis!' snapped Rachel. 'That's none of our business.'

'Why not?' Mavis turned to her colleague. 'That's the sort of thing the detectives need to know.'

'What is?' Bowen bit a chunk out of his snack. 'Lovely scone, by the way.'

Mavis beamed at the compliment. 'Besides, it was you that told me, Rachel.'

'Can you explain?' Sara asked the reluctant woman.

'Not much to tell.' Rachel shrugged. 'Family were having a little problem recently. Nothing serious.'

'Oh, come on,' said Mavis. She leaned forward conspiratorially. 'I've seen it myself sometimes. Mrs Simpson and that daughter of hers. Had some kind of falling out a few months ago. Hardly been on speaking terms ever since.'

'You're such a gossip, Mavis,' said Rachel. She pulled her lips flat and tight in disgust. Sara wondered how they managed to work together if the café manager thought so little of the cook. Mavis must have a very thick skin, or maybe Rachel didn't like anyone very much. 'You shouldn't listen to her.'

'You said you'd heard them in that old barn fighting like cat and dog.' Mavis drew herself up to her full height, which still wasn't very high.

'Rachel? Is that what you heard?' asked Sara quietly. She got a reluctant nod in reply.

'Something about Mrs Simpson not buying them a house, like she promised,' continued Mavis, obviously determined to finish her accusations. 'Then, you said she said the business made no money, and she couldn't. Gave me a shock, that did. Because when I went home, I talked to my husband, and he said I could give up if I wanted to. No good if they can't pay our wages. And then this happened.' Mavis waved out of the window in the direction of the burned-out barn. 'Convenient, eh?'

'Mavis!' Rachel almost shouted. 'You be careful what you say.'

'Well,' said Mavis, appearing to run out of steam at last. 'Just saying.'

'You think this could have been deliberate?' Sara took charge. 'In what way?'

'In no way,' said Rachel sharply. 'If it was deliberate, it had nothing to do with the family. Like that fire out the back.'

'The one on Willmott's field? That was certainly deliberate.'

'And all these others on the news,' carried on Rachel furiously.

'Insurance,' muttered Mavis to Bowen. Her voice was loud enough to carry.

Rachel let out an inarticulate, furious cry. 'How can you be so ungrateful? When we've both worked for this family for years. Paid us even when they couldn't pay themselves.'

Mavis looked ashamed and mumbled as she dropped her gaze to the work surface. 'I know.'

'And when it's all so tragic!' Rachel flung the tea towel she'd been clutching into the sink. She swung away through the open kitchen door and marched angrily across the yard towards the parked cars.

'Tragic?' Mavis looked at Bowen in confusion. 'It's just an old barn.'

'There was someone in there,' said Sara slowly. 'I'm afraid they died.'

Mavis dropped her mug with a clatter. 'I'd no idea.'

CHAPTER 30

The air conditioning in her little car was noisy. Claudia didn't want to be overheard and shut the car door as she searched her handbag for the card the police detective had given her. DC Mike Bowen. She dialled his mobile number, only turning off the welcome cool wind when he answered.

'I don't know if you remember me,' she said after she'd given her name. 'From Coles Construction?'

'Of course.' Bowen sounded friendly enough. 'Did you remember something else?'

'Not as such.' Claudia hesitated. The DC had asked about the moped when he'd seen it in the yard at work. All the same, she wasn't sure how she felt about reporting Kyle like this.

'Something that you think is important?' Bowen prompted.

'It might be. Do you remember Kyle Atkins? His uncle, Eric Beatty, sat in with you.'

'Seventeen-year-old with a floppy fringe,' said Bowen with a ring of humour. 'Had one of those myself, back in the day. What about him?'

'I think you noticed his moped in the yard?'

'It was damaged,' replied the detective. The humour had gone from his voice now. 'In fact, we were wondering how that happened.'

'He should have been at work today but hasn't turned up. I asked his uncle. He's taken the bike back to *Scoot! Rural* to get it repaired. I thought you ought to know.'

'Bugger,' said Bowen quietly. 'We wanted another look at that. Hold on, can you?'

Claudia heard him speaking to someone else, and after a moment, a woman spoke. 'Hi, it's Detective Sergeant Hirst. You say Kyle has taken his moped to be repaired? Where?'

Claudia recognised the DS who'd been at West Ruston village hall on the night of the fire, and at the meeting at Howards. 'It's a rural access scheme called *Scoot! Rural*. Their workshop is on an industrial estate near Aylsham.'

There was more off-phone discussion before Hirst returned. 'Do you think he's there now?'

'Eric, his uncle, seemed to think it would take most of the morning.'

'If we were to go to this place, would his uncle be free to meet us there?'

'I doubt it. I could go instead.'

'That might be all right,' said Hirst doubtfully. 'Can you go right now?'

Claudia said she would. Checking through the site fence, she saw Eric bending over a small digger covered in oil and soot. If she told Eric about this, would he blame her for getting Kyle into trouble? Would he call Kyle and warn him the police were on their way? On the other hand, did Kyle have something to hide? Curiosity got the better of her, and she headed to Aylsham without speaking to Eric.

The shortest route was cross-country through the lanes. It still took Claudia more than half an hour to reach the industrial estate, and several more minutes searching the identical internal roads with their blank-faced units before finding *Scoot! Rural.* The row of shiny mopeds parked outside gave it away.

DS Hirst had beaten Claudia to it and was already deep in conversation with a middle-aged man. The detective towered over him as he sat on a moped seat, wiping his dirty hands on a cloth. He wore stained red overalls, with the top falling open to reveal a dirty grey T-shirt beneath. Hirst was dressed smartly and wore chic sunglasses. It wouldn't do to get those things dirty, suspected Claudia, although the woman's shoes were practical and heavy-duty. She didn't look happy.

'Eric was busy,' Claudia explained when she joined them and introduced herself. The man nodded at her. 'So I came myself. Is Kyle all right?'

'Not here,' said Hirst. She sounded exasperated. 'Andy here doesn't know where he is.'

The man smirked at the detective's frustration. It sounded like he was exaggerating his Norfolk accent to make himself less easily understood. 'I'm not his keeper. B'int my lad. Just a cus'omer.'

'The moped that he brought in,' began Hirst. She stared into the dark entrance to the workshop. Claudia looked too. The bright sunlight outside made it look like a black hole. Her eyes couldn't adjust quickly enough. 'Is that still here?'

'Why would you want to know?' Andy was obviously enjoying himself.

'Well now, let me see,' said Hirst. The woman bent forward, deliberately invading Andy's personal space without actually touching him. Claudia held back a smile. 'Because this may be a murder enquiry. That moped could be evidence. And you're being obstructive. Makes me wonder why.'

Andy lost his nerve first. He nodded towards the workshop door. 'It's in there.' His accent was far less exaggerated now.

'Have you done anything to it?' asked Hirst.

'Not yet,' replied Andy.

Hirst stepped back and gestured at the entrance. 'Can you show me, please, sir?'

Andy shrugged in a sulky way before jerking his thumb. 'Ladies first.'

Hirst strode towards the roller shutter door. When Claudia stepped after her, Andy muttered to her, 'Bloody foreigners. Why should we help them?'

Claudia flinched, taking care to put a couple of steps between them. She wasn't sure what the man meant and didn't want to seem to be condoning anything he was implying. Some people were just born to be difficult.

Kyle's bright-red and black moped was on its stand at the back of the workshop. A younger man stood nearby with tools in his hand and mouth open.

'Have you started on this one?' asked Hirst brusquely. The young man shook his head and pointed at a dark blue model surrounded by bits.

'Give us a chance,' said Andy. 'It's only been here half an hour.'

'That's all to the good,' said Hirst. 'Don't do anything. I'll have to arrange for forensics to come and pick it up. It needs to be examined properly.'

'What on earth do you think you'll find?' demanded Andy angrily. He pushed past DS Hirst and grabbed the bike by the handles to swivel the free front wheel.

'Now we'll need your DNA and fingerprints,' said Hirst. 'You've been handling it.'

'He got run off the road and into a hedge.' Andy pointed to the scratch marks on the front guard.

'Is that what Kyle says?' asked Claudia. The two antagonists turned to look at her. She flushed with embarrassment. 'Lucky he wasn't injured.'

'What do you expect to find?' snapped Andy. 'It's not like there's anywhere you can hide stuff on one of these things.'

The young man dropped his spanner with a clatter. Claudia jumped. Hirst turned to look at him. Clearing his throat, the youngster pulled at the seat of the moped he was working on. With a click, it pulled up to reveal a small storage area.

'Well, how convenient,' said Hirst. She stepped towards Kyle's moped. Before she could reach it, Andy pulled at the

143

seat. It swung up. Inside was a small, bright-green plastic fuel container. Andy looked at Hirst and then at Claudia.

'Spare fuel?' he hazarded.

Across the forecourt, a moped approached at its best speed. With a scuff of tyres, it drew up outside the workshop door. The engine was turned off.

'Yeah, that's great,' said a voice. Claudia recognised it, even if Hirst wouldn't. It was Kyle. 'Can I borrow this one until mine's been fixed?'

CHAPTER 31

It looked as if Kyle would do a runner when he saw Sara coming out of the sun-darkened workshop interior. She watched his hand reach for the starter and his face flush red. His helmet was in his other hand. It had left damp marks around his head and face. Sara raised her warrant card.

'You're not in any trouble, Kyle,' she said. 'I'd just like a quick word with you.'

'I don't have to talk to you,' he said mutinously. Sara knew this had been made clear to him, so it didn't sound as street-smart as Kyle might have wanted it to. 'Not on my own.'

'I'm here if you need me,' said Claudia. Kyle looked over at her in surprise. She hovered near the roller shutter door. Andy stood a couple of paces behind.

'Me too, son,' said the workshop manager.

'That good enough?' Sara asked. She kept her tone neutral. No point in spooking the lad. He frowned, then nodded. 'I've spoken to your mum this morning, and met your brother.'

'You leave my mum out of this!' snapped Kyle. 'And Ryan. He might be a little shit, but he's a kid.'

'I only have a couple of questions. Are you willing to answer them?'

'Don't know,' mumbled the young man. 'What are they?'

'Where were you on the night of Wednesday, the second of August?'

'At home, with my mum. Watching telly.'

'All night?'

'Until I went to bed. And the other question?'

'Why did you bring your moped in to be mended today?'

'Busted it, didn't I? Got run off the road and through a hedge.'

Sara heard Claudia shuffle behind her. When she glanced round, Sara could see the woman looked uncomfortable.

'Thanks for that,' she nodded. 'Kyle, I'll need to get a proper interview and statement from you. With your mum, or another adult if you prefer. We'll be in touch to arrange a convenient time.'

With a nod, Sara turned her back on Kyle. Andy strode past her. 'Come inside the office and we'll do the loan paperwork for the new bike.'

The pair vanished. Sara stood close to Claudia, speaking in a low voice so she couldn't be overheard. 'Do you agree with what Kyle's saying about the accident?'

'Not entirely,' replied Claudia. She looked thoughtful for a moment before deciding to explain herself. 'He might have been run off the road — only, would it have happened twice?'

'What do you mean?'

'When I first saw that moped out at the West Ruston site on Tuesday morning, it was already damaged. In the yard, the morning after our fire, it looked worse than before.'

Sara looked at the moped parked at the back of the workshop. 'You think there's more damage now? Can you show me?'

'I can't be sure,' said Claudia. 'I don't think the wing mirror was broken then.'

They walked quietly over to inspect the moped. The younger mechanic had vanished. His tools and some broken parts lay beside a fan on a nearby workbench, waiting for his attention. It allowed them to look over the moped alone until a toilet flushed and the youngster reappeared.

'Can you get a tarpaulin or something?' Sara asked him. 'Cover this up for now?'

He nodded and vanished again.

Finding the petrol container was intriguing, Sara acknowledged. On its own, it didn't prove much. If he wasn't careful, riding the bike on rural lanes might leave him short of fuel with a long drive to the nearest petrol station. Carrying a top-up might be prudent. On the other hand, how good was any seventeen-year-old lad at forward thinking?

'Do you need me anymore?' Claudia broke into Sara's thoughts.

'No, thanks. We'll give you a shout to get a formal statement about this soon.'

Sara followed the office manager outside and waited until she'd driven off. Then she rang the office. Luckily, it was Aggie that answered. Sara explained that she was impounding the moped and wanted it collected by the forensic team.

'We need them to go over it to see what, if anything, they can find,' she said. '*Scoot! Rural* will just have to put up with it.'

'I'll sort out the necessary paperwork.' Sara could hear Aggie scribbling on her notepad. 'Should we do the same with Faye Rushworth's moped?'

'I don't have enough grounds for that. Not yet. Any news on her missing husband?'

'I'm afraid not,' sighed Aggie. 'Oh, and DI Edwards says he'll meet you at three o'clock for the post-mortem.'

'Anyone else with us?'

'No. Ian's out chasing Kyle Atkins' alibi for the night of the West Ruston fire,' said Aggie. 'Mike's still at the herb place taking statements.'

And enjoying scones, thought Sara. She wasn't going to tell Aggie that. It might make her jealous.

'If you haven't had a chance to check your emails, the fire officer's report on the barn is through.'

'Anything of interest? Just the outline, if you don't mind.'

'The fire was started deliberately. Accelerant splashed around the front of the barn doors. Seems to have caught quickly. Got into the thatch, as might be expected.'

'And the back?' asked Sara. She tried to imagine the building she had seen on their initial visit. There had been no reason to go round the back of the building then. She remembered Faye's moped parked in the gap between the farmhouse and the old barn. There'd been two cars in the same space, which hadn't left much room to walk to the rear of either building.

'There's a small back door. It had been locked and barred from the outside. Half a dozen windows, all of them boarded up. It would have been hard to get out. They found the victim there.'

'Anything else I should know before the PM?'

'Well, I was going to raise this at the afternoon meeting,' said Aggie. She lowered her voice so far that Sara had to put a finger in her free ear to catch what she said. 'It doesn't add up.'

'What doesn't?' Sara knew better than to question Aggie's logic.

'You told us at yesterday's meeting that Mrs Simpson claimed to have heard someone out there.'

'Or she'd seen someone.' Sara couldn't quite remember. She'd not had much sleep recently. 'Something odd about that?'

'Depends where Mrs Simpson sleeps in the farmhouse,' said Aggie carefully. 'It might not be clear when you look from the ground. But if you look at the site on a satellite map, the barn is at a slight angle to the house.'

'So?'

'The front door of the barn wouldn't be visible from most of the bedrooms. And if Mrs Simpson sleeps at the back, she wouldn't be able to see anything in the yard.'

CHAPTER 32

It had been several months since there had been any cause for Sara to visit Dr Taylor's post-mortem suite. She was watching from the observation room. Up on the first floor, it gave her and DI Edwards an overview of the lab below through a panel of glass windows. The room was rarely used and had that musty smell from lack of ventilation. Sara preferred the clinical cleanliness and scent of bleach in the examination room. Dr Taylor preferred them out of his way. This afternoon he had insisted that they use the upstairs room. DI Edwards stood next to her, chewing a soft, strong mint like they'd had to in the old days to cope with the smell of the cadaver. It was only a habit now, as the smell from the lab didn't reach the observation room.

The doctor stood by the metal table, waiting for them. Whatever was on the table was covered in the usual white sheet. The shape of the body beneath was unusual. It looked too short, as if the victim was incomplete. Something bulged, lifting the cloth high. A technician was working with his back to them on a bench at the far end of the room.

'You both ready?' asked Dr Taylor. Without waiting for a reply through the intercom, he lifted back the sheet.

Sara gasped. The forensic team had removed the victim directly from inside the barn to the private ambulance in a body bag. This was her first view, and it was shocking. Despite their often violent ends, the victims they investigated in death usually looked like any other deceased person. When rigor mortis had subsided, the morticians could lay the person out on the dissection table, ready for investigation. There was absolutely no chance of that for this victim.

The man lay on his back, and his skin was burned black. His arms were pulled up as if trying to defend himself. The victim was unmistakeably male. His appendages lay crisply on display between his legs, which were drawn up and flopped open from the hips. There were a few signs of clothing, such as the metal rivet button from a pair of jeans or shorts. It stood proud like an inverted belly button, only in a lower place. There were bulky folds on the victim's upper arms, which may have been the sleeves of a jumper or top pushed up. The head was thrown back, the neck arching and the mouth open, displaying soot-blackened teeth.

'You both okay?' asked Dr Taylor. He glanced up at them. 'That's why I didn't want you down here. Believe me, you don't want to smell this.'

'Why are his arms raised?' asked Sara. 'Was he trying to protect himself?'

'It's called the boxer pose,' said Dr Taylor. 'The fire got very hot where he was lying. That causes the soft tissues to contract, making the skin tear open. Next, the fat layer, muscles and internal organs will shrink. All of that makes the extremities pull up.'

'His head is pulled back,' observed Edwards.

'Muscles in the back of the neck are stronger than the front. In life, they develop more because they control most of the weight of the skull as we stand upright.'

'Poor sod,' said Sara. She felt nauseous for once. 'What a way to die.'

'The forensic team will confirm things with their report on the scene,' explained Taylor. 'My best estimate is that the victim was trapped inside when the fire started at the front door. You know that he was found near a smaller back door? Presumably, he was trying to get out before the fire got too bad.'

'It was locked from the outside,' said Edwards. 'Why didn't he try elsewhere?'

'There were piles of junk near the front doors. They would have caught fire quickly, cutting off that route. The fire officer's report should confirm my theory.'

'They'd been cleaning out the barn,' Sara reminded Edwards. 'Perhaps it was piled there waiting for a skip.'

'That would make sense.'

'So, our victim was trapped near the back door. The fire moved up into the thatch, then among the piles of junk at ground level. The heat would have been tremendous. So would the smoke.'

Dr Taylor stood to one side of the body before lifting aside a thick flap of burned skin above the ribs. The body underneath showed shockingly clean colours. A yellow layer of fat was still attached to the underside of the blackened and taut skin. Then, the white of rib bone, the pink of muscle and, finally, the purple-pink of the lungs. The pathologist pointed to the still squashy tissue.

'It's not unusual in such a situation for the victim to die of smoke inhalation before the fire reaches them.'

'Burn to death or cough to death,' murmured Sara. 'What a choice.'

'Depending on the type of junk in the barn, there's also the possibility of poisonous gases. Old sofas, for example, can give off noxious fumes at high temperatures. Either way, mercifully, our victim would have been unconscious or, more likely, already dead by the time the fire reached his body. He wouldn't have known about that part of it. All the same, it's a horrible death.'

'Can you tell the cause?' asked Edwards.

'I've got my technician doing some tests on tissue samples.' Dr Taylor indicated his helper, who hunched over a microscope concentrating on whatever was on the slide beneath. 'My money is on smoke inhalation.'

'Why is he so badly burned?'

'Burning thatch fell inside the building. I think that's what did all this surface damage to the body.'

'Do you know who it might be?' asked Sara. 'Apart from being a man?'

'That much is obvious, isn't it?' Taylor shook his head. 'I've taken DNA samples and sent them off for analysis.'

'Forensics took an old toothbrush for samples of Darren Rushworth's DNA. Did you get that?'

'That's gone off too. Unfortunately, it will take a day or two for the results to come back, as you know. We can hardly ask any family member to try and identify them from this.'

'What about dental records?' Sara looked at the victim's head. The skin was pulled tight, the jaw wide open as if the man were shrieking in agony. His teeth looked dirty but unbroken. 'Any chance?'

'I've asked my tooth fairy to come over,' said Dr Taylor. 'The forensic odontologist. You may not know her, as she's based in Cambridge. Said she'd try to get here this afternoon. I'll get on to local dentists to see if anyone knows him.'

'So all we have to go on is that he's male?' asked Edwards.

'Not quite. I can estimate our victim was about six feet tall. From the skin under the burning, he was Caucasian, and from the state of his teeth, he was in his thirties. The tooth fairy will be more accurate on that front. I would also say that he was fit and active. There's good muscle definition under this damage. He had earrings. Three on this side, two on the other. He also had a pair of lip piercings, one upper, one lower.' Dr Taylor pointed to the sides of the skull. 'Amazing that cheap jewellery survives, isn't it?'

Sara thought hard about her visits to Wild Thyme. She'd only seen Darren once, and very briefly at that. Hadn't he had lots of piercings? 'And his nose?'

Taylor bent to examine the victim's shrivelled nostril. 'Yes, there was a nose ring. It's gone, but the hole in the cartilage is still apparent.'

'I think Darren Rushworth had several piercings.' Sara looked at Edwards, who nodded in reply. 'We'd better ask Mrs Simpson if he ever visited a dentist.'

CHAPTER 33

The day dragged and dragged. The forensic team worked in the barn until teatime. Jean and her two ladies kept them fed and watered as they worked hard to clean the kitchen until it was ready for food preparation again.

Faye had managed to sleep for a couple of hours then stumbled exhaustedly over to the café in the middle of the day. Jean was seething when DC Bowen insisted on talking to her. Although her daughter was willing to speak to the man alone, Jean hovered nearby, cleaning a table that was already spotless so that she could overhear the conversation. It was hardly discreet, and DC Bowen turned his back to Jean.

She watched as Faye repeatedly shook her head or shrugged at DC Bowen's questions, looking increasingly confused as he persisted. He kept referring to a notebook, then carefully watching Faye's reactions when he said something. Jean was surprised when Faye led the detective to look at her moped. After that, Faye broke down in tears, prompting Jean to interfere.

'Isn't that enough for now?' she demanded angrily, hoping her disgust at the man was apparent. 'If you don't have news of Darren, you should leave us alone.'

She led Faye to the café kitchen, leaving her in the care of Rachel and Mavis. When Jean returned, the detective was running his fingers over some scratches on the side of the moped. 'What now?'

He ignored her question. 'Can you confirm your movements on the night of the fire?'

Jean repeated what she'd already told DS Hirst. At least she'd cared how Jean was during that terrible night and put out the search for Darren. This man's persistence was maddening.

'Can you think of anyone who might bear you or the herb farm a grudge?' he asked.

'Not at all,' Jean insisted. 'I've never sacked anyone in thirty years of business. We pay the staff fairly and our bills on time. Why would someone do this to us?'

'We have to consider all the possibilities,' said Bowen. 'No rivals? What about family problems?'

Jean was furious now. 'I'm sure I have no idea what you mean by that.'

'A family member who thought they should have inherited something? Or thought they weren't being listened to? A row or feud?' He smiled at this last. 'I once knew of a family that fell out over a teenager taking the last biscuit in the packet when grandma thought he shouldn't have. Didn't speak for five years. Of course, it wasn't really about the biscuit.'

This attempt at humour failed to amuse Jean. With a scowl, she assured him they were a small family, and everyone was on good terms. When he gave a quizzical look, Jean doubled down and refused to provide him with any further details about Faye or their few relatives. The man was not only unkempt, he was also nosey and suspicious.

Must go with the job, I suppose, Jean thought later. *I wish he would leave us in peace and concentrate on other people.*

She was grateful when the whole bunch packed up for the night and left. Mavis and Rachel agreed to come the next morning to continue clearing up. The wooden display tables in the yard were covered in a jumble of damaged pots. The ones nearest the old barn were charred where the fire had scorched the painted legs and tops. Even the jaunty payment shed looked bedraggled and sooty.

Both the forensic team leader and the fire investigation officer gave her permission to reopen if she wished to.

'We've finished what we need to do, though you might want to give it a few days,' the fire investigator advised her. 'There will be a few ghouls who'd love to look over the site, I'm afraid. The interest wears off after a while. You'll need to get that barn isolated for safety reasons.'

'What do you mean?'

He looked the building up and down. 'A builder should put a security fence around it. Perhaps some netting. To stop people trying to go inside. It will be a health and safety issue if you don't.'

Faye walked up and down the small garden to the rear of the farmhouse, still reflexively redialling Darren's number to listen to his voice. Jean sat in the kitchen in despair after they'd all gone. How on earth was she going to deal with all this now? Apart from the personal worry, there was the barn to be covered up, the display area to be restored and another supermarket plant order due out soon. The weight of her almost seventy years felt heavy. Her back twinged and her legs were stiff and sore. Her stomach growled, warning of a possible problem if she didn't eat soon. Was it all really worth the effort?

When her mobile rang, she grabbed it, hoping for news. It was Kevin Howard.

'Mum and I just wondered how you were,' he said carefully. 'It must be a terrible time for you. Is there anything I can do? Would you like to stay with us? Get away from the place for the night?'

'That's very kind,' said Jean mechanically. There was no way she could leave. 'I don't suppose you know any builders, do you?'

'Yes, I can recommend someone. He does work around the factory and glasshouses for us. What do you need?' Jean explained about securing the barn. 'I'll give him a ring now, if you like. See if they can come over tomorrow morning?'

'Could you? There are so many things to worry about.'

'Why don't you let me deal with that for you? It's not a problem, and I'd like to be of some help. Have you heard any more from Darren?' Kevin's voice trailed away.

'I'm afraid not.' Jean felt tears coming. 'I'll see you tomorrow, hopefully.'

She left the phone on the table as she stretched her aching back. Leaning wearily on the edge of the kitchen sink, Jean looked into the car park, empty of all vehicles except her old car and Faye's moped. The smell from the charred building seeped into the kitchen through the open windows. It permeated the whole house. What they needed was a good rainstorm to clear the air. When her phone rang for a second time, she glanced at the screen then grabbed it quickly. The number belonged to the lady detective.

'DS Hirst, do you have news?' she demanded before the woman could get beyond her greeting. 'From the post-mortem today?'

'I'm sorry, not yet.' Hirst sounded cautious. 'Would you like me to arrange some support for you and Faye? A family liaison officer might be helpful.'

'No, I don't want any more strangers here. Was there anything else?'

'Just another question, I'm afraid. Can you tell me if you and your family use a local dentist?'

'Er, yes, we do.' The question threw Jean. What did they need to know that for? 'It's in Wroxham. On the main road, beyond the boatyard and the vets. I think it's called Wroxham Dental Surgery.'

'And you all go there?'

'Yes. Why?'

'I'll pop round tomorrow to see how you are,' said the detective before she signed off. When Jean turned, Faye was standing by the kitchen table.

157

'Why would they be asking about dentists?' she demanded hysterically. 'My God, is the body that badly burned they need to see dental records?'

'I'm sorry, love,' said Jean. She reached towards her daughter to hug her. 'I just don't know.'

'It has to be,' sobbed Faye as she collapsed against Jean. 'It must be the only way to identify the body.'

'Try not to think about it. Try to wait.'

'How can I? My darling. My Darren. What if this is him? If he's dead, it's all my fault!'

CHAPTER 34

Nothing Sara could have done or said would have prevented Jean Simpson from realising that asking about their dentist was not good news. Of course, it was not uncommon for the police to send requests around the various practices in the area asking for possible matches. But dentists were busy people, and the replies sometimes took days, even for a murder victim. Sara needed to to short-circuit a general callout and the wait for DNA results. Dr Taylor's tooth fairy had produced a decent impression of the victim's teeth, and Sara was on her way to collect them before taking them to the waiting dentist in Wroxham.

She was so preoccupied that she failed to notice when Dante spotted her leaving. He caught up with her before she got to the stairs at the end of the corridor. She was extracting her car keys from her handbag when he tapped her arm.

'Don't go,' he said, pulling her to a halt.

'I'm on the way to the mortuary,' she told him. 'It's urgent.'

'I'm sure. Can't you spare me a minute or two?'

Sara huffed a bit before nodding. 'Yes, of course.'

'I have to ask,' he began. Sara could see that he was angry with her. It made her uncomfortable, and she moved away. 'What have I done wrong?'

'What do you mean?'

'You haven't been to stay with me for a couple of weeks. Now you won't answer my messages or calls. Am I really that bad in bed?' Dante drew a deep breath and glanced around to ensure no one was listening. 'Look, I don't want to do this here. Can we have dinner tonight? We need to talk.'

'I can't.' Sara shook her head and spluttered out what she knew were excuses. 'This case is really difficult. We're all up to the eyeballs. I'm on my way to try and identify a victim.'

'I'm just about to knock off. Why don't I come with you?'

'There's no need. I have to go straight home after my visit. Someone is waiting for me.'

Dante folded his arms. 'What sort of someone?'

'Please don't make something out of nothing,' she rolled her eyes. 'It's just a workman. A gardener, to be precise. Gilly arranged for him to tame that wilderness at the back of the cottage.'

'Gardener? I'm guessing an older chap with a pipe and a trowel,' said Dante acidly. Sara recoiled at the look on his face. 'If Gilly knows him.'

Sara longed to tell him to mind his own business. He was bristling with barely controlled irritation. She wasn't about to admit that the man was young, handsome and ripped. Nor that Dante would have reason to be jealous if he saw the effect that Adie Dickinson was having on Sara.

'He's just a workman. Don't get all uptight about it. I have to go. Dr Taylor is waiting for me.'

'Uptight!' spat Dante as she rattled down the stairs. 'You owe me an explanation.'

She waved her hand without actually agreeing.

I've got to deal with this, Sara thought, as she drove to meet the pathologist. *I should never have got into it in the first place.*

* * *

The impression was a pair of moulded plaster-of-Paris teeth, upper and lower jaw. It felt weird to carry the things in a small plastic container knowing they belonged to a dead man. Sara placed them carefully in the glove box of her car. She didn't want the things grinning at her from the passenger seat like a skeleton's dentures.

The surgery was easy enough to find. It was a 1930s detached villa on the main Norwich Road through Wroxham. There'd been a building boom between the wars when retiring to the Broads had become fashionable. Bowen had once told her that famous old-time British film stars had homes on the riverside back in the day. Large by modern standards, these days the houses were often split into flats or housed businesses like the surgery or the vets a few doors down.

It was after six when Sara pulled into the little gravel car park. There was a light on in reception, although the sign on the door said 'Closed'. When she knocked, a middle-aged woman in a dentist's uniform appeared to let her in. Sara produced her warrant card.

'I was expecting you. I'm Mrs Pearson,' she said, leading Sara through a door into a corridor. 'Come this way.'

Several white doors opened off the corridor. There was a strong smell of cleaning fluid, and the place looked immaculate. Sara could hear her shoes squeaking on the lino. Mrs Pearson was wearing crocks, which made no noise at all as she walked. Pushing open a door, she ushered Sara inside.

'This is my surgery,' Mrs Pearson said. 'There are three partners here. The person you mentioned on the phone is my patient. Do you have the impressions?'

Handing over the box, Sara looked at the room. There was the standard dentist's chair, with various gadgets, bowls and overhead lights. A range of cabinets lined one wall, with storage cupboards above. A computer blinked in the far corner, showing a patient's records. Sara wasn't at ease in a dentist's chair like most people. She shifted uneasily.

'Done by the forensic odontologist from Cambridge,' she said, feeling the need to justify their work.

'Judith McCloud?' asked Mrs Pearson in surprise.

'Yes, I believe so. Why?'

'Then they'll be perfect. That woman is a true legend in the world of odontology.' The dentist picked up a tatty buff file. The name *Darren Rushworth* was written in red pen across the top. 'I got the old records out. We're computerised these days, but you can't beat the X-ray flimsies for identifications.'

'You look after the whole family?'

'Mrs Simpson and Faye have been with us for years,' nodded Mrs Pearson. 'Darren joined us when he married Faye. Jean insisted. His mouth was a bit of a mess, to be honest. His lip piercings were poorly done and had caused some damage. Better now, though.'

She double-checked the file with the screen, then pulled out a pair of small square X-ray sheets. Clicking on a light box, the woman slid them into the holder and looked at them closely. Taking first the upper impression, then the lower, she turned them to study various angles in comparison to the X-rays. Finally, she returned them to the container and clicked on the lid.

'I'm sorry,' said Mrs Pearson. She looked sad as she turned to Sara. 'In as much as I can be sure, these impressions match our X-rays. I believe this person is most likely to be Darren Rushworth. You can see the damage I had to repair from the piercings. I take it that this is not good news.'

'We can't identify him any other way until the DNA results come back,' said Sara. 'May I take these X-rays? Then I can send everything to Mrs McCloud for final screening.'

'Of course.' Mrs Pearson put them in an envelope for her.

'Thank you for your time. I'll let my boss know.'

It wasn't until she was back in her car dialling DCI Hudson that it hit her. The victim was Faye's husband and Jean's son-in-law. Someone would have to deliver the news to those two women, and she was almost on their doorstep. Hudson was bound to tell her to do it. They all hated that job more than any other, and she would have to do it alone.

CHAPTER 35

As expected, DCI Hudson told Sara to visit Faye and Jean immediately on the strength of the dentist's identification. Her boss insisted there was no need to wait for the DNA or Cambridge to confirm it. The unexpected thing had been DI Edwards volunteering to go with her. She parked in the supermarket car park with a takeaway coffee to wait for him.

'I'm worried about this,' Sara told the DI when they met. 'I know it's a difficult decision. If we leave it for the DNA results, they could say we kept them waiting too long. But what if Mrs Pearson is wrong?'

'Everyone expects DNA these days,' agreed Edwards. 'Not so long ago, a confirmation from a dentist was as good as a fingerprint and sometimes all we had.'

'Poor things,' she said as they climbed into their cars. 'This is going to be awful.'

When they arrived, the gate to Wild Thyme Herb Farm was closed with a chain and padlock. Rather than wasting time with it, they left their cars in the lane and walked across the gravel car park to the farmhouse as the evening shadows were lengthening. Sara could see Mrs Simpson at the kitchen window as they approached. She opened the front door to them before they needed to knock. Her face was drained of all colour, and her hand trembled on the door lock.

'Come in,' she said quietly. 'Faye is in the living room.'

They followed her into the living room, where Faye stood by a sofa, twisting her hands together and breathing quickly. Sara knew that although Edwards was there as her moral support, he would leave her to break the bad news. She waited until Mrs Simpson reached her daughter before speaking.

'I'm very sorry to bring you this news,' said Sara as carefully and clearly as she could. The words stuck in her throat for a second, and she swallowed hard. 'Dental records show that the victim in your barn fire was your husband, Mrs Rushworth.'

'You think it's Darren?' wavered Mrs Simpson. 'Oh, God. Please, no.'

Sara paused, waiting for the news to sink in and the reaction to start. Faye stared at her wide-eyed. She stood immobile, not responding, when her mother wrapped her arms around her in a hug. When Mrs Simpson tried to turn her towards the sofa, Faye's body was so rigid the older woman couldn't even move her shoulders.

'Perhaps you should both sit down,' suggested Sara to Mrs Simpson. Faye suddenly pushed her mother away.

'Can you tell us any more?' asked Mrs Simpson. 'You said the dental records. Is that absolute? Are you sure?'

'I'm afraid we don't have the DNA results yet,' explained Sara. 'Unfortunately, the dentist agrees with our post-mortem examination. We considered it best to let you know immediately rather than wait for the lab to complete the DNA test.'

'Could they be wrong?'

Sara watched Faye begin to sway gently.

'It's possible,' said Sara softly. 'But it's highly unlikely. We expect the DNA results to confirm the identification.'

When the collapse came, it was Mrs Simpson who fainted and not her daughter. Sara had been so busy watching the younger woman, waiting to catch her if she went over, that she missed the signs in the older woman. Mercifully, she went backwards on to the squashy sofa. Edwards darted forward to check Mrs Simpson's pulse while Sara strode to help Faye. The sudden movement of her mother fainting brought Faye's attention back from whatever dark place it had been in. She looked quickly at Edwards bent over her mother, then back at Sara.

'How can you be sure?' she demanded. Her voice was breathy and high. Sara hoped she wasn't going to hyperventilate and faint as well. 'I want to see him.'

Sara simply didn't know what to say to this. The image of the burned man with his raised fists and silent scream was fresh in her mind. She didn't know if they could even loosen the muscles by cutting to lay him out. Even so, the charred facial skin rendered it impossible to identify the man visually and was deeply distressing. No matter what Dr Taylor said about the victim being unconscious or already dead when the body began to burn, the sight was the stuff of endless nightmares if it was a loved one. Not to mention the smell.

'I really don't think that would be a good idea,' murmured Sara.

'You'll need someone to identify him,' urged Faye. 'They always do on the television. Who better than me?'

'It would be better if you waited for the DNA results.' Sara knew this was only delaying the issue.

'I want to do it,' Faye insisted.

Mrs Simpson groaned a little as she came round. DI Edwards was patting her hand. 'It's okay, Mrs Simpson. You're not alone. Faye, come and help your mother.'

His natural tone of command was enough to make Faye move, and, pushing Edwards aside, she sat beside her mother. As she helped her mother to be more comfortable, Edwards stepped away to join Sara, his back to the women. Catching her eye, he shook his head and made a cutting gesture at his throat. Sara understood immediately what he meant. When the two women stopped fussing, Sara sat in the armchair opposite them.

Faye took a couple of deep breaths. 'It's okay, Mum. I'll deal with this. Well?'

'Of course, if you insist, we can arrange a visit to see Darren,' Sara explained. 'However, the dentist's records and the DNA test are more than sufficient for an identification.'

Having to care for her mother seemed to have helped Faye, at least for the moment. Squaring her shoulders, she looked directly at Sara. 'Why don't you want me to see him?'

'I'm afraid the fire did a lot of damage.'

'I wouldn't be able to recognise him, is that what you mean?'

'I'm sorry. I don't think you would.'

Mrs Simpson moaned as she tried to sit up. 'Faye? What is she saying?'

'I'll explain later,' Faye tried to assure her mother. 'DS Hirst, I would like to make it clear that I would still like to visit my husband. It's all my fault, and I want to apologise to him.'

Startled, Sara tried to reply. Mrs Simpson cut her off. 'No, Faye. No. That's not true. It's not your fault. It's mine.'

CHAPTER 36

Sara worried all the way home about the confessions of the two women. In her opinion, they were just expressions of guilty emotions and were unlikely to have any bearing on the fire. All the same, she would need to scrutinise both women even more closely.

Despite what she had told Dante, Sara hadn't expected Adie to be there when she got home. He had left the key with Gilly as requested. The garden did indeed look a mess, as he'd warned, but she was too emotionally drained to worry. She rang Gilly and arranged for her neighbour to let Adie in the following morning, as Sara needed to leave early.

Sara was the first one in when she reached the office. The morning catch-up meeting was due to begin at eight, and she wanted to be in before that to get her thoughts together. Checking the local news websites, it seemed there had been no more major fires overnight.

The meeting convened on time. Aggie sat at her desk while Bowen perched proprietorially on the front edge of it. DC Noble typed at his computer keyboard until his attention was required. Sara turned her chair round to look at the incident board. DI Edwards was leaning on the outside wall of his office. DCI Hudson stood in front of the whiteboards, marker pen in hand, the picture of office-based efficiency in her crisp blouse and suit trousers.

It's obvious you don't go out in the field much anymore, thought Sara, looking at her boss.

'The number of fires is settling down,' Sara began. 'The slight drop in temperature seems to have stopped the worst of the spontaneous outbreaks.'

'What about this meeting you went to?' DCI Hudson asked.

'No one came forward with any more unreported fires,' replied Sara. 'Claudia Turner at Coles Construction agreed to organise an observation rota, which began last night. She also told us about the damage to Kyle's bike.'

'I can't help wondering why,' murmured Bowen. 'What's in it for her?'

Sara silently agreed with him. Was Claudia Turner just a busybody? Or did she get a vicarious buzz from helping the police? She intended to keep an eye on Coles' office manager.

'Let's get out and take a full statement from her,' instructed Hudson. She wrote up the action on the board. 'Find out about this rota and get a copy, just in case. Bowen can do that. How are we doing with the moped?'

'Forensics are transporting it this morning,' said Aggie. 'They're taking it to Snetterton for a full examination.'

Hudson wrote another note on the board. 'Did we check Kyle's alibi for the fire at West Ruston?'

'I did,' said DC Noble. 'Claimed he was drinking with a few mates, which, given that they are all under eighteen, made it difficult to get them to admit it.'

'And did they?'

'In the end.' Noble grinned. 'Apparently, one of them pinches cans or bottles from his dad's shop, and they meet on Belaugh Common. It's between their home villages. They have a sort of den there among the trees. I went for a walk and found the place. It's a real mess, full of empty drink containers and the butts of what I assume to be joints. I brought a few in a bag in case we need them.'

168

'Did you believe them, Ian?' asked Sara. 'Or were they just looking out for their mate?'

'On balance, I'd say I believed them.'

'We need to get a DNA sample from Kyle,' said Bowen.

'We need to be careful because of his age.' Hudson wrote more actions on the board. 'We also need an official statement from him about his movements on all the dates of the other fires, including the unreported one at Howards. Let's make an appointment to do that. Aggie, if his mother or uncle can't be with him, we'll need to arrange for a responsible adult to attend.'

'And the duty solicitor?' Aggie scribbled a note on her pad.

'Indeed. What about his mother? Do you think she could be doing this?' asked Hudson. She looked at Sara and Bowen. 'She certainly has reason to hate Willmott. What did you think when you met her?'

'Unlikely, I'd say.' Sara glanced at Bowen, who nodded in agreement. 'It's been years since the accident, and I'm not sure she would be happy riding that moped. She didn't look very secure on her pushbike and doesn't have a car.'

'There's the younger brother, Ryan,' suggested Bowen. 'He's only thirteen. According to his mother, he knows nothing about his father's death. I'm not so sure.'

'Too young to be riding the moped,' dismissed Hudson.

'Tall enough,' Bowen persisted.

Hudson wrote a note on the list. 'Bear him in mind. How did you get on with the Wild Thyme staff?'

'I've put their statements online,' answered Bowen. 'It's the gossip that's more interesting. The cook, Mavis, is adamant that Faye and her mother haven't been getting on recently. We saw some of that on our first visit.'

'What about these confessions from last night?' Hudson looked at Edwards.

'I doubt they will be useful,' Edwards grimaced. 'They're not official, and any decent solicitor would claim they only said it because of the shock.'

'I know it will be difficult for them, but we need official interviews with both mother and daughter. Ask about all the fire dates we're looking at, not just their movements that night. You never know. Sara, I'd like you to do that.'

'I'll go with you,' volunteered DI Edwards. 'They know me a little.'

Sara nodded and glanced at Bowen. 'Mrs Simpson isn't so keen on Mike. I have no idea why.'

'No need to sound so sarcastic,' replied Bowen. He puffed his cheeks out in mock offence, then grinned as they laughed at him. 'I'm a nice kinda guy.'

'Any more news from Dr Taylor?' asked Hudson.

'His report should be here this morning,' said Sara. She'd already checked her emails, but it was too early for the results. 'I left him a message last night to confirm the dentist's identification of our victim.'

Hudson turned to look at the list of fires. 'Apart from Belaugh Manor Farm, are there any other connections we're missing?'

They all stared at the list of fires. Noble moved over to the map and scrutinised it. After a moment, he turned to them and, looking apologetic, offered his opinion.

'Thatched roofs,' he said with a shrug. 'At least with the later ones. The third fire at Willmott's place involved an abandoned cow shed. I checked the fire report photos and it had a thatched roof. In this heat, they're really dry.'

'I thought they were good for thirty-five years when they were laid,' said Bowen.

'Yes, when they're maintained. All three buildings on our list are thatched and have been unused for some time.'

Sara perked up as it suddenly made more sense. 'Mr Willmott said they had thought about selling the cow shed for conversion into a house, but it was too dilapidated.'

'The old pub at West Ruston had been empty for over three years,' added Noble. 'The site manager told me that on the night of the fire.'

'And the barn at Wild Thyme had long been used for storing junk,' added Sara. 'All of them had decaying thatched roofs, making them easier to set fire to.'

'So, the fire at the cow shed was just an attack on Mr Willmott?' Hudson reasoned. 'But it showed our arsonist that they got a better thrill from burning old thatch. After that, they looked for old buildings in a similar state to get their thrills?'

There was a murmur of general agreement until DI Edwards spoke from the back of the room.

'I can see why we're looking at Kyle. He fits the bill of the average arsonist. What I don't understand is why he would burn the barn at Wild Thyme. It's not as easy to get at as the other two. He could have been seen, and there's no connection with that family or access through work. It seems an odd choice. Though whoever set the fire at West Ruston would have needed to be able to climb over the security fence.'

'You think we might be looking at two arsonists?' asked Hudson. She looked at Edwards through narrowed eyes. 'That would complicate things. Although Mrs Simpson's family seems to be in crisis as much as the Willmotts are.'

'Why would you burn down your own barn?' asked Sara. 'Insurance?'

'One of the staff did suggest that, didn't they?' said Bowen. 'Said the business was on rocky ground.'

'Aggie, how are you getting on with looking into their finances?' Hudson looked at Aggie.

'I got the order signed off.' Aggie nodded. 'I'm waiting for the copies from the bank. It's the weekend, so they won't be fully staffed.'

'What about revenge for this argument?' asked Sara. 'That would put Faye or Jean in the frame, wouldn't it?'

'Might depend on how bad the rows were,' suggested Bowen. 'So far, neither is willing to admit they've fallen out.'

'Insurance or revenge, both are decent motives,' agreed Edwards. 'Even so, was Darren Rushworth's death just an unfortunate coincidence? A terrible accident? How did he get into the barn if it was locked up?'

'Or maybe the fire was meant to kill him,' said Hudson firmly. 'Either way, the fact that the fire was set on purpose means that this is at least manslaughter and possibly murder.'

CHAPTER 37

Claudia had been enjoying a leisurely Saturday morning when DC Bowen called her. She was sitting on the sofa in a lightweight faux-silk dressing gown, sipping an iced tea and watching some chefs giggling at one another on the television. Her life was hardly the stuff of dreams these days. When she'd still been married, Saturdays were for going to Norwich and meeting her girlfriends for shopping and lunch. As the marriage was breaking down, it had been the best excuse for getting away from her snoring, farting husband before he woke up with a hangover. Claudia had taken on the house when they had split up, extending the mortgage to buy out the man she had once loved. Each month was a struggle, but she was proud to think she was slowly winning. Saturdays with the girls were now a rare treat, as was any other social contact outside work.

'I would need to call out the security guard to get into the office,' she explained to Bowen. Claudia looked round the half-empty sitting room in dismay. She rarely allowed any visitors because the bastard had taken half the furniture as well as half her money. At least it was clean. 'I suppose you could come to my house.'

'I'll be about half an hour,' said Bowen.

Which gave Claudia time to shower, dress more professionally, and plump up the two solitary cushions that made her sofa more comfortable. Piles of DVDs leaned crookedly against the wall. Stacks of books from the town's charity shops attested to her love of historical fiction. Her work bags were stuffed in the corner, the laptop in its padded case.

The kettle was on in anticipation when the detective rang at the door. There wasn't much milk left. Claudia sniffed it suspiciously. It seemed to pass the test. She wouldn't go shopping again until tomorrow morning at the low-cost supermarket.

'Tea? Coffee?' she asked, leading DC Bowen to the tiny living room. Claudia watched him as he surveyed her home. Beyond the pair of narrow French windows was a small patio area with tall wooden fences on three sides, where Claudia kept a handful of pots which she carefully watered and tendered.

'Nice place,' said the detective with a smile. 'Tea would be good, thanks.'

'Put it on the floor,' she advised him as he accepted the mug of tea from her moments later. There was no coffee table. 'Don't worry about it.'

'You been here long?' he asked.

'Six years,' she replied. Bowen looked surprised. 'I know. It looks like I've just moved in, doesn't it? Divorce.'

'Ah,' he nodded understandingly. 'I've just remarried myself, and at my age! You never know, do you?'

'I suppose not.' It was a vaguely comforting thought. Perhaps she wouldn't always be on her own.

Claudia sat beside him on the sofa and pulled the laptop on to her knee. 'You said you'd like a copy of the rota for the night observations? I can forward you a copy if you let me have your email. I don't have a printer at home.'

'Here you go.' Bowen handed her one of his cards. She typed the email address carefully and sent a copy.

'Done. I hope it helps.'

Slurping his tea, the detective opened a tablet and logged into something. He turned it for her to look at.

'It's taken me a while to enter the twenty-first century,' he apologised. 'These days, we can take your statement and sign it off on this. Is that all right with you?'

Claudia agreed it was. It took about fifteen minutes for Bowen to type up her brief statement about Kyle's moped with two fingers. His hunt-and-peck technique drove Claudia crazy, though she felt it would be rude to offer to type it herself.

'Did you think there was further damage when you saw the bike at *Scoot! Rural*?' he asked, squinting at the screen.

'On balance, yes, I think so.'

'What do you think of Kyle?'

Claudia was a bit surprised by the question. She took time to consider her answer. 'To be honest, I don't really know him that well. I didn't know Eric was his uncle until you visited. Kyle seems like a nice young man. Doesn't say much to me, except when I went near his bike the other day. That was a bit odd.'

'In what way?'

'He didn't like me looking at it,' she explained. 'It was parked next to my car. It was hard to miss. Jamie Waller pointed out the damage to me.'

'Jamie Waller?'

'The site manager at West Ruston, if you remember.' Bowen grunted an acknowledgement. 'Eric and Kyle were attached to the site before the fire. Eric is still there, helping Jamie assess the damage. Kyle's been moved on to a job at Paston.'

Bowen nodded, making more notes on the laptop. 'So, Kyle didn't want you inspecting his bike?'

'Got a bit upset,' she nodded. 'Eric intervened before he could get too mouthy. He didn't look very happy when I turned up at *Scoot! Rural* either. Didn't like your sergeant being there, or her taking the bike in for tests. What do you suspect him of?'

'We follow all lines of enquiry,' said Bowen swiftly. 'Getting evidence is the key, hence my visit to you. Here you go.'

He handed over the tablet for Claudia to read the statement. When she nodded her agreement, he proffered a stylus pen. 'You can scribble on the little pad there to sign it.'

It was awkward to do, and as he leaned over to show her where to press, his foot knocked the mug flying. Dregs of tea spattered the carpet, and he shot up with a muttered curse.

'I'm so sorry, how clumsy of me.' He grabbed the mug and wiped at the marks with a handkerchief rapidly pulled from his pocket.

'Not to worry,' she said with a sigh. The carpet was that beige colour that came with most new houses, and the stains probably wouldn't show up that much.

Bowen continued to fuss at it for a moment. Standing up, he handed her the offending mug and frowned. 'I really am sorry. Look, can I say something?'

'Yes, I guess so.' Claudia felt wary.

'I remember this.' The detective waved at the room. 'How it is when you get left on your own. I've been lucky to meet someone new, and when I moved in with my Aggie, we amalgamated two homes. We have lots of extra stuff, like coffee tables and bookcases. I could drop some bits off for you?'

She was taken aback and hesitated before answering. 'Do I look that poor?'

'Not at all,' he rushed on in embarrassment. 'I just thought it might be useful. It would help us out, actually.'

Claudia smiled at him as she accepted. It felt nice to have someone helping her for once. 'That would be kind.'

'Just don't tell anyone at work,' he grinned. 'That would ruin my reputation as a grumpy old bugger.'

'Your secret is safe with me.'

CHAPTER 38

Despite it being Saturday morning, Kevin Howard had turned up early at Wild Thyme with his friendly builder. The man sucked his teeth a lot as he wandered around the outside of the barn. After taking a hard hat from the back of his van, he went inside alone to assess the damage. Jean took Kevin inside for a cuppa.

'Thank you for doing this,' she said as the young man settled at the kitchen table. 'It's one less thing for me to face.'

'I'm glad to be able to help,' he replied. 'Any news?'

'The police came last night. They confirmed the victim was Darren.'

'I'm so sorry.'

'They had to check his dental records to be sure. The body was so badly burned.'

Jean turned away to hide her tears, pretending to make tea for them both. She was cross with herself for breaking down the previous night. It wasn't like her to give in to weeping, let alone faint. How could she have left Faye to cope with all that?

Of course, the two detectives had pricked up their ears when both she and her daughter had claimed to be at fault. Faye claimed a major row had erupted at his parents' house, culminating in Darren walking out. He'd driven off in their car and never come back. Jean confessed that she had once promised to buy them their own house but had never followed through. 'Maybe us all living together wasn't ideal. That's what I meant when I said it was my fault. Every couple should have their own space.'

The detectives had exchanged glances but passed no further comment. When they left, she'd persuaded Faye to eat something before they both went to their rooms. Jean had made no attempt to go to bed, however. She'd stood by the window in the moonlight, racking her brains for over an hour. How had her son-in-law ended up trapped in the barn? His car wasn't in the car park, and Faye still had his work keys. Unable to settle, Jean had taken a large flashlight and walked around the entire property, checking everywhere a vehicle might be hidden. Then she'd walked the circle of narrow lanes that surrounded them. It had taken her over an hour, and she hadn't found the vehicle anywhere. So how had he ended up in there? Why hadn't she heard him?

'Have you had any breakfast?' asked Kevin.

Jean turned round and looked at him blankly, her whole body beginning to shake. She had forgotten to eat again. He guided her to a chair and held her hand until the trembling subsided. She was grateful for the human contact.

The man was obviously loving and caring. His mother was so lucky. Why didn't Jean have a loving child like him? Why hadn't Faye married Kevin? They could have amalgamated the two businesses. Wild Thyme herbs could have been on the shelves of every supermarket in the country. Why had Faye fallen for the tattooed man with piercings who wasn't local and had strange ideas? Jean felt anger rising from the pit of her stomach.

Kevin dropped her hand suddenly when they heard feet on the stairs. He smiled briefly at Jean as he moved away to finish making the drinks.

'Kevin!' Faye sounded surprised to see him. 'What are you doing here?'

'I brought a builder to look at the barn,' he said over his shoulder. Jean sensed his reluctance to face them. Faye came over and looked out of the kitchen window.

'Yes, it will need seeing to,' she agreed. 'Surely it could have waited though?'

'It has been suggested that we can't reopen with it as it is now,' said Jean carefully. 'It would be a health and safety hazard.'

'Reopen?' Jean watched as Faye gripped the edge of the porcelain sink until her knuckles went white. Her daughter gazed steadily outside. 'Naturally, that would be your first concern. You could at least have left it until after the funeral.'

'That might take a while,' said Kevin quietly. 'With the police being involved and all.'

Faye didn't acknowledge him.

'My main concern is that nobody gets hurt,' said Jean, struggling to keep her voice steady. 'It's falling apart.'

'I think it's too late for that, Mother,' said Faye sharply. 'Someone already has been hurt by it. My husband. Remember him?'

Kevin clattered mugs of tea on to the table. 'Here you go. I'll just see how the builder is doing.'

Faye waited until he shut the kitchen door before she turned on her mother with blazing eyes. 'Did you do this?'

'What?' Jean was astounded. Her mouth dropped open.

'Did you set fire to the thing? For the money, I mean. It would be like you.'

'Jesus! What do you think of me?' Jean demanded. 'I might ask you the same thing! Where have you been going in the middle of the night all these weeks? Riding off on your bloody moped and vanishing for hours. Have you been starting all these fires around here? Did you get a taste for it?'

'Did I set fire to the barn? Why would I do that?' Faye's voice grew dangerously quiet. 'Why would I murder the man I loved? You were the one that hated him.'

'I didn't hate him!' yelled Jean. 'I loved him. More than you ever did. He was just a rebellion with you. Something to

179

beat me up with. Someone you thought I would disapprove of. Well, you were wrong.'

'This isn't all about you, Mother.' Faye looked icily at her mother, realisation dawning on her face. 'My God! You fancied him, didn't you?'

'Don't be ridiculous!' Jean was incandescent now. 'That's obscene. I'm nearly seventy.'

Faye turned away with a snarl and looked across the car park at Kevin's retreating back. 'Oh, look. How wonderful. Those detectives are back.'

CHAPTER 39

'What do you think about those two so-called confessions from last night?' asked DI Edwards as he drove them through Wroxham and over the river bridge.

'Spur-of-the-moment guilty reaction,' replied Sara. 'Sounds like they both have personal things they haven't resolved. None of it amounts to a confession of deliberately killing Darren, though it might be what they have been arguing about.'

'Is it something in the air around here?'

'Making families dysfunctional?' Sara smiled and shook her head. She watched the road for a moment. 'Do you think all these fires are tied together?'

'If they are, and I'm not sure of that, then Darren's death was probably accidental. If they're not, perhaps the herb farm one was all about killing him.'

'Aggie says that we need to check what room Jean Simpson sleeps in,' said Sara, flipping through her notebook. 'I should have done it by now. This heat is making me slack.'

'Why?'

'She wonders if Mrs Simpson would have been able to hear or see anyone in the yard at night. The barn and the house are at an odd angle, apparently.'

DI Edwards swung in at the gate to Wild Thyme. A car and a builder's van stood in the car park already. He stopped in the centre of the car park where they could see both buildings. Two men stood deep in conversation by the barn wall.

'The barn turns away from the farmhouse at the far end,' said Sara, pointing at the now derelict building. The gap where the main doors should have been faced the sales area. The café was behind them, and the farmhouse stood at right angles to the lane outside. 'I reckon both front and back doors are only visible from certain upstairs rooms.'

Edwards parked the car, and Sara walked along the barn wall, glancing back at the farmhouse.

'You need to be careful,' shouted one of the men.

When she reached them, Sara could no longer see the house. The barn obscured it from view. She reached into her trouser pocket for her warrant card.

'No need, DS Hirst,' said Kevin Howard. He introduced the second man as the builder whose van Edwards had parked next to. 'We're here to see what needs to be done to make the building safe before Mrs Simpson decides what to do with it. I said I'd help sort it out. The least I could do for them.'

Sara raised an eyebrow. 'That's very kind of you.'

Kevin smiled at her scepticism. 'We've been friends for years. My parents knew Jean and her husband back when they started the herb farm. I went to school with Faye. We've looked out for each other for decades. Are you getting any further with those fires?'

'We're working hard on it,' Sara assured him before rejoining Edwards, who was waiting impatiently for her. She paced the distance between the barn and the farmhouse while he knocked at the front door. Jean's car and Faye's moped were parked at the far end of the car park, leaving the gap clear.

The gravel was dark with soot. Burned reeds from the thatch lay around in damp lumps. There was less damage at the back of the barn. Long ropes of thatch hung down, partly obscuring half a dozen windows, three on the ground floor, three above. All of them were covered with old, thick wooden shutters and nailed closed with planks. The small door had a wide metal bar across it, with a large padlock to keep it in place. It was clear that no one was welcome to go inside this way. It was no wonder Darren hadn't been able to get out. Looking towards the farmhouse, all Sara could see was the end wall. Two normal windows faced the barn with a side door between them. There was another long window through which Sara could see the staircase inside the house. The easiest way to see the back of the barn would be from the stairs, perhaps from the upper landing. It wouldn't be possible to see the double doors at the front of the barn where the fire started.

Faye Rushworth let them in. 'Mum's in the kitchen. Go through.'

Jean Simpson looked tired. All this was clearly taking a serious toll on her. Faye seemed to be in charge. She told them to sit at the table, and when her mother offered them tea, she snapped, 'Let's just get this over with, shall we, Mother?'

Sara watched as Jean flinched and subsided back into her chair. 'Of course.'

'So, what do you want?' asked Faye. Her tone was sour, her dislike of Sara and her boss all too clear. Perhaps it was because they had brought the bad news yesterday. Sara decided to let Edwards take the lead.

'We need to talk to you about your movements on the night of the fire,' he began.

'You know already,' Faye interrupted. 'I was with my in-laws. Mum was here. She saw the fire and called 999. I didn't even know until the next day.'

'We also need to know your whereabouts on certain other evenings,' said Edwards calmly. Sara knew he wouldn't stay calm for long if Faye remained uncooperative. Her boss pulled a list from his coat pocket, which he offered to Jean.

'We were here.' Faye slapped her hand on the list, pinning it to the table. 'We're always here. We never leave.'

'Not even to go out for a drink? Meet friends?' persisted Edwards. He tried to pull the list free. Faye suddenly lifted her hand, releasing the list which nearly ripped in half from the sweat on her palm.

'We don't have any friends,' she hissed. 'Just this bloody business. It's never-ending.'

'Mrs Simpson?' asked Sara quietly. 'Are you unwell?'

The mother was watching her daughter in amazement. Her chin was wobbling, her distress all too obvious. When she spoke to her daughter, her voice was breathy and faint. 'We have to help the police. It's our duty.'

'No, we don't.' Faye looked at her mother, her lips twisted with exasperation. 'God knows, you watch enough of those bloody detective things on the television. It's up to them to prove something. We don't have to help them.'

'Don't you want to find out what happened to your husband?' Sara was perplexed. She'd had Faye down as the newly bereaved wife trying to cope, and her aggression as simply shock. What was the woman afraid of?

'That's your job.'

'We know that,' said Edwards, his patience wearing thin. Mrs Simpson began to sway in her chair. Sara stood up and moved to her side, thinking she might be going to faint again.

'Can I take you to your room?' she asked, reaching to hold the woman's arm. 'Do you need to lie down?'

'Oh no you don't.' Faye stood and grabbed at her mother. 'I'll see to her if necessary.'

The pair stared at each other over Jean's head. Faye's face was knotted with anger. Sara tried to keep her manner neutral.

'I think I would like to lie down,' came the faint voice of Mrs Simpson.

With difficulty, Faye pulled her mother up from the chair.

'Can't I help you?' begged Sara.

'No. You don't get to touch her. You don't get to go upstairs or see our rooms or anything else. Not without a search warrant.'

Sara felt her mouth open in surprise. Faye managed to get her mother on her feet and supported her out of the door.

'I warned you,' she heard Faye say to her mother as they went up the stairs. 'We said too much last night. Tell them nothing, or they'll try to blame us for everything. They always do.'

As they reached the first landing turn, Jean stumbled and fell onto the next step. Sara rushed to the door. 'Please, let me help.'

'Go away!' shouted Faye. 'Leave us alone.'

Mrs Simpson's eyes closed, and her body slumped forward as she lost consciousness.

CHAPTER 40

Mrs Simpson came round after a few seconds. Groaning softly, she allowed Faye to take her upstairs after refusing to let Sara call for an ambulance. 'I just need to rest,' she insisted. Sara felt helpless as she watched them struggle. It wasn't just Faye's unexpected outburst; the atmosphere told her something was wrong. Her copper's radar was pinging insistently. DI Edwards joined her from the kitchen.

'I think we should go outside for now,' he suggested. Sara followed him reluctantly to the car park, carefully closing the front door behind her.

Edwards walked over to inspect Faye's moped. Glancing across, she saw that Kevin Howard was watching them. Was he being protective or just plain nosey? She followed Edwards as he walked around the bike. It was a jaunty red colour with a black seat and looked to be the same model as Kyle Atkins'. It was also damaged. There were scuff marks on one side as if Faye had dropped it on the floor, and there was an aroma of petrol. Sara checked the fuel cap. Whoever had fastened it last had forced the screw thread, and the cap stood proud on one side. That might account for the smell.

'There's a storage space under the seat,' she told Edwards. She found the catch at the rear. It was locked.

The crunch of gravel warned her that someone was approaching. Sara let go of the catch as Faye and Kevin Howard strode towards them. Faye obviously felt the need for reinforcements.

'What are you doing?' she demanded.

Edwards pointed to the scratch marks. 'How did you get these?'

'I had a bit of a fall. Several weeks ago. I haven't had time to get it seen to.'

'Is this machine from *Scoot! Rural*?' asked Sara.

Faye frowned. 'No. What's that? I bought it from a bike dealer near Norwich.'

'With a small loan from me,' said Kevin Howard. 'Before you investigate Faye's accounts and make something out of nothing.'

Sara was sure he was blushing. Did he carry some sort of candle for Faye Rushworth? If so, that was another complication for this already dysfunctional family. Facts, that was what they had to hold to. What were the facts?

Sara looked at her boss. 'Sir?'

'Get it taken in.' DI Edwards gave a curt nod, then turned away. He walked briskly towards the damaged barn. 'Call Aggie to get the paperwork sorted out.'

'What does he mean?' demanded Faye.

'I'm afraid I shall have to arrange for the machine to be taken to our forensic team's facility at Snetterton for examination. You should consider it impounded and not use it until we've finished.'

'How dare you!'

'It's a possible material piece of evidence in a police enquiry,' said Sara as patiently as she could. Faye was beginning to aggravate her as well as Edwards. 'I'll make the call now. It should be picked up in the next few hours.'

'That doesn't give you the right—' began Faye, stepping forward.

'It does.' Kevin Howard pulled Faye's arm to hold her still.

'We also need to take formal statements from yourself and Mrs Simpson,' Sara carried on undeterred. 'You can agree on a time to come and give us voluntary statements. Otherwise, we will be forced to interview you under caution, which means being arrested.'

Faye gasped. 'My husband is the victim here. I'm the victim too.'

'In either case,' said Sara, ignoring the interruption, 'you would be advised to have your own solicitor present.'

'I don't have one.' Faye turned to Kevin Howard. 'What are we going to do?'

'I'll ring mine,' he assured her. 'He'll help. You'll have to do this.'

Faye visibly deflated. Her shoulders sagged and her head hung forward. 'They'll blame us.'

'There's no reason to think that.' Kevin tugged at her again. 'I'll look after you now. You and your mum. We have to trust the system if we're ever going to know who killed Darren.'

Sara held out a card with her contact details for Kevin to take. Sometimes, she reflected, the system wasn't as kind or as fair as it should be. 'Give me a call later on today.'

Kevin nodded and grabbed the card. Sara left them in peace.

Edwards was talking to the builder when she joined him. 'Will you have to demolish it?'

'Depends on the insurance company,' the man said. He scratched his chin as he thought. 'Sometimes it's cheaper for them to demolish and replace. Sometimes they want to preserve older buildings. It might be listed, and it would be possible to rebuild. There's enough wall. I'll put a fence around it to keep people out.'

'Will it be a long job?'

'Always is when the insurance people get involved,' he replied. Edwards nodded in agreement.

Sara's phone vibrated in her pocket. The screen told her it was DC Noble.

'Hey, Ian. What have you got?'

'They've found Darren Rushworth's car,' he told her. 'Local patrol saw it in a layby not far from Wild Thyme. At Belaugh Common. And you'll never guess.'

'You're right,' said Sara, smiling, 'I won't. What about it?'

'The layby is about twenty yards from where Kyle and his chums have their underage drinking den.'

CHAPTER 41

Jean lay on her bed and counted. She'd dismissed Faye with a flutter of her eyelids and a promise to sleep. Clearly, her daughter wanted to argue some more with the two detectives, which was fine by her. She felt that her performance on the stairs had been worthy of an Oscar. She'd managed to convince everyone, even her daughter.

The kitchen door slammed. She couldn't hear footsteps on the gravel from her muggy bedroom, although raised voices sometimes reached her. She counted to one hundred, got up and put on her slippers, then checked out the window by moving aside the drawn curtains very slightly. She was grateful to see that there was no one in the back garden or beyond the hedge that marked the boundary.

Holding her breath and turning the door handle slowly, Jean peeked along the upstairs corridor. It was clear. Stepping out cautiously, she tiptoed to the top of the stairs. If she crouched down, she could see through the rails of the banister along the back of the barn. Earlier, she had spotted that female detective looking around at the rear of the building. Now there was no sign of anyone, not even the builder. Her knees cracked as she stood up. An ache in her head pulsed, warning Jean to breathe properly. She felt terribly thirsty again.

'And the moral is, don't get old,' she whispered. Jean waited a minute, which felt like an hour, until she was sure the house was empty. There were no voices inside. No sounds of people moving around. No radio or television playing.

Watching out of the long window, Jean descended the stairs as quickly as she dared. These days she had to pay attention. She walked unsteadily along the corridor at the centre of the house. The kitchen door was open. She would be unlucky for anyone in the car park to see her passing. Next to the kitchen was a laundry room. Although it was at the front of the house and lit by a big window, a pale-coloured blind was kept pulled down most of the time. Her husband, Malcolm, had got a builder to convert the room from a walk-in pantry just a few months before he had died. Jean had been grateful then and was even more grateful now. The blind was down. No one in the car park would be able to see in.

A crumpled pile of clothes sat in a basket on top of the washing machine, waiting to be put inside. A pair of trousers, a T-shirt and a grubby pullover lay on the bottom. Jean hadn't had time to sort this out since the night of the fire, and now it was beyond urgent. She dragged the items out and sniffed them. There was a strong smell of smoke.

She realised it was simple luck that had prevented her from catching fire along with the barn. Poor Darren had not been so lucky, even though she'd rung the fire brigade as soon as she'd realised. How could she have known that he was in there? How had he got in? She bit her lip to hold back the horror of her memories, to keep herself in the present.

Holding the items in her trembling hands, Jean was unsure if she should wash them or burn them or throw them away somewhere. There was no time to decide. Outside, she heard the crunch of gravel as a vehicle moved off. The back door opened, bringing the sound of voices. Jean looked around her wildly. She was supposed to be in bed.

'You'll have to do it,' she heard Kevin Howard say.

'I know,' replied Faye. Her daughter sounded resigned. 'I hope Mum has dropped off. She needs to rest as much as I do.'

'I'll try my solicitor; I have his mobile number.' Kevin's voice retreated as he went into the kitchen. Faye followed him. Jean could tell by her footsteps moving from the hall carpet to the tiled floor.

Jean grabbed a plastic carrier bag and pushed the clothes inside it. Screwing it up tightly, she stuffed it into the tiny gap between the washing machine and the tumble dryer. Squatting down, she pushed it as far back as she could, almost trapping her arm. Her skin squealed painfully against the metal sides as she pulled her arm free. Jean sucked in a hasty breath and stood up to listen.

She'd moved too quickly. Her head began to swim as she heard the kettle boiling and Kevin talking on the phone. The pair in the kitchen didn't seem to have noticed the noise. Jean put one hand to her forehead, where sweat was running into her eyes. She put the other out towards the washing machine to steady herself. Her hand didn't meet the comforting cold of the machine's metal lid. It grasped at the plastic basket which stood on top. Her head was spinning. The room was turning. The basket tipped treacherously downwards. Jean felt her weight unbalance and her knees crumple as she slipped after it.

The basket crashed to the floor. Jean collapsed on top of it. The last thing she remembered was the door banging open and Faye screaming for help.

CHAPTER 42

Darren Rushworth's car was an old Ford Fiesta, long past its prime and covered in rust patches from years of neglect. It stood in an unofficial passing area, carved out of necessity into the verge by local vehicles using the narrow lane. A blanket of dust had settled on it over the last few days. Noble assured them that a forensic team was on its way to look it over. Sara climbed the bank on the other side of the lane to check out the local countryside, turning slowly to take in the view.

'Which way to the herb farm from here?' she asked DI Edwards when he joined her. The top of the bank was wide, and the earth was packed solid from the weeks of drought.

'That way?' suggested Edwards, pointing across the fields. The common with its trees and scrubby undergrowth was behind them. Farmers' fields spread out in front of them, full of tall cereal crops. The occasional burst of bright yellow indicated oilseed rape ready to be harvested. Sara hated the cabbage-like smell of that stuff. A hedge line was visible in the distance. 'I guess that's an official footpath.'

A swathe had been cut back or sprayed with chemicals to create a footpath which headed across the wheat field. Further along the lane, Sara spotted one of those wooden markers the local council favoured for showing rights-of-way.

'Who does this belong to?' she wondered.

'Belaugh Manor Farm,' said Noble from the lane below them. 'I checked it out while I was waiting for you. That's a local footpath. It comes out on the lane that goes past Wild Thyme, about halfway between Willmott's farmhouse and the herb nursery. If you were modestly fit, you could walk there in about fifteen minutes.'

'Presumably, local people would be aware of it? Ramblers? Dog walkers, and all that?'

'It looks well used, so I would think so.'

Sara sat on the brittle grass and began to tap at her mobile. Edwards scrambled down to inspect the vehicle. It didn't take her long to find a website detailing routes in the area. One showed a circular walk. It ran from a car park by the distant Wroxham Broad, around the lanes and across the common. The route took it to Wild Thyme for the café (highly recommended), then back to the beginning. Six miles.

'I'd say it was likely to be very well used,' she said to DI Edwards. She showed him the walkers' map.

'Goes past the lads' drinking den too,' said Noble. He squinted at the screen, pushing the map back and forth to be sure.

'And these youngsters have been going there in the evenings to hang out?' she asked him. 'The same ones that gave Kyle his alibi for the night of the West Ruston fire?'

'It's the perfect weather for it,' he nodded.

'Let's assume Darren Rushworth parked here to hide his presence at the herb farm from his mother-in-law,' mused Edwards. 'He's young and fit. He could have easily walked over there to let himself in.'

'And the lads might have seen or heard him park up,' suggested Sara.

'It's only twenty yards that way,' said Noble. 'If it was getting dark, they would have noticed his headlights. Want to see it?'

The drinking den was tucked into a dense area of low-growing bushes and brambles in the middle of a circle of trees. It was high enough to provide a wind break and prevent an occupant from being seen so long as they were sat down. The trees were mature, their branches forming a thick canopy which shut out the glare of the sunlight. Dappled light illuminated the leaf litter below. In the middle, a ring of flints marked out a burning pit. It was full of ash and melted bits of plastic. The youngsters had arranged some random logs into a circle around the firepit. A trail of empty tins and bottles formed an outer ring, the litter reaching back into the bushes. Unless you were prepared to scythe through the outer brambles, the only entrance was a low gap in the undergrowth. It was its own little universe. Sara had to drop to her hands and knees to get inside. Choosing a log, she sat on it to survey the den.

It was nowhere near as private as the young men presumed. The smoke from the firepit would be easily spotted. If they stood up or walked around, they would be clearly visible. The well-walked public footpath was only a few yards away.

When Edwards had said all this, Sara replied, 'I don't think it's about secrecy. It's about privacy. Their own space to do and say what they like. How many of them usually come?'

'It varies,' said Noble. 'Up to seven in the group. Schoolmates. All in the same year group. Some already working, like Kyle. Some at sixth form.'

'So just larking about and trying out drinking,' nodded Edwards. 'I get you. It's an interesting age.'

Sara turned away to hide a smile. It was hard to imagine Edwards as a seventeen-year-old rebelling against the system, even in a minor way. She'd never asked him how old he had been when he'd joined the police, but she would bet Bowen a fiver that their boss had been a career policeman in his head before he'd ever left school.

'I don't understand what Rushworth was up to,' said Edwards. 'I know they'd had a fall-out, but why go back in the middle of the night? Why didn't he take his keys?'

'Maybe he just forgot them,' answered Noble.

'Was he looking for something he didn't want his mother-in-law to see him taking?' suggested Sara. 'Something she would have objected to them having?'

A forensic van pulled up in the lane. The sound of the engine was clear in the heat of the day. When Sara stood up, it was easy to see the white panels through the trees. They crawled out again to greet the officers.

'Easy enough to see the headlights,' she said to Edwards as they headed to the layby. 'Why would they think a car was there?'

'Is this area known for dogging?' asked Edwards with a shrug. Sara couldn't resist a smirk.

'No, sir,' said Noble with a grin. 'Not that I've heard. They might think it was a couple and come out of the den to watch for a laugh?'

'Or they might think it was the police on to them,' suggested Sara. 'Perhaps someone had complained about them? They wouldn't have admitted that to you, would they?'

'If Kyle was here that night, he could have followed Rushworth to the herb farm,' said Edwards slowly. He sounded worried. 'Then set the place on fire. That would make it deliberate.'

'And murder,' agreed Sara. 'Still seems unlikely to me. The pyromania thing I can understand. It's like any addiction. But he had nothing against Rushworth as an individual, did he?'

'Not that we know of,' said Edwards. 'That doesn't mean he didn't have a reason to hate him.'

CHAPTER 43

Sara and Edwards left DC Noble to deal with the forensic team. With some difficulty, Sara found the dead-end lane that took them down to the cottages where Kyle Atkins lived.

'It might not be that far from Wroxham,' said Edwards as they climbed out, 'but it feels remote, doesn't it?'

Sara agreed. When she knocked, there was no answer from the Atkins house. 'I'll try at the back.'

She led Edwards down the dirt track at the side of the house, where she had seen Michelle emerge with her bike. The old-fashioned machine was leaning against the end wall. A broken gate was propped open in the middle of a rickety wooden panel fence, and a pair of local council rubbish bins stood nearby. They heard a metallic crash from the garden.

'Oh, Kyle! Not like that.'

'Mrs Atkins?' called Sara from the gate. 'It's DS Hirst. Can we come in?'

There was no reply, so Sara went in anyway. Michelle looked up, flustered by their sudden appearance. She held a pile of junk in her arms, an old plastic toy truck balanced precariously on the top. Kyle was standing by an old shed at the bottom of the garden. He held a garden spade in one hand and a hoe in the other. Both had seen better days. Next to him lay a pile of metal wire that might once have been shelves and now lay in a vibrating heap. The sound of some pottery breaking came from inside the shed.

'Sorry, Mum,' called a young male voice. 'I dropped it.'

'It's all right, Ryan,' called Michelle. With a heartfelt sigh, she gave up the struggle and her pile of stuff slipped forward and crashed to the floor. 'Bugger it.'

'We're sorry to disturb you,' said Sara. She held up her warrant card. 'Do you remember me?'

'Yes, of course,' said Michelle. 'Do come in. We were just trying to get some stuff together that we didn't need anymore. For a car boot sale. Ryan needs some new . . . oh, never mind.'

Sara introduced DI Edwards. Michelle invited them to sit on a set of well-used plastic chairs near the back door. A round table with wobbly legs had a garden umbrella shoved down the central hole. It gave some shade from the sun, which was now high overhead. The umbrella had the logo of a local brewery all over it. Sara wouldn't ask how it came to be in their garden, rather than at a pub.

'Can you join us, Kyle?' asked Edwards.

The young man laid the garden implements against the pile of metal with a clang and slouched over reluctantly. He slumped into one of the dirty chairs. Sara watched the shed until Ryan emerged, curiosity getting the better of him. He leaned against the doorframe, and the whole building shifted slightly under his weight.

Now Sara saw the two brothers together, it was clear that Kyle had a maturity that Ryan lacked. It wasn't just the four years in age difference. Ryan was nearly as tall as his brother, but he hadn't grown into his height yet. He looked gangly and uncoordinated compared to Kyle, who was developing the strength and muscles of an outdoor worker. Kyle's face had a look much older than his years. A sign of early responsibility, perhaps. That might explain his need for a bolthole to hang out with his mates in. He stared at the two detectives with suspicion.

'We met at *Scoot! Rural*,' Sara began.

'I know,' replied Kyle quickly. 'I don't have to speak to you—'

'Actually, you do,' interrupted Edwards.

'Kyle,' said his mother sharply. 'Be polite.'

Kyle shuffled in his seat and glared at Edwards. 'Not without a solicitor.'

'And/or an appropriate adult with you,' agreed the DI. 'We only want to make an appointment to interview you, Kyle. You can do that voluntarily at a prearranged time.'

'Don't wanna,' said Kyle. He sounded unexpectedly like a toddler.

Still not entirely grown up, then, thought Sara.

'Or we can do this the hard way,' said DI Edwards. He put his open warrant card on the table as if warning the young man.

'Why don't you come in on Monday morning,' Sara cut in. 'If you can get into Wroxham Station with your mum or uncle, we could take a statement then. We can arrange for a duty solicitor to be there if you don't have access to one.'

Michelle snorted. It was half laugh and half anger. 'How would we afford a solicitor? I can't even buy Ryan new football boots. What's this all about?'

'You know we've taken Kyle's bike in for examination?' Edwards turned to Michelle. Sara could see he was growing impatient with the entire family.

She nodded. 'Good job the scheme gave him another one. This is beginning to sound like harassment to me.'

'We need to talk to you about the bike and other things, Kyle.' Sara was glad she'd sat between her irascible boss and the bristling, protective mother.

'He can't come in Monday,' snapped Michelle. 'He's got work. So have I. How can I pay my bills if I don't work?'

'There isn't any choice in the matter,' snapped Edwards. 'Either Kyle comes in voluntarily, or I'll have to charge him and take him in for an interview anyway.'

There was a momentary stunned silence. Kyle's mouth dropped open in surprise. Sara heard a wooden squeak. Ryan had suddenly stood up, and the shed relaxed back into place.

'You can't do that!' gasped Michelle. Her voice rose angrily, panic clearly etched on her face. 'He'd have a police record. You'd ruin his life before it's even started.'

'Best you come in of your own accord then,' said Edwards.

'Kyle,' called Ryan. Sara watched his brother flinch. 'Don't go.'

'Shut up, little shit,' snarled Kyle. He pushed the plastic chair back, its legs dragging noisily on the baked ground. Standing straight, he turned slightly to look at Ryan. 'Keep quiet. It's got nothing to do with you.'

Michelle didn't seem to know who to speak to first. Her eyes darted between the two boys. She settled on the elder brother. 'Kyle! Don't call your brother names like that.'

Edwards stood up to face Kyle. The young man looked him bravely in the face.

'I know what you think I've done,' he said. 'Well, I haven't. I'll come in on Monday. I've got nothing to hide.'

CHAPTER 44

To show willing, Claudia had put herself on the rota. Norfolk born and bred, and a country girl at heart, she had no fear of being out in the lanes at night. Even so, she wished Jamie Waller was with her. He'd claimed to be busy when she had suggested it to him at work yesterday. Claudia couldn't help but wonder if he'd been embarrassed at her request, as if she'd asked him out on a date and he'd thought it unmanly or something.

It was still very warm. The heat of the day had barely dissipated from the roads. She'd set off at half past eleven, radio off, air conditioning on. Unlike the others, she included the building site at West Ruston. Pausing there briefly, she peered through the fence from the driving seat. There was no sign of life.

The participating farms and small businesses were all within a five-mile area. Each observer was left to make their own route, though all agreed to cover each other's properties at least once when it was their turn. Claudia ensured she drove past the lane that turned down to Kyle Atkins' house. Despite the removal of Kyle's bike, she couldn't help feeling that the police were barking up the wrong tree with the young man. Jamie Waller clearly disagreed with her.

Maybe that was why she was starting to feel defensive of the apprentice.

Claudia had chosen her route by consulting an old county road map and her memory. The scuffed black book lay open on the seat beside her. It was proving harder than she'd anticipated now that it was night-time. There were no clouds and only a tiny sliver of moon. These back roads were dark as only a country lane could be, with no illumination, natural or manmade. She shimmied across the main Wroxham Road. So far, she hadn't seen a single vehicle since leaving North Walsham. There were some lights on in the house at Wild Thyme Herb Farm.

Hardly surprising, she thought, *given their news*.

The herb farm stood at a crossroads. Claudia paused, engine running. If she turned down past it, the only other place Claudia could check down there was Belaugh Manor Farm. Since Thomas Willmott had been at the meeting, she felt she should take a look. It was another dead end, with a small car park for walkers and boaters down by the river where she could turn round. Hopefully, no one would be using it at this time of night. If they were, Claudia smiled to herself, she would just ignore them.

The lane narrowed once she got past the farm. Hedges rose up on both sides. Pottering slowly, Claudia looked to either side of her. There was an old pair of barns on one side and Belaugh Manor Farmhouse on the other a little further on. No signs of light or life at either of them.

When she reached the gravel car park, Claudia was relieved to find it empty of couples shagging in cars. Turning her vehicle to leave, she paused with the window down and the engine off. She could hear the water moving gently, the occasional grumpy duck quack and a slight breeze moving in the rushes on the riverbank. There was no cruiser mooring on this bend of the river, so no holidaymakers drinking or creating a fuss. It was just her and the natural world for a few minutes, their little secret. It gave her a thrill of pleasure. It was small moments like this that kept her going.

Winding the window up, she drove slowly back up the lane towards the crossroads. Being a cautious driver, she halted, despite there being no traffic. With a cursory glance, she began to move off when something flashed in front of the car. Her foot slammed on the brake pedal as shock made her squeal.

'What the hell?' she said. Her voice sounded loud in the quiet of the car interior. Claudia wound down her window and squinted into the night. To her right, a moped engine puttered away from her. By the sound of it, someone was pushing the thing as hard as it would go. Either the bike had no lights on, or the rear lights were broken. If she hadn't caught the sudden gleam of metal in her headlights, Claudia doubted she would have seen it until it was too late. 'Now what?'

If she followed it, her headlights would give her away. And she had no intention of driving around without her lights on. It was far too dark.

'Who the hell was that?' she whispered to herself. The engine was fading. Racking her memory, Claudia decided that if she followed them, this road would turn out not far from Hoveton and the high school. The shock was settling into pure adrenaline. What if this was the fire starter? Had they already done something? Were they on their way to do something? Was it just someone going home from the pub?

There was only one way to find out. Claudia turned after the bike. She remembered this stretch of road. It ran straight for hundreds of yards, so she put her foot down. Before long, there was a lane turning off to the right. Pulling up, Claudia turned off her engine and momentarily listened through her open window. Sure enough, the moped engine sounded to be coming from down there. It still had quite a lead on her. She had no idea where the lane went. Pressing her starter button, Claudia turned after it.

'You ought to ring someone,' she muttered, then giggled at herself. 'Listen to you. Who would believe you, and what would you say?'

A common, studded with trees and undergrowth, loomed out of the dark on her right. It didn't give her any more sense of direction or place than before. This lane was even more narrow than the one down to the river. She slowed the car to navigate the random twists and turns. After a couple of miles, the common ran out, and the lane reached the B-road, which led to the Junior Farm near Hoveton. Somehow, she had gone round all sides of a square. Claudia turned off her engine again to listen; it tinked as it cooled. It was the only sound. The bike must have got away from her.

Claudia picked up the ancient road map and flicked on the car's interior light. After a hasty search, she found the lane she must be on. There was only one more place on her visit list: Howards food factory and growing houses. They had their own security guards. Would it matter if she didn't go that way? Going back into Hoveton and on to the main road would be easier. She yawned, despite the fresh air coming through the window.

The noise, when it came, was behind her. It was a sort of *whump*, like a distant explosion. Loud enough to startle Claudia. Not close enough to feel dangerous. She poked her head out of the window. It had definitely come from along the lane she had just driven down.

Claudia climbed out of her car and craned to look. In the distance, she could see a yellow light. No, not light. Flames. Red and yellow, streaking up into the sky. Someone had set fire to the common! The thing they all feared was happening again. Grabbing her mobile, Claudia dialled 999. She had difficulty describing her whereabouts to the call centre, as it was so remote. As she stuttered details, her trembling finger stabbing at the faded page in the atlas, Claudia heard running feet.

'Who's there?' she shouted, nearly dropping her phone in fear. 'Who are you?'

There was no reply. The feet skidded to a halt before the runner reached the circle of light created by Claudia's car.

'Come and help me,' called Claudia. 'I've called the fire brigade. I need to tell them how to find us.'

Then she heard a crashing and stamping as whoever it was climbed the roadside bank and ran, stumbling, through the cornfield beyond.

CHAPTER 45

DI Edwards threw up his hands in despair after the conversation with Kyle and his mother. They had reached the car park outside Wymondham HQ in double-quick time, Edwards driving wordlessly and rapidly with pinched lips. Sara recognised the look on his face and waited for him to speak.

'Why does everyone have to be so difficult? Too many bloody cop shows. They all think they know better than us.'

Sara silently agreed with him. His temper was not improved when Kevin Howard rang to say that Jean had been taken to hospital and that his solicitor wasn't available until Monday. Could they come in then? She expected the DI to explode any moment.

Instead, he dropped his head on to his hands where they clutched the car's steering wheel and groaned. 'Isn't the murder of this man important enough for them?'

'He didn't say why Mrs Simpson was in the hospital. Perhaps it's serious? Shall I ring A & E?'

Edwards nodded. 'Then call Aggie and get her to arrange the duty solicitor for Kyle Atkins' interview. Can we do that tomorrow?'

'Only if we get them to Wymondham. Hoveton is shut at the weekends. That's why I said Monday to his mother. They have no transport either.'

'Bloody budget cuts,' snapped Edwards, slapping at the steering wheel. 'What can we do tomorrow?'

'Erm,' Sara hesitated. 'Noble is keeping an eye on the fire brigade website. We're waiting on the forensic reports. They might come through tomorrow. Anyway, the DCI is away for the weekend. So it's up to us.'

Edwards' shoulders fell, and he pulled a defeated grimace. 'For God's sake. All right, I give up. Let's go home. Monday looks likely to be a long one.'

Taking him at his word, she transferred to her own car and drove home, only to be disappointed to find that Adie, the gardener, had already finished for the day. At least that left a quiet evening to enjoy a bottle of wine in the garden. Thinking time. A chance to face up to her private life, such as it was.

Sara accepted that she had made a serious mistake ever getting involved with Dante Adebayo. Gratitude or fear of being alone wasn't a good enough reason to stay with him. A handsome and pleasant man on the outside, it had seemed a good idea at the beginning. Now he was showing signs of a seriously bad temper, and several other officers had commented on his lack of control.

Unable to make her mind up, and despite her confused thoughts, she took herself to bed and fell into a deep sleep until Tilly head-bumped her awake at seven o'clock.

'Hungry, eh?' she said quietly. Giving the creature a fond stroke, Sara slid out of bed and wandered to the kitchen. 'What am I going to do?'

The cat was too busy enjoying her breakfast to pay attention to her human mother. She didn't even look up when Sara unlocked the back door and went to sit in the garden to drink her coffee.

Adie seemed to be making good progress. Although the ground was rock hard, piles of dirt and debris were everywhere. Small stakes with string wrapped round them marked out various areas. Some of the larger shrubs had been trimmed to more manageable sizes. The skip was already needed. The image of the young, powerful hippy in his hemp shirt and cargo shorts played in her mind. The idea was an aphrodisiac. It sent a frisson of excitement jingling through her body. Tilly wandered through the door and hopped on to the spare chair with a hoarse miaow. Sara rubbed her head.

'This is ridiculous,' she said out loud to the cat. 'I can think of this gardener and feel like that. Yet when I think of Dante, I see that look on his face, and all I worry about is how to avoid his company.'

The cat mewed again.

'Yes, I know. That's what I ought to do.' Sara laughed at herself. 'I think I already am a mad cat woman. Talking to you like you can answer me.'

Settling on the chair for a morning wash, the cat gave her what could only be classed as an old-fashioned look. With a burst of determination, Sara went inside for a shower. She gulped down some cereal and was on the way to Dante's house before eight o'clock.

The roads were already busy as early risers drove their families towards the coast for a day at the beach. Sara was grateful that they were mostly going in the opposite direction. It took nearly an hour to reach Dante's estate and to be sure she'd found the right street and house. She had to knock several times to wake him up.

'Sara, to what do I owe this pleasure?' he asked when he saw her. His tone was hardly welcoming, his eyes were barely focused, and his jaw opened with a huge yawn.

'I'm sorry, were you working last night?' Sara stepped past him and into the lounge.

Dante followed with a shuffle. He flopped on to the sofa, looking exhausted. 'Until four. Give me a minute, then I'll make a drink.'

'No need.' Sara sat opposite him and folded her hands so he couldn't hold them. Now that she was here, what had seemed so simple at home in the garden now felt awfully complicated. 'Look, this isn't easy.'

'What isn't?' Dante frowned.

'What I've come to say.' Sara paused, waiting for him to be awake enough to follow her. She watched as his expression changed from sleepy to antagonistic. 'I'm sorry.'

'Why?' He pursed his lips. Clearly, he wasn't going to help her.

'This situation between us.'

'It isn't a *situation*,' he said. 'I, at least, thought it was a relationship.'

'So did I, to begin with.' Sara felt horrible. 'I've enjoyed our time together. But there are so many difficulties.'

Dante let his head roll back on to the sofa. He looked at the ceiling for what felt like an age, then back at Sara. His eyes flashed with anger. 'There wouldn't be so many difficulties if you would only agree to move in with me. Or let me move out to live with you.'

Sara stiffened. 'We've been through all that. I like living in the countryside. I like having my own space. I said so from the start.'

'I see.' He looked to be only just keeping his anger contained.

'Then there's the issue with work,' she stumbled on. 'You know they don't really approve of relationships between staff.'

Dante snapped upright. 'What, like the one between Mike Bowen and your civilian admin. You remember, the couple whose wedding we went to.'

'They were worried about it for ages. Thought they might lose their jobs if anyone found out. Ended up asking for permission from Personnel, for God's sake.'

'And this *situation* between us isn't worth taking a risk on?' Dante held up his hands as Sara opened her mouth to speak. His voice rang with sarcasm, and his upper lip curled with derision. 'Don't bother. I don't need your explanations. You've obviously made up your mind. Your career is more important than how I feel about you. I get it.'

'I don't think you do,' said Sara as she stood to leave. She felt threatened by the look on his face and the tension in his body. She'd be bracing for an attack if this had been a suspect. It was time to go. 'I'm truly sorry. This isn't working for me.'

'Get out,' said Dante. He thumped his fists into the sofa cushions. 'Just leave.'

As Sara opened the front door, she heard him yell, 'And good luck with your inspector's exams, you miserable bitch. I hope the promotion is worth it.'

CHAPTER 46

There had been a paramedic, a volunteer from Wroxham, he'd said, followed by an ambulance ride. A lengthy wait in A & E, followed by tests and X-rays. Faye had sat with Jean as she lay on a trolley in a stuffy corridor. They barely spoke to one another during the many hours they were there. Finally, a harassed-looking doctor came to discuss the results.

'How long have you had diabetes, Mrs Simpson?' she asked kindly. Faye stared at Jean in amazement.

'Eighteen months,' admitted Jean.

'Are you on medication for it?'

'Metformin.'

'I think you should go back to your doctor. You need a new assessment and possibly to move on to insulin injections.'

'When had you intended to tell us that little nugget?' demanded Faye as they left the hospital.

'I've been managing it,' replied Jean. 'I didn't want it to add to your worries.'

Faye looked at Jean as though her mother was an idiot. 'Happy to bully us for other reasons, though. Why not tell us you were unwell?'

Jean didn't have the energy to reply.

'My God,' breathed Jean when she eventually lay on her bed at home. 'Could things get any worse?'

The answer, of course, was yes. Completely exhausted, Jean slept in until mid-morning on Sunday. Feeling less than refreshed, she dragged herself down to the kitchen. The sun was already blazing through the windows. Dirty pots lay in the sink and on the worksurfaces. Struggling to find the energy to put on the kettle, she spotted Faye talking to Kevin Howard in the yard. Whatever they were saying seemed to be rather heated. In the lane outside, she could see the roof of a vehicle recovery lorry heading slowly away. With a deep sigh, Jean slumped into a chair and pulled out her tablets. Two tablets, twice a day, it instructed, and now they were not enough. Jean levered herself up to get a glass of water. She had barely swallowed them when the backdoor slammed.

'I thought you were resting,' snapped Faye, halting suddenly in the doorway. Kevin Howard hovered behind her. 'Here, let me sort the kitchen out. Kevin, why don't you sit there?'

Kevin did as he was told. Jean sat at the table, allowing her daughter to bustle about the place, making drinks and loading the dishwasher.

Not before time, she thought.

A mug of tea was plonked in front of her, slopping half the contents onto the table. Jean frowned. Kevin got the same treatment. His attempt at thanks was brushed aside. A plate of toast, a butter dish and a jar of jam appeared some minutes later. Jean slowly loaded the bread and tried to chew a small piece. Finally, her daughter sat next to her at the table. Faye rolled an offcut of burned toast between the fingers of one hand until it was a pile of crumbs. She held her right hand on her lap, hidden under the table. Jean pushed the plate away from her.

'Thank you,' she said. Faye looked at her mother. Her face was pinched and white. 'Faye?'

'You've missed quite a lot while you've been asleep,' said Faye.

'Such as?'

'The washing machine isn't working properly,' complained Faye. She pursed her lips angrily. Jean knew that whatever else was on the list, it was human nature to start with the smallest annoyance. 'I put the clothes in from the basket. They washed but didn't spin. I don't know what's stopping it. Now they're sopping wet and I'll have to wring them out by hand.'

'We can get someone out to look at it,' said Jean wearily, hoping that the carrier bag of clothes down the side of the machine hadn't caused the problem. She really needed to get those things into the bin. To change the subject, she looked pointedly towards the hand hidden under the table. 'What have you done to your hand?'

Faye kept the hand on her lap. 'I cut it, looking round the barn this morning.'

Jean saw Kevin wince as Faye said this. 'We can get someone to look at it tomorrow. At the doctor's, maybe?'

'No, we can't. We have to give statements to the police,' Faye went on. 'We've got to turn up at Hoveton in the morning.' She gestured at Kevin. 'Kev has found us a solicitor.'

'I don't think you should be there without legal help,' he said apologetically.

'That's a good idea. Thank you for arranging it.' Jean nodded. Her voice was quiet, almost as if she was speaking to herself. 'We had to expect that. It can't be helped.'

'Then my moped was stolen overnight,' said Faye.

Jean looked up in surprise. 'I thought the forensic people were going to come for it?'

'I stayed here after you went to the hospital,' explained Kevin. 'They never turned up or rang. I gave up at seven and locked the house up.'

'Was it here when we got back?' asked Jean in confusion. They'd taken an expensive taxi from the hospital to get home. It had been late evening and she'd little recollection of their arrival. Her main concern had been getting into bed, not checking the vehicles in the yard.

'I think so,' said Faye. 'I went straight to bed once you were settled. I didn't look.'

'Two men came in a truck this morning.' Kevin seemed to be watching Faye carefully. She messed with the pile of crumbs to avoid his gaze. 'They were obviously expecting it to be here.'

'That's when you realised it was missing, Faye?' Her daughter nodded, avoiding Jean's look as well. Those crumbs must be fascinating. 'We need to report it stolen to the police.'

'We should,' agreed Kevin. Jean hadn't been asking him, and she looked at him in surprise. 'Perhaps you could tell them in the morning at the interview?'

'Not meaning to be rude, but why are you here?' Jean asked him.

He blushed. 'I came round to see how you both were. How you'd got on at the hospital.'

'That's kind of you,' Jean conceded. 'And you were here when the men turned up?'

Kevin nodded. 'They weren't happy.'

'No doubt we'll be accused of something else now that it's gone missing,' said Faye. Her voice was starting to sound hysterical. 'They'll get us for something in the end.'

'Faye?' Jean reached out to try and take her daughter's hand. Faye snatched it away. 'Where has all this come from? What do you have against the police?'

Faye began to sob. 'I loved my husband.'

Kevin shifted uneasily in his chair. 'We know that.'

'I'd do anything for him.' Faye carried on as if Kevin hadn't spoken. She stared at the pile of crumbs on the table for what felt like an age before taking a deep breath. 'He has a police record. And so do I.'

Jean was stunned into silence. Kevin's eyes widened.

'We were arrested at the climate protest in London. Unfairly prosecuted for trying to save the planet. And I can't begin to describe how vile my treatment was while I was locked up.'

CHAPTER 47

Claudia had waited at the end of the lane until the fire engine turned up. It had been her 'patrol' that had spotted the fire, and she'd been the one to ring it in. A police car arrived moments later. An officer took her details and told her to go home. They'd take a statement later, he'd said.

For once, she'd managed a lie-in. Perhaps it was the late night or the stress. Or both. Either way, Claudia had shopped at the low-cost supermarket before preparing her lonely Sunday lunch. She was picking at a healthy but unappealing bowl of salad when her mobile trilled from the living room.

'Hello?' said Claudia cautiously. She didn't recognise the number.

'Ms Turner? Mike Bowen here,' said the familiar voice. 'My wife and I wondered if you would be free about five-ish? We could drop off some things for you if you'd still like them.'

'That would be fine.'

As soon as he'd gone, Claudia felt her housekeeping pride rising, despite the heat. Dumping tins of soft drinks into the fridge to cool, she swept the little backyard and dug out her old third-hand vacuum. It sputtered and clunked as it sucked up the dust from the carpet.

The doorbell rang fifteen minutes before she was expecting her visitors. She smiled to see that the avuncular detective had got there early. The shape showing through the frosted glass in her front door looked taller than she expected, but it was still a surprise to find Jamie Waller on her doorstep when she answered. He looked embarrassed.

'Hello, Jamie,' she said.

He shuffled his feet uncomfortably. 'Can I come in?'

'Sure.' Claudia smiled. 'I'm expecting another visitor in a few minutes.'

'Oh. Right.' Jamie looked around her living room at the piles of books and DVDs.

'Can I get you a drink?'

'Erm. No. I just wanted to ask . . .' Jamie's voice petered out.

'Yes?' Claudia's heart began to thump in expectation until the sarcastic demon on her shoulder warned her that this would be about work.

'About last night.' Jamie muddled on. 'I'm sorry I couldn't come with you. I was going out with my mates. To the pub. Birthday bash. You know.'

A night at the pub would have been very acceptable to Claudia. Not only could she not afford it, she felt awkward doing it alone. 'Did you have a good time?'

Jamie nodded. He blushed a bright crimson. 'The others had taken their girlfriends. So, I could have invited you. I'm sorry. I thought it was just the lads.'

Claudia wasn't sure what to make of all this.

'Would you like to go next time?' Jamie stumbled on. 'Or on our own? I mean, would you like to come out for a drink with me?'

He released a pent-up breath and smiled.

'I'd love to go for a drink with you,' said Claudia. Not about work, after all. Much better than work. She smiled in return. 'Would you like to stay for a cold drink now? I have some stuff in the fridge.'

'Lovely,' said Jamie as he finally relaxed. 'How did it go last night?'

'It was a bit weird,' she began as the doorbell chimed again. 'Excuse me.'

This time it was Mike Bowen. His wife stood by their car, watching and smiling, the hatchback door standing proud at the rear.

'Take anything you like,' he said, leading her to peer into the boot.

A pair of metal folding garden chairs with a small round table were balanced on top of a lovely 1950s coffee table. Underneath them lay a pair of pine bookcases. A small, comfy-looking armchair was squashed up against the rear of the front seats, and a couple of wicker bedside tables had been stuffed into the armchair seat.

'You don't have to have them, my dear,' said the woman. 'Only, if you could use them, we'd be grateful to you for taking them.'

Claudia smiled and held out her hand. 'I'm Claudia. Thank you so much. I'll take the lot, if that's all right with you.'

Bowen recruited Jamie to help carry the items inside, and ten minutes later, all four of them were sitting on her little patio sipping cool drinks.

'No need for thanks,' said Aggie. 'Glad to see them being used.'

'And we won't tell anyone at your work,' Claudia assured her.

Aggie's eyes twinkled, and a smile pulled at the corner of her mouth. 'We wouldn't want anyone thinking Mike's gone soft.'

'There is one thing I'd like to tell you about.' Claudia turned to Bowen. 'How do you find out about the fires you've been investigating?'

'Usually, the fire service sends us a report if they think something's suspicious,' he replied.

'I think you should check the reports in the morning when you get in,' said Claudia. 'You'll find one with my name on it.'

'Go on?' Bowen sat up to pay more attention.

'You saw that I put myself on the rota? I sent you a copy.'

'To be honest, I haven't looked at it yet.'

'I said I'd do last night.' She put her drink down. 'It's not like I go out on a Saturday.'

Jamie cleared his throat and whispered so only Claudia could hear, 'Sorry.'

'And you saw something?'

Claudia told Bowen about her decision to follow the moped. 'Then a fire suddenly started like an explosion. And I heard someone running. I rang 999 and they sent a fire engine.'

'No police in attendance?'

'Yes, a police car came along after the fire engine. He only took my details.'

'No one took a statement from you?' Bowen frowned. 'You didn't tell them about the person running away?'

'They didn't give me a chance.'

'It seemed suspicious to you?'

Claudia nodded. 'Something went up with a bang and started a fire. I can't help but wonder what happened to the moped. Did they pull off into the trees?'

'That's possible,' agreed Bowen. 'Do you think they realised they were being followed?'

'I don't know. I think the rider set fire to it. I think that's why they were running away.'

CHAPTER 48

Sunday had felt long and full of self-recrimination for Sara. She had sat in the garden with Tilly and demolished a bottle of wine, avoiding everyone and not answering her phone. Whether it was the sun or the wine, she woke up on Monday morning with a headache. Paracetamol took the edge off.

'Serves me right,' she muttered as she drove to Hoveton Police Station.

Hoveton and Wroxham were an unusual pair of villages. Sitting on either side of the River Bure, with boatyards lining both banks, they were full of shops and cafés. The difference between the two was jealously maintained by some residents, which Sara understood; there were closely guarded differences between traditional areas of London like Stepney and Poplar, which had been joined into Tower Hamlets in the 1960s. Despite its name, Roy's of Wroxham, which claimed to be 'The World's Largest Village Store', stood in Hoveton. Sara often used it for food shopping, and the part-time police station stood next to the food hall. She was pleased to see that two spaces had been coned off and parked in one of them. A police boat on a trailer occupied two other spaces; the Broads Beat boat patrol was unique to the Norfolk force. As she signed in, she was surprised at the chat and laughter coming from the office to one side of the building.

'We only have one interview room,' explained the uniformed constable on the desk. He glanced over his shoulder at a partially opened door. 'The Broads Beat will be going out soon, so it will be quiet after that.'

'Will you be here to sign people in?'

The young man grimaced. 'Yeah, I drew the short straw. I'll be here. Got a list of people you're expecting?'

He clearly regretted not having a day on the water, chugging about the rivers and Broads in the sunshine. It was the sort of day out that people paid good money for. Sara gave him the names, which he tapped into the computer, then he showed her the room and the recording equipment. With a great deal of banter and amusement, half a dozen other officers hooked up the boat on its trailer before heading to wherever they would be launching. DI Edwards pulled in moments after they had gone, followed by the duty solicitor. After plying them all with tea, the young constable settled in the other office with a bored look.

When Kyle Atkins arrived, he was accompanied by his mother and his uncle for good measure. He looked both worried and annoyed as he accepted a handshake from the solicitor. His mother was ashen-faced, while Eric Beatty looked furious. DI Edwards started the recorder and explained his rights as someone giving a voluntary statement.

'As you know, Kyle, we have impounded your moped, and it is being tested by the forensic team,' Edwards began. The duty solicitor scribbled on his notepad. 'Why do you think we've done that?'

Kyle shrugged and began to say 'no comment' when his uncle prodded him in the arm.

'You tell 'em what we agreed,' prompted Eric Beatty.

'You think I've something to do with these fires,' he mumbled.

Edwards laid a sheet with a typed list of dates on the table for Kyle to read. The solicitor leaned in to note the dates on his pad. 'These are all the dates we're interested in.'

'That's the fire at West Ruston,' said Kyle. He pointed with his finger. 'I've already told you about that.'

'I agree that you have,' replied Edwards. 'We spoke to your friends, who confirmed you were at Belaugh Common with them that evening. What about these others?'

Kyle squinted at the paper, then handed it to his mother, who scanned the list.

'I can't be sure. Most nights in the summer, I'm either at home with Mum or meeting my mates, like I already said.'

'Mrs Atkins, do any of these dates mean anything to you?'

'It's like Kyle said.' His mother shook her head, and her voice took on a defensive tone. 'He's a good lad and spends time with Ryan and me in the evenings. What if he does meet up with his mates sometimes? They aren't doing any harm.'

Sara jumped in before Edwards could get into underage drinking or dope smoking in their woodland den. 'Kyle, why did you have a petrol container in your moped?'

'No comment,' said Kyle. He looked at his uncle.

'Go on, Kyle, read them what we agreed,' urged his uncle.

Kyle stood momentarily to drag a folded, scruffy piece of paper from his jeans pocket. The duty solicitor held out his hand and waited until Kyle dropped it on the table in front of him. He slumped back into his chair to watch the solicitor. After reading the paper thoroughly, the solicitor turned to Kyle's uncle.

'You helped to write this statement?'

Eric Beatty nodded.

The solicitor turned back to Kyle. 'I would advise you that you don't need to say anything like this, or read out or give this paper to the police. I don't think it's in your best interests.'

Beatty huffed in aggravation. 'I told him. Best to say what he wants to say. Then there can't be no mistake.'

Sara waited with bated breath, grateful that Edwards kept silent for once. The solicitor handed the paper back. Kyle hesitated as he read over the words again. Finally, he decided and held it up high enough to read it.

'I, Kyle Atkins, do hereby state that I've got nothing to do with these fires around the area. I have no reason to cause this damage and do not know the people whose places have been attacked. I spend my days at work with my uncle and evenings with my mum or my mates. They can swear that. I damaged my moped when I was run off the road by a Range Rover on my way home from work two weeks ago. I went into the hedge and fell into the ditch. Signed: Kyle Atkins.'

'But you do know them, don't you, Kyle?' asked Sara quickly before anyone else could intervene. 'Thomas Willmott of Belaugh Manor Farm is your grandfather. Your father was working for him on the farm when he was fatally injured.'

'How dare you!' Mrs Atkins said in outrage. 'You only know that because I told you. How dare you turn that against us?'

'We also checked the accident reports,' said Sara to Kyle's mother.

'Plenty of reason to dislike the man.' Edwards pressed on. 'Plenty of motive there.'

'Rubbish!' Kyle went bright red. 'I can't remember the last time I saw the old bugger, and I haven't spoken to him since Mum told me about the accident. I don't blame her for not wanting anything to do with him. It don't mean I've set fire to his places.'

'What about the building site at West Ruston?' asked Sara. 'You know your way around that.'

'It's my job.' Kyle looked at his uncle for support. 'Wouldn't have no job if it wasn't for Uncle Eric. Why would I do that to us both?'

'I warned you,' urged Beatty. 'Don't answer no questions. Just read what we agreed.'

'And what about the herb farm, Kyle? Did you set fire to that too?'

Kyle's eyes grew wide with panic. 'Why would I do that? They were nice to me. Gave me a Saturday job in the summer when I was at school. I like Mrs Simpson.'

'I think it's time we took a break,' interrupted the duty solicitor. He closed his pad and stood up.

'Kyle, did you see anyone on the night of the fire at Wild Thyme?' Sara asked urgently. 'Someone who parked near your den on the common?'

Kyle looked at the solicitor, then checked with his mother and uncle. They all shook their heads.

'No comment.'

CHAPTER 49

Before they left the herb farm on Monday morning, Faye rang the doctor and booked a visit for Jean. When the receptionist heard what the hospital had said, they gave her an emergency appointment.

Her daughter's revelation of having a police record had shocked Jean. Still, she didn't feel that being arrested at a Climate Action demonstration merited Faye's clear hatred of the police in general. It left Jean wondering exactly what had happened to her daughter after her arrest. Faye admitted having had to pay a sharp fine, as had Darren. They had never asked Jean for the money, and she had no idea how they had found the hundreds of pounds necessary to deal with it.

Unsure of her ability to drive with all her worries and woozy head, Jean accepted Kevin Howard's offer to take them to the police station. He introduced his solicitor, Toby Byatt, in the tiny car park outside. In his mid-forties, Mr Byatt looked calm and collected in his smart grey suit. He exuded an air of efficiency, which Jean immediately liked. He looked like the sort of man she would be happy to trust. As they entered the station, Jean's head began to swim again.

It was explained that they were each to be interviewed. Jean told them about the theft of Faye's moped, and DS

Hirst noted it disapprovingly. The officer behind the desk entered it on his computer with lazy fingers.

When the detective sergeant led Jean into the interview room, she must have looked ill, as Byatt asked for a glass of water for her. The place had no windows and was airless in the heat. She sat gratefully on a chair with Byatt next to her. The two detectives sat opposite, with a desk between them. The inspector's explanation of her rights during the interview went straight over her head. At a nod from the DI, Hirst laid a list of dates in front of her.

'Can you tell us where you were on all these evenings?' she asked. Her tone was even, with no hint of accusation. Jean picked up the page and looked at the numbers. They made no sense to her. Byatt gently extracted the sheet from her shaking hands and copied the dates into a notebook.

'I'm sure my client will be able to furnish this when she has had time to check her appointment diary,' he said, returning the sheet.

'Probably don't need to,' mumbled Jean. Her tongue felt thick in her mouth, and she sipped from the plastic cup of water. 'I don't go far these days, unless it's to the supermarket.'

'So, you would have been at home on most or all of these evenings?'

Jean nodded slowly. 'I think so.'

'Would you have been alone?' asked Hirst.

'Err, Faye and Darren were there almost as much as me.' She hesitated. 'They go out occasionally to see his parents or friends.'

'You share a house?'

'We do.'

'Do you share all the accommodation with Mr and Mrs Rushworth?'

'Like the kitchen?' Jean frowned in concentration. 'Is that what you mean? We do share that. They have their own bedroom and bathroom, of course.'

'What about the living room? Do you, for instance, watch television together or socialise in the evenings?'

'Sometimes.' Jean knew she needed to be careful. Where were these questions leading? 'They have a sitting area in their bedroom with a television and stuff. We don't always want to watch the same things.'

'Can you be sure they were with you in the house all these evenings?' Hirst pointed to the list. Jean nodded. 'Would you be aware if either of them left?'

Jean thought of the recent nights with their extreme heat and her subsequent lack of sleep. She had heard one or other of them moving around sometimes, which was hardly surprising. They were probably as restless as she'd been.

'I don't know,' she said evasively.

'Mrs Simpson, do you recall when we first met?' asked Hirst.

'After the fire in the field behind us,' replied Jean. 'Why?'

'You said you were woken by Jake Willmott,' said Hirst. 'That you and your son-in-law went round to check out the problem.'

'That's right.'

'Where was your daughter that night?'

And there it was. They were trying to trap her into incriminating Faye. Perhaps her daughter was right.

'I'm not sure.'

'She didn't go to inspect the fire with you?'

Careful, Jean thought. 'We've all had difficulty sleeping in the heat. Perhaps Darren didn't want to wake her.'

'Can you remember if her moped was there?'

'No, I can't remember. It was dark, and we were hurrying.'

DS Hirst looked at the DI, who took up the questions. 'Mrs Simpson, can you tell us in your own words about the night of the fire at your barn?'

Jean looked at Byatt with a mute appeal. He whispered to her that she didn't have to answer any questions she didn't wish to.

'It's all a bit of a blur,' she said vaguely.

'Let's take it step by step, then,' he said quietly. 'Who was in the house that night?'

'Only me. Faye and Darren had gone to visit his parents.'

'Did you lock up the house? Close all the windows?'

Jean nodded, then corrected herself. 'I didn't close my bedroom window.'

'Because of the heat?'

'Yes.'

'Where is your bedroom?'

'At the back of the house.'

'At the back?' DI Edwards confirmed. 'Even with the window open, would you be able to hear someone in the car park at the front of the house?'

'A car would be unusual.' Jean was getting muddled. 'I think I would have heard that.'

'And did you hear an unexpected vehicle?'

'I can't remember.'

'What alerted you to the fact that the barn was on fire?'

'I'm not sure. Look, why are you asking all this? I've said it's all a blur.'

'We've looked at the sightlines of the barn from your home,' he continued. Jean felt him relentlessly and logically move forward, and her heart jumped with nerves. 'I think it would be impossible to see the front of the barn from your bedroom at the back. So, what was it that alerted you to the fire?'

'The noise,' Jean hazarded. 'Yes, that's it. I heard a noise, like a little explosion. Then the sound of a moped driving away.'

'A moped like the one your daughter rides?'

Jean opened her mouth to answer, then snapped it shut. She'd trapped herself with a stupid lie. She glanced at Toby Byatt, then said, 'No comment.'

CHAPTER 50

If Sunday had been long, Monday morning felt torturous. Neither Sara nor DI Edwards had been able to get anything else from any of the interviewees. In fact, Sara was sure they had lost Mrs Simpson's trust during the interview. Faye had been an altogether different prospect. She sat next to Toby Byatt with her face set like stone. Every question was answered with the professional criminal's standard response of 'no comment'. She had refused to check the list of dates or give her DNA and fingerprints. Perhaps the mother had picked up her hostility from the daughter. It was all very frustrating.

'There's not enough evidence to merit an arrest to interview under caution,' DI Edwards confirmed to the team when they met back in the office. Only DC Noble was missing.

DCI Hudson sat at the front of the office by the whiteboards twiddling her marker pen. 'Why do you think the young lad read out this statement?'

'The duty solicitor tried to stop him,' said Sara. She handed the note to Hudson. 'It was so obviously full of holes. I think this uncle, Eric Beatty, persuaded the lad to do it.'

The handwritten note was in an evidence bag. Hudson fastened it to the whiteboard with a piece of tape. 'Let's see what other information has come through over the weekend.'

'Mrs Simpson had an impromptu visit to the hospital,' offered Edwards.

'Apparently, it was a diabetic hypoglycaemic attack,' said Sara. 'I don't think that helped her this morning. She looked worn out.'

'Did we know she was diabetic?' asked Hudson. Sara shook her head.

'Okay, let's be careful with her. Bowen?'

'I spoke to Coles' office manager Claudia Turner over the weekend,' he said. 'There's a copy of the rota if anyone wants it, and I put her statement about Kyle's bike on the system. However, she told me something interesting, which we checked out this morning when we got in.'

'There was another fire on Saturday night,' said Aggie. She approached the map on the board, brandishing copies of the fire officer's report, and stabbed at it with her finger. 'At Belaugh Common. It started about fifteen metres into the woods from the lane where we found Darren Rushworth's car.'

'Deliberate?' asked Hudson.

'Definitely,' Bowen carried on. Sara smiled at the couple's double act. They were almost finishing each other's sentences these days. 'The seat of the fire was actually a burned-out moped. Started with petrol, the same as the other fires. Forensics are giving it the once-over now. Number plates are gone, but they rang over with the chassis number.'

'It belonged to Faye Rushworth,' said Aggie with a note of triumph.

That made Sara sit up. 'Who had a huge plaster on her right hand this morning when we interviewed her. Could be a burn.'

'It sounded too convenient that they reported the moped stolen this morning,' murmured Hudson.

'Why would she burn her own bike?' asked DI Edwards, although the question was rhetorical. 'What evidence did she want to get rid of?'

'That's not all.' Bowen frowned at Sara. 'Claudia had put herself on this vigilante rota. She spotted and followed a moped because it had no lights on. Lost it on the lane, then heard the fire start. As she rang for the fire brigade, she heard someone running away. They must have seen her car because they veered off the road into the field and thrashed off into the night.'

'That's where Ian has gone.' Aggie went back to her desk.

'DC Noble's gone to look at the new fire scene?' asked DCI Hudson.

'To see if he can find anything out about this runner,' confirmed Bowen.

'Good. Have we seen any forensic reports?' asked Hudson. Aggie nodded. 'Check them out, will you, DS Hirst?'

Sara nodded and flicked open her email account while DI Edwards explained more about their interviews. There were several reports to get through.

'So, none of them was prepared to volunteer DNA or fingerprints?' asked Hudson when the DI finished.

'I don't know how far that would get us,' said Edwards. 'You'd expect to find evidence of them at the different fires. They work or live there. Kyle's traces will be all over the bike; he uses it every day. Same with Darren Rushworth in his car.'

'Indeed. Anything new?'

'Dr Taylor has had DNA confirmation that the victim is Darren Rushworth,' Sara began. She read from her computer screen. 'Also, he died of smoke inhalation, so the damage to the body occurred after death.'

'That's a mercy,' said Aggie quietly. Sara silently agreed and moved on to the next file.

'Rushworth's car has been checked for DNA and contents.' Sara nodded towards Edwards. 'As the boss says, only what you'd expect. Hold on . . .' She read more quickly. 'It says they can confirm the fingerprints in the car are from both Darren and Faye Rushworth. How do they know that?'

'This heat is making us all stupid,' DCI Hudson said quietly. 'Please tell me someone checked to see if any of our suspects already had a bloody record.'

A stunned silence was eventually broken by Aggie typing furiously at her keyboard. 'Both of them have records. The

Met arrested and charged them following a Climate Action protest outside Parliament last year. Got in a fight with some uniformed officers. Jeez! You should see the size of the fine the court dished out. Oh my! Look at that.'

Bowen dodged around the desk to look where Aggie was pointing at her screen. He whistled softly.

'After they were released on bail, Faye Rushworth made an official complaint. Said one of the arresting officers touched her inappropriately.' He read on in silence for a short while. 'The complaint was dismissed as a tactic to try and get out of her charge.'

'I bet that went down well,' said Hudson. 'No wonder she doesn't trust the police. Knowing the Met, I bet they found additional evidence to ensure she got the maximum fine after that.'

'Ma'am! You can't say things like that,' objected Sara. Anger made her stand rapidly and move forward. 'Just because we've made a mistake doesn't mean we should make accusations against the Met.'

Hudson turned on her. 'Then that's two things we'll have to make sure we keep to ourselves, right? Incompetence from two police forces. I know you used to work at the Met, but you don't anymore. Perhaps you'd like to go back?'

Sara stared at Hudson with her mouth open. Bowen sucked in a sharp breath. Edwards waded in. 'No need for that, DCI Hudson. What's the matter with you?'

Hudson glared at him. Then she suddenly backed down. 'I'm tired. It must be the heat.'

'That's how mistakes get made, isn't it?' suggested Edwards. Hudson took the chance to save her dignity.

'Yes, it is. Have we missed anyone else?' she asked. 'What about Kyle or any of his family? Or any of the Willmott clan? Get on to that, Aggie.'

'Yes, ma'am.'

'Hirst? What else?'

Sara settled reluctantly at her computer again. She was still smarting from the crack about her former force. 'The

Wild Thyme fire was started with accelerants and probably clothes at the base of the double wooden doors on the front of the building. Accelerant was thrown around to make it spread faster. Ah, this explains one thing.'

'What?' asked Edwards.

'They found the door lock among the debris. It had been broken. That's how Darren must have got in. The lock didn't work. And there was an attempt to put out the fire with a fire extinguisher. Forensics have obtained partials from the extinguisher, confirmed as Darren, Faye and two others.'

'Two?' Hudson checked.

'Yes, ma'am,' Sara read on. 'One set that matched others which were commonly found in the area. Jean Simpson, probably. The other set is unknown on this report.'

'What did you find out about the Wild Thyme finances? Aggie? Bowen?'

'Not in very good shape,' said Aggie. 'The statements came through this morning. The first impression is that they are persistently on the edge of going under. Summer income is better, of course. Seems to me that they rely heavily on their supermarket bulk sales for most of their profit. They only seem to have two large regular customers. It's precarious.'

'Then Mrs Simpson wasn't exaggerating when she told us there wasn't enough money to buy Faye and her husband their own place?' asked DI Edwards.

'I doubt they would even get a mortgage or a loan.'

'Are they insured?' asked the DCI.

Bowen nodded. 'Regular payments out to NFU Mutual, which I assume are insurance premiums. I'll do a check with the company.'

'So, one of them could have set fire to the barn to claim on the buildings insurance,' said Hudson.

'Not an uncommon motive,' agreed Edwards.

'Have we checked Faye Rushworth's alibi for that night? If her husband had gone out, have her in-laws vouched for her? Could she have followed him?'

'How? He had the car, and her moped was at the herb farm,' said Sara. She was still reading the reports. 'Taxi, maybe?'

'Bowen, can you follow up with the in-laws, please,' instructed Hudson. 'Why did he go back to the barn? Was he looking for something? I think we need to bring Faye in again. Grounds for arrest?'

'Suspicion of setting the fire at the herb farm?' suggested Sara. 'And destroying evidence by burning the bike.'

'Good enough,' agreed the DCI. 'Interview under caution. Try to be as polite as you can. She is the grieving widow here, and we don't want another complaint from her. We need another talk with young Kyle as well. Grounds, anyone?'

'Hang on. There's a report from Kyle's bike too.' Sara flash-read the report. 'And the joints from the den. Got DNA from the joints and fingerprints from his bike.'

'Smoking a bit of pot isn't really a good reason to bring him in again,' said Edwards. 'He can easily claim personal use.'

'This is a good reason,' said Sara. She pointed at the forensic report on her screen. 'There are three sets of fingerprints on the bike. The predominant set is a match for the unknown visitor to Wild Thyme.'

'Kyle was at the herb farm fire?' asked Edwards in surprise.

'It would appear so.'

'Good enough. Let's have him arrested and questioned under caution,' instructed DCI Hudson. 'Aggie, arrange a neutral appropriate adult to be there, and drag back the same duty solicitor if you can.'

'I think we need to treat this with kid gloves as well,' said Sara cautiously. 'His prints were only found on the fire extinguisher.'

CHAPTER 51

There'd been a voice message for Claudia on her work phone when she'd arrived at Coles to start the new week. Kyle Atkins' mother said he would be late for work because he was 'helping the police with their enquiries'.

'I still think they've got the wrong person,' Claudia muttered as she deleted the message.

She'd left a reply on Mrs Atkins' mobile telling her to send Kyle into the yard when he was finished. Claudia doubted they would keep the youngster for very long. He turned up at half past eleven, and she sent him into the warehouse for the rest of the day to help with shelf tidying. Claudia watched him sorting boxes of plumbing spares from her office window. With a sigh, she returned to her computer, where she was starting the extensive paperwork for the insurance claim at the West Ruston site. The housing association was undoubtedly doing the same with their insurers. It was likely to be a large amount of money, and Claudia suspected much negotiation would be needed to make the insurance companies share the responsibility or pay up.

The heat may have technically subsided today, but her office still felt like a Mediterranean beach. The fan drubbed on the floor by her desk, and the door to the next office was wide open in an attempt to get some air moving between the three staff.

'Lunchtime soon,' she said as her stomach grumbled.

Squinting in concentration at some particularly small print on the insurance document, Claudia suddenly heard raised voices from the warehouse. She had barely sat up to look around when heavy feet pounded up the metal stairs.

'You need to come, quick!' called the warehouse manager. He looked furious. He beckoned to her with both hands and stood with his legs apart as if poised for a fight. 'They're taking Kyle away.'

It took Claudia a moment to comprehend what the man was shouting about. Then she rocketed from her chair and rushed out to meet him.

'What? Who?'

'The police!' he was shouting. 'They're arresting Kyle. What's he supposed to have done? He's only a kid.'

He's seventeen, thought Claudia. Her rubber-soled sandals clattered on the metal steps as she ran down them. There was no sign of Kyle or anyone else in the warehouse. *He has different rights. If only I knew what they were.*

The manager followed her, pausing to shout over Claudia's head, 'You leave him alone!'

'Not helpful,' she called over her shoulder.

'Then do something, woman. You wanted to be in charge.'

Claudia bridled at the sexism. She didn't need reminding that she was a woman in a man's world right now; it only served to undermine her. Jumping down the last three steps, she catapulted past the plastic bins of spares at a run and out into the work yard.

A marked police vehicle and a large black SUV stood side by side in the middle of the space. Kyle stood in the centre of a group of people, only one of whom Claudia recognised: DS Sara Hirst. It was a pity that Mike Bowen or his friendly wife weren't there.

'DS Hirst,' she called, marching rapidly over to join the group. 'What's going on?'

Claudia looked round the group until her gaze halted at Kyle, and she realised he was handcuffed. At least his hands were in front of him, not behind his back. With a jerk of disgust, she faced the tall DS and pointed.

'Is that really necessary?'

'Kyle needs to come with us and be interviewed,' the DS replied. 'Under caution.'

That sounded really serious to Claudia. 'You only spoke to him this morning! He visited you voluntarily. You didn't arrest him then, so why now?'

'That was then,' said the DS. Her face looked grim and determined. 'This is now.'

'Kyle? Do you need any help?' Claudia turned her attention to the youngster. His head was hanging down and his shoulders were sagging. 'I'll ring your mother or your uncle. Or both. Would that help?'

Kyle nodded. A woman Claudia didn't know stepped forward. She sounded friendly, if a little earnest. 'Kyle isn't alone. I've been designated his responsible adult, at least for now.'

'I'm not sure what the hell that means,' replied Claudia. 'I don't know why you have to do this, especially in such a public way.'

'Just doing our job,' said Hirst.

'This way.' A uniformed officer pulled Kyle's arm, moving him towards the police car and putting his hand on Kyle's head to protect it as he was pushed into the back seat.

'Don't say anything until you have help,' Claudia called after him. She turned on the responsible adult. 'He needs a solicitor. Don't you dare let them interview him without one.'

'It's already been arranged,' the woman assured her. 'He met Kyle this morning and will meet us at Wymondham.'

'Why Wymondham?'

'It's police HQ.' The responsible adult darted a glance at DS Hirst before leaning towards Claudia. She spoke in a half-whisper. 'I'll try and get them to put him in the family suite, not the adult interview room. Get on to his parents. He's lucky to have family support.'

Car doors slammed, engines fired up, and the two police vehicles powered out of the yard. Claudia watched them kicking up dust as they retreated down the parched road that led out of the industrial estate. Her heart was pounding and she was shaking with anger.

When she turned to go back to her office, Claudia realised that an audience had developed. The warehouse staff were standing silently in the doorway. They looked like a lynch mob blocking her path to the office. Behind her, she heard someone approaching across the concrete yard.

'What was that all about?' asked Mr Cole.

'Damned if I know,' said Claudia. She turned to face him, holding up her hands in defeat. 'Something to do with these fires, I assume.'

'Get on to our legal people. I'll authorise a solicitor for him. Won't have my staff treated like that.'

Then Mr Cole walked back to his office, leaving Claudia to get past the cowboy posse.

CHAPTER 52

Faye went with Jean to her appointment with the doctor. A simple test showed the hospital doctor was right, and more extensive blood tests were booked. It wasn't surprising to Jean that her blood pressure was also through the roof. They booked a visit to the diabetic nurse for her introduction to insulin.

'You need to look after yourself better,' said her doctor.

'I do my best,' Jean reflected gloomily.

When they got home, Kevin was consulting with the builder in the yard. A team of half a dozen men had arrived early that morning, erected a safety fence and put up warning signs everywhere. The men had already pulled down the remaining thatch. One was gathering it to throw into a skip. The rest were beginning to rake up the burned rubbish inside what was left of the barn.

Faye plonked a plate of toast on the kitchen table in front of Jean. 'You mustn't let yourself get hungry.'

'I shouldn't eat sweet things either,' replied Jean. She put butter on the bread, then ate it without any jam. It felt like cardboard in her mouth and was hard to swallow. Faye began to unload the dishwasher.

'Can I ask you something?' asked Jean. Faye looked up at her, hot plates balanced in her hands.

'You can ask,' she replied cautiously. The plates were dumped unceremoniously on the worktop.

'I see what you mean about the police,' Jean began. 'They were trying to trap me into saying something that would incriminate us.'

'You didn't tell them anything, did you?'

'I don't think so.' Jean threw the cold toast back on to its plate. 'I can't be sure because there's so much you're not telling me.'

Faye snorted. 'There's nothing to tell.'

'Yes, there is. I know you were upset about the house, but why did you threaten to leave?'

'We'd had enough of being treated like that.'

'Like what?' Jean was genuinely bewildered.

'Like unpaid servants. Having no privacy. Not even being able to make love without thinking you were in the bloody room next door listening to us.'

Jean paused to consider this. 'I think I understand that.'

'Big of you,' said Faye. She turned away and stacked the plates in an overhead cupboard. 'We thought you were enjoying the voyeurism. Old folks sleep lightly, or so they say.'

'This old folk sleeps like a log,' Jean assured her. 'What did you have a row about when you got to his parents' place?'

Faye stopped what she was doing and gazed out of the kitchen window. She stood motionless for so long that Jean thought she hadn't heard the question. Finally, she turned to look at her mother.

'We argued about leaving, and the barn,' she said. Her daughter's eyes bored into her.

Jean suddenly felt inspired. 'Did you want to turn it into your own home? Do a conversion on it?'

Faye shook her head. 'No, nothing like that.'

'Then, what did you fight about? And why did Darren come back to the barn in the middle of the night?'

Before Faye could answer, the sound of two cars arriving made her turn to check out of the window.

'The bloody police are here again,' she snapped. 'Stay here, Mother. I'll deal with them.'

Jean had no intention of obeying her daughter. Levering herself up, she hurried after Faye, who was already striding across the gravel, ready for a confrontation. Kevin ran to catch up with her. Jean's heart was pounding with the effort of moving so fast. She needed to be there, whatever was going on.

'What now?' Faye demanded as she reached the officers.

A pair of officers in full uniform appeared out of a police car. Jean recognised another in plain clothes as DI Edwards. Where was the tall, helpful girl when you needed her?

Mind you, Jean's mind ran on in overdrive, *she was part of that fiasco this morning. You can't trust her.*

She was panting by the time she reached the group. Edwards held up his warrant card.

'Faye Rushworth, I am arresting you on suspicion of tampering with evidence in a murder enquiry,' he said. His voice was clear and precise. 'I am also arresting you on suspicion of starting a fire which caused a fatal injury.'

Jean gasped. The shock held Kevin still, his eyes wide. Faye looked the DI up and down. Turning to her mother, she said sarcastically, 'See, Mother? I told you they'd find a way to fit one of us up with this.'

DI Edwards began to rap out her rights. Faye held out her hands, wrists together, waiting for the handcuffs. When Edwards finished, he looked at her hands. 'Do you want them on? Or are you coming willingly?'

Faye shrugged and let her arms drop to her sides. 'I no longer care.'

Jean swung round to speak to Kevin. He had already moved away and was punching at his phone.

'Don't say anything to anyone,' he called to Faye. 'I'll get Toby Byatt immediately.'

One of the uniformed officers began to lead Faye towards the car. Jean reached out to stop her.

'Mrs Simpson, please don't interfere,' said DI Edwards quietly. 'It doesn't help your daughter.'

'Where are you taking her?' she demanded. Fury made her shake, or perhaps it was another of those hypo things the doctor had gone on about.

'To our main offices in Wymondham,' replied the DI. He glanced at Kevin Howard, who was now talking rapidly on his phone. 'If you want your own solicitor there, we will wait to interview your daughter until he arrives.'

Jean walked as quickly as she could to the car, where Faye sat in the back seat. 'Kevin is getting that solicitor to meet you there.'

'It's okay, Mum,' said Faye. Her eyes closed wearily as she leaned back into the seat. 'I knew they'd blame me. And do you know what? Without Darren, I don't care if I live or die. What does it matter?'

The officer closed the car door, and Jean watched helplessly as the two cars pulled out of the car park.

CHAPTER 53

Sara followed the police car back to the Wymondham HQ. Kyle Atkins was placed in the family room, with a uniform officer outside the door in case he decided to try and leave. The team had to wait for the duty solicitor to arrive, so she went upstairs to the office. Edwards and Noble were still missing.

'How is he?' asked DCI Hudson.

'The responsible adult is with him,' replied Sara. 'I offered them both a cuppa, which Trevor is sorting out for them. Otherwise, he's not saying anything.'

'I've had a phone call,' said Aggie. She waggled her note-pad with a name and phone number on it. 'Says he's a legal advisor to Coles Construction and has been told to come and represent Kyle.'

'Is he on his way?' Hudson grimaced when Aggie nodded. 'Then we'll have to wait until he gets here. Stand down the duty one, will you?'

With a nod, Aggie picked up the phone.

'Financials?' Hudson moved on to DC Bowen. He was smiling.

'I spoke to NFU Mutual, and they confirmed the payments were for buildings and contents insurance,' he nodded.

'Apparently, the barn is valued at £200,000, and they've already been contacted by Wild Thyme about making a claim. I've put in the formal request for a copy of the policy.'

'What about the contents of the barn?' asked Sara. 'Did you ask about them?'

'The contents' value was minimal,' Bowen shook his head.

'There must have been something of value in there if Darren Rushworth went back for it in the middle of the night.'

'Something easily carried?' suggested Bowen. 'He was on his own.'

'Buried pirate treasure perhaps,' said Hudson sarcastically. Sara and Bowen shared a rueful glance. 'Let's ask the wifey when we talk to her. What about the in-laws?'

'They said that Faye was there all night.' Bowen checked a note on his pad. 'At least they heard her in the bedroom when they went to their own bed, and apparently, she was still there when they woke up the next morning.'

'Exactly what I'd expect them to say,' said Hudson.

Sara was reading more carefully through the forensic reports when DI Edwards came in.

'I've put Faye Rushworth in Interview Room One,' he told them all. 'Waiting for her solicitor to get here. Shouldn't be too long.'

'How did she take it?' asked Sara.

'Resigned to it all, I'd say,' replied Edwards. 'Told her mother she didn't care anymore. Want to have a look?'

She followed the DI to the viewing room. Faye Rushworth was sitting at the table, one arm across her stomach supporting the other. She was picking at the broad plaster strapped across her right hand. Her face looked passive. There was no spark of interest in her eyes. It wasn't even the deliberately dumb expression Sara had seen so often when a young criminal was determined not to say or show anything, despite being guilty as hell about something. The woman looked exhausted.

'Wonder what's under there?' mused Sara. 'Cut or burn?'

'Tenner on burns,' Edwards shrugged.

'Not taking that one. The odds are too good on your side.'

Faye stretched back in her chair, raising her arms above her head, and yawned. They heard a knock at the interview room door, and Sergeant Jones leaned into the room.

'Fancy a cuppa while you wait?' he asked.

Faye looked surprised at the offer. A plastic cup of water stood untouched on the table. She glanced at it and then nodded to Jones.

'Milk? Sugar?'

'No sugar, thanks. Do you have soya milk?'

Sara laughed at the expression on the genial, old-school sergeant's face. He paused to consider the question as if the answer was of the utmost importance.

'I don't,' he said finally. He usually made his visitors' cuppas in a little kitchen area behind the front desk, where the options were builder's tea or Earl Grey as a concession. 'I can ask in the canteen if you don't mind waiting.'

Faye smiled at this. 'I'll wait. It's not like I'm going anywhere, is it?'

Jones nodded and vanished as the viewing room door opened. DC Noble stepped in behind them, holding a large evidence bag.

'How did you get on at the fire site?' asked DI Edwards.

'I worked out where Ms Turner would have stopped her car. It didn't take me long to find where our runner had gone up the bank and through the field.'

'You been taking tracking lessons from the Lone Ranger? It's too dry to find footprints.'

'No, sir,' said Noble. He looked confused, which made Sara smile. After all this time on the team, Ian still didn't always spot the DI's quirky sense of humour. 'It was easy, really. The bank is hard as nails. The crop beyond is so dry it's already like straw. Whoever it was trampled through the stuff and left a clear trail heading directly towards the public footpath. Just call me Tonto, sir.'

Then he grinned, and Sara revised her opinion. He held up the evidence bag.

'This got pulled off in the middle of the field. Either they didn't realise they'd lost it, or they were too panic-struck to go back for it.'

'It couldn't have been dropped by a previous walker?' asked Sara.

'Doubt it, sarge,' replied Ian. 'It was too far from the main hiker's path.'

'You had a good look at it?'

'Of course. It's a black zip-up hoodie from one of the cheap chain stores.' Noble held up the evidence bag. 'A woman's size *large*.'

CHAPTER 54

It was inevitably going to be difficult, which was why Sara had made her decision on Sunday. It gave them both a day to at least begin to come to terms with the situation. Even so, she felt her cheeks flame and her body sweat even more than they already were when she walked into Dante as she left the viewing room. DI Edwards ran into the back of her, sandwiching her between the two men. It was far too embarrassing.

'Watch where you're going,' said Edwards, skirting round the pair. 'That was nearly a motorway pile-up.'

There are no motorways in Norfolk, she thought inconsequentially. 'Sorry.'

'My fault, DS Hirst,' said Dante. Both his body and his tone were stiff. He stepped to one side, unwilling to meet Sara's look, and strode away down the corridor. She heard the viewing room door close behind her.

'Are you okay?' asked Noble quietly. She nodded. 'I thought you two were . . . well, you know.'

'Not anymore,' she told him. 'And that's why. It's just too difficult if you go out with someone at work.'

'Aggie and Mike seem to manage, though I'm glad my girlfriend isn't in the business. Shall I take this to forensics?' He rattled the evidence bag with its hoodie.

'Leave it until we've spoken to her,' she suggested.

Like buses, solicitors were either missing in action or came along two at once, she reflected, when Trevor Jones rang up to say both suspects were now in conference with their legal advisors.

'You tackle the lad,' DCI Hudson instructed Sara. 'Take Noble with you. I'll take the woman. Bowen, you're with me. Bring the bag.'

A glance over her shoulder confirmed to Sara that DI Edwards was glowering at being left out. Aggie was cutting him a conciliatory piece of cake.

'It's not as if she's even met any of them,' he complained.

'I think she may be smarting a bit.' Sara picked up her notepad. 'After all, we did make a fairly classic rookie error over checking the national database for previous.'

'She'll stuff it up,' he said gloomily. He pushed some cake into his mouth and held up both thumbs in approval, making Aggie smile. Sara left them to it.

It was crowded in the family room. Kyle was hemmed in on the sofa by the female responsible adult on one side and a solicitor Sara didn't recognise on the other. He stood to introduce himself as Lee Smith, then squashed down again next to Kyle. Sara thought the man looked uncomfortable with his long legs bent upwards and elbows cramped at his sides. He was trying to balance a laptop on his knee. It slid slowly towards his stomach, only to be pushed back up and begin its journey again.

She turned on the recording machine, introduced Noble and explained what would happen next.

'Kyle, do you understand why you are here?' she began.

The young man rubbed dramatically at his wrists. 'Because you arrested me.'

'Do you remember we took the bike you left at *Scoot! Rural* in for forensic tests?'

Kyle looked at Lee Smith, who nodded. 'Yeah. So what?'

'Obviously, it was covered in your fingerprints and many other traces.'

'No shit, Sherlock. It's mine.' Smith held up a warning hand, and Kyle subsided.

'Indeed,' agreed Sara. 'It was also covered in lots of other things. Such as earth and grass from various places.'

'I told you I got run off the road. So what?'

'What about the container of spare petrol in your seat locker? Why do you have that?'

Smith looked at Kyle with raised eyebrows. Kyle leaned sideways and whispered to Smith, who made a note on his laptop. It jiggled distractingly.

'Uncle Eric,' said Kyle. 'He told me to do it in case I ran out on my way to work.'

Noble nodded and smiled. 'Sounds like a good idea.' Kyle flicked a glance at him but didn't respond.

'There were two sets of fingerprints on the fuel can. One set is yours. We don't recognise the others.'

Kyle looked at Sara mulishly. Smith whispered to him, and he nodded. 'No comment.'

Here we go, she thought. 'The same prints appear on the bike itself. Still no idea?'

'No comment.'

'Kyle, are you the only person to ride or handle that bike?'

The young man chewed his lip for a moment. 'No. Andy at *Scoot! Rural* wheeled it into the workshop the other day.'

'We've already arranged for his prints to be collected. Did Andy handle the petrol can?'

Kyle shrugged.

Sara pushed on. 'Do you know if anyone else handled the bike or the can?'

'No comment.' Kyle shuffled his bum in discomfort, making the sofa cushions sigh.

'Are you sure?'

Kyle looked at Lee Smith, then glared at the ceiling for inspiration. 'All right. I'll tell you. It was Ryan.'

'Your little brother?'

'He's not so little. Thirteen now. He wanted a ride on it, just to see if he could. So, I let him take it up and down the lane a few times. Little shit damaged it as well.'

'How?'

'Fell off it, didn't he? Slapped it down on its side on the bloody gravel.'

'Why haven't you told us this before?'

Kyle snorted in derision. 'Because he's underage, ain't he? You gonna charge me with that an' all? It was only in our lane. No one ever comes down there.'

'When was this, Kyle?'

'Few weeks ago.'

'Has he used it since?'

'No bloody way. Little shit.' Kyle's lips curled in disgust. His eyes flicked around the room before settling on the coffee table in front of the sofa.

'Would Ryan have handled the petrol can?' asked Sara.

'Don't see why.'

'I'm afraid we'll also have to get his fingerprints to eliminate him.' Sara nodded to Lee Smith. 'I'll make the formal arrangements for protection. Could you be there, Mr Smith?'

'Yes, of course.'

Kyle relaxed as Sara gathered up her notepad and pen. 'One more thing, Kyle. Can you explain why your fingerprints were on a fire extinguisher outside the burning barn at Wild Thyme Herb Farm?'

Kyle looked at the solicitor in panic before hissing, 'No comment.'

CHAPTER 55

As DI Edwards predicted, the outcome of DCI Hudson's interview with Faye Rushworth had been a string of 'no comments'. Sara had at least persuaded Kyle to give his fingerprints and DNA; Hudson had drawn a blank on that front as well.

'She has no choice, of course,' said the DCI. She sounded petulant, which made Sara turn away to hide a smile. 'The pair of them can have a night in the cells to see what they'll be facing. We'll re-interview in the morning. Everyone can bugger off home.'

Sara knew it wouldn't go well with either solicitor when the DCI refused police bail to both suspects on principle. The principle being that she was pissed off with them. It had been a thoroughly unprofessional day from Hudson, Sara reflected as she drove home.

The sound of a shovel hitting solid ground filtered into the kitchen when she walked through her cottage. Adie was still working. Dropping her bag on the garden table, Sara walked down the path to find him. He'd made great progress. Piles of dead weeds and undergrowth stood like a guard of honour on either side of the path. The beds behind them had been turned over, despite the solid texture of the ground.

She wondered how he'd managed it and glanced around for a pickaxe.

'Good evening,' she called as she passed the rickety shed. Adie had almost reached the fence between her garden and the field beyond. He looked up at her with a smile that made her body fizz with excitement. A multi-coloured floppy hat sat low on his head to keep the sun out of his eyes. 'I'm pleased with how far you've managed to get. Are you?'

'Not bad.' He stabbed the spade into a freshly turned piece of earth, which spat a gout of dust at him. He pulled off the hat to wipe the sweat from his forehead. 'I think this will have to be a two-part project, though.'

'Okay. When will you finish for the evening?'

Adie glanced at the sun as if telling the time. 'Another half hour?'

'Would you like to stay for a cold drink or some supper?' Sara cringed at the crassness of her words. Talk about being forward. 'Then we could talk about it?'

'A drink would be great,' he said. 'I'm expected at home for dinner at seven.'

'Alcohol or not?'

'Not, thank you.' Adie pulled out the spade. 'I don't do booze.'

'Okay, see you soon.'

Sara returned to the cottage and showered, as much to get rid of her anxieties as to get rid of the sweat. When Adie appeared, she had a jug of iced orange juice and two glasses waiting on the garden table.

Looking far too needy, she scolded herself silently. She listened as the hippy gardener washed at the kitchen sink.

'This is kind,' he said. They sat in awkward silence for a moment, sipping their drinks.

'What did you mean by a two-part project?'

'That depends on what you want to do with this.' Adie waved at the garden. 'It's a big garden for someone on their own. I take it you're not a keen gardener.'

'I don't know,' replied Sara. She contemplated the long, thin space. 'It's mostly that I don't have time because of my job.'

'What do you do?'

Sara was surprised that Gilly hadn't already given the man Sara's life story. 'I'm a copper. Detective sergeant.'

'Oooh! You investigate murders?' Adie sounded impressed.

'Yes, sometimes,' she smiled. 'The job is usually much more prosaic than that. It's not like it looks on the television.'

'Are you doing that now?'

'I can't say.'

Adie looked puzzled for a moment, then comprehension dawned. 'I see. It's still an ongoing case?'

Sara nodded. 'What about you? Is this your full-time job?'

'Sort of.' Adie turned away to gaze at the garden. 'Actually, I'm training to be a landscape gardener, so it's back to college in September.'

'College?'

'Specialist place over the Cotswolds.' He grinned at her raised eyebrows. 'I'm a mature student. Anyway, I only got into it because we have such a huge garden at home. Someone had to look after it, and there was no money. Then I found I really liked it.'

'Where's home?'

'Richmond Hall.' He laughed to himself. 'Sounds impressive, doesn't it?'

Living in a stately home of some sort. That explains his accent, Sara thought. 'I guess it does.'

'You're right to be cautious. It's large, of course, but very run-down. When Father died, he left us with loads of debt, not to mention the death duty. Mother is doing her best with bed and breakfast lets, which bring in some money. My brother sends funds when he can, although he has a family to look after. Bit of a nightmare, in truth. Mother refuses to sell.'

Sara sipped her juice and thought about her own father. Although he'd been absent for most of her life, he had left her with the security of this cottage to live in or sell as she saw fit. It had set her up financially for life, and she would always be grateful.

'How do you know Gilly?'

'Mother, naturally,' said Adie. 'She's an ace networker regarding local things and people.'

'What do you mean about the garden?'

Adie blushed red under his suntan. 'I don't want to sound like I'm trying to get more money from you.'

'Tell me anyway.'

'Well, there isn't much you can do with the planting this late in the year,' said Adie. His enthusiasm grew as he spoke. 'You only asked me to clear it up for you, which is fine. It could be a lovely space with sequential colour rooms, water features and loads of other possibilities. You need to replace the shed, so why not a combined garden room and shed? This patio area would have a low-maintenance pot-based herb system. You could recycle old boards to make raised beds. I know of a 1930s greenhouse that could be reused.'

Suddenly his voice faded away. He dropped his gaze to his juice glass.

Sara hadn't understood a word that he'd said, apart from replacing the shed. His enthusiasm was as catching as his good looks.

'Sorry, I get carried away. That would be expensive.'

'That's the sort of thing you want to design?'

'When I'm qualified. I'd better get going.' He swigged his glass to empty it. 'Thanks for the juice. Will you be here in the morning?'

'Only if you're early,' said Sara. 'I'm due in at half past seven.'

'No problem. Have a good evening.'

She waved casually to his retreating figure, waiting until she heard the front door close before searching for Richmond Hall on her mobile phone.

'Did you notice one thing?' she asked Tilly when the feline joined her at the garden table. 'He never mentions a girlfriend or wife.'

CHAPTER 56

After arranging the solicitor for Kyle and ringing both Eric Beatty and Mrs Atkins with the news, Claudia struggled through the rest of the day. She tried to keep her mind on the insurance claim in front of her without success. She'd begun the evening by arranging her books and DVDs on to the new shelves. Choosing from among her favourites, she'd stretched out on the sofa to watch a rom-com. At some point, she must have dozed off because the strident ringtone of her mobile jerked her awake. She sat up and hit the answer button.

'Hello?' Claudia didn't recognise the landline number and was naturally cautious.

'Is that you, Miss Turner?'

'Oh, hello, Eric,' she said. 'Is something wrong?'

'I'm at my sister-in-law's place,' said Eric. Claudia unpacked the comment for a moment and came up with Mrs Atkins. 'We're really worried.'

'About Kyle? Didn't the solicitor turn up?'

'Yes, he did, thank you.'

'How is Kyle coping?'

'We don't know. They've kept him in overnight. Said they would be speaking to him again in the morning.'

Claudia was shocked. 'Didn't the solicitor object?'

'He did,' said Eric. His voice wavered as if he was trying not to cry. 'We went to the place in Wymondham to see Kyle. The man tried to get him bail while we were there. They said no.'

'Poor Kyle.' Claudia sighed with frustration. 'For what it's worth, Eric, I don't believe he's responsible for any of this.'

Eric stuttered his thanks, drew in a ragged breath and continued. 'It's not Kyle we're worried about now. It's Ryan.'

'His younger brother?'

'Yes. You see, he've gone missing.'

Claudia nearly fell off the sofa in surprise. 'Ryan? When? What? Sorry, I'm confused.'

'We got back from the police place at teatime,' explained Eric. 'His mum and me. Told Ryan what was going on. Well, you can't keep the lad wondering, can you? He started shouting and cursing. Said it was all his fault. He'd set fire to Manor Farm, and they shouldn't blame Kyle.'

Eric paused to catch his breath.

'And then?'

'Then he ran off. I went after him, but he was too fast for me. I let him go 'cos I thought he was just upset. Wanted to be on his own.'

'When was this?'

'About five o'clock. We've not seen him since. I'm really worried. He was heading towards the river.'

'Have you called the police?'

'Of course. A couple of hour ago. They weren't very helpful, couldn't wait to get me off the line. We've bin waiting and wond'ring, then I remembered you spoke to that detective who came to take our statements.'

'DC Bowen,' confirmed Claudia. 'I have his card somewhere.' She stood up, feeling decisive.

'What if he's gone to the river to throw himself in?' stammered Eric. 'He was so upset.'

'Right. I'll ring DC Bowen, then I'm coming round there.'

Digging Bowen's card out of her handbag, she dialled him as she pulled on some jeans and a jumper. It went to voicemail three times before he answered on the fourth.

'Yes?' Bowen sounded curt.

'I'm so sorry to bother you,' began Claudia as she shoved her feet into a pair of socks. 'I think we're going to need your help.'

She rapidly explained about Ryan's confession and disappearance.

'That's five hours ago,' said Bowen. 'He's only thirteen, yes? I'm going to get on to the boss and see what she says. He needs finding.'

'I'm heading to Mrs Atkins' house.' Claudia strode back to the living room, looking for her car keys. 'I'll let you know if I hear anything else.'

* * *

Sara was grateful she'd only had one glass of wine when her mobile rang and Mike Bowen told her about Ryan. She made a quick coffee in her travel mug, pulled on walking boots and hurried to her car. It was likely to be a very long night.

It was pitch black and getting late. The moon was just a sliver, providing little light. Stuffing a pair of torches into her jacket pocket, Sara powered her SUV on to the road and set off for Belaugh. When her hands-free console warbled, she stabbed at the button on her steering wheel.

'DS Hirst?' It was DCI Hudson. The woman sounded rattled.

'I'm on my way, ma'am,' Sara assured her. 'Mike already rang me.'

'I've called out the troops. Search parties will meet at Belaugh Common. I'm concerned he might harm himself or set fire to somewhere else. You go to the mother's house and find out what direction the little bugger set off in.'

'Yes, ma'am,' replied Sara. She punched angrily at the button to end the call. Little bugger, indeed. Confused and panic-struck, more like. Or frightened? Or guilty? Had he really started all those fires? Was he Darren Rushworth's murderer? Her spine froze with fear as she rounded the corner at the Walton Road junction and sped towards Marlham.

'Concentrate,' she muttered to herself. It wouldn't be helpful if she caused an accident. 'Find out what was said first. You don't have all the facts.'

* * *

Claudia's car was small and not very high-powered. Even so, she pushed as hard as she dared. She felt guilty.

'I should have done more,' she told herself. 'Kyle is innocent, and they still arrested him. They might never have even thought about him if I hadn't told them about his bike. Now his little brother has run away.'

The turning area was already full when Claudia reached the end of the lane with its three cottages. She carefully steered her little car onto the verge out of the way. She recognised the black vehicle belonging to DS Hirst. Another large blue car was next to it, and a marked police car with its blue flashing lights still on.

She could see a family of holidaymakers in the end cottage. Making no attempt to disguise their interest, a man and a woman stood in the front garden watching proceedings. The woman held a toddler in her arms. The child blinked dreamily as it looked around in confusion.

'The gang's all here,' she said sarcastically as people emerged from the side passage by Michelle Atkins' cottage. There was Hirst and Bowen. And wasn't that the DI she'd met? Edwards, wasn't it? Hirst was talking to Eric Beatty as they walked.

'I'm pleased to see you,' said DC Bowen when he reached her car. 'This could be a difficult night. Can you go and sit with Mrs Atkins? She won't let us bring in a family liaison officer. She's in a state, I'm afraid.'

'That's hardly surprising,' said Claudia. She locked her car before heading around the side of the house.

* * *

'Where does this path go?' asked Sara. She'd extracted what information she could about Ryan from his terrified mother and uncle and relayed it to DCI Hudson. Eric Beatty pointed as he walked in front of her.

'Down the side of the fields, behind Manor Farm and out at the river.'

It was hard to see anything in this light. Sara trained her torch onto the earthy footpath, set rock hard by the weather. Dust kicked up from Beatty's feet. He wasn't as young or as fit as the officers were. He was already panting. Sara reached forward and tapped him on the shoulder.

'Mr Beatty.' She pulled him to a halt. 'I can go faster with the officer here. Can you wait for Ryan at home? You have my number, don't you?'

Beatty sagged in defeat. 'You're right. He doesn't have anyone else, see? Just us.'

'We just need to make sure he's safe,' Sara assured him. 'Are there any turns off this path to avoid?'

'No. A couple of stiles, but no turnings.'

'I'll call if I find him,' she promised. Then she strode away quickly, the uniformed officer working hard to keep up behind her.

It might have been a mile or more. They climbed the two stiles at either end of a field of oilseed rape, then crossed a field of some corn crop, which rustled as they powered past. The field ended in a tall hedge, and for a moment Sara was confused about how they could go any further. She swung her torch beam left and right until she spotted a trimmed gap in the hedge. A wooden council way marker leaned crazily on the far side of it.

They walked through, and the land changed immediately. Despite the months of heat and lack of rainfall, it was boggy underfoot. The path clung to a slightly higher strip of land where walkers had kept the way open. To the sides of the little spur of land, her torch caught patches of bullrushes. Beyond that, she glimpsed what she thought must be the beginnings of a reed bed.

'Careful,' called the officer behind her. 'We're almost there.'

He was right. Twenty yards or so away, Sara could see the glistening oily blackness of the River Bure sliding serenely through the dark. Reaching the bank edge, it crumbled slightly under her impatient feet. She shone her torch along the bank in either direction.

'It's a dead end.' She was almost shouting in frustration. 'Where the hell did he go from here?'

'Into the river?'

'I bloody well hope not,' said Sara. She swung her torch across the water. 'Please, God, let's hope not.'

CHAPTER 57

The new moon was waxing in the sky. Just a couple of days old, there was little illumination. Despite the minor light pollution from Wroxham, Jean could see a sky full of stars from her seat in the courtyard. Unable to sleep, she had given up lying on her bed, made a cup of tea and wandered across to the café with it. A security light had flicked on when she approached. After she settled in her seat, her lack of movement allowed it to go out again. Without her glasses, the buildings around her were blurred, dark shapes. The broken body of the burned barn was irregular and easiest to identify. To her right, the dark bulk of the café loomed closest. Gazing at the wooden and glass-panelled walls, Jean wondered if they could ever reopen now.

'I'm sorry, Malcolm,' she whispered to the ghost of her husband. 'I've mucked everything up, haven't I?'

She waited for some reply or word of comfort from beyond the grave. But Jean was a practical woman. None came; none was expected. She was just trying to give herself some hope. Hunching up her shoulders, she crouched over her mug to extract warmth. It wasn't that the night was cold. It was more that the action was familiar.

'I've hurt too many people,' Jean said to herself. 'Starting with you.'

Their marriage had been happy by most people's standards. The herb farm had been Malcolm's baby, his big idea. He loved it and pursued its growth with vigour. The house and land belonged to Jean's family. She had inherited it when her father died. During one of their very rare arguments, Jean accused Malcolm of only marrying her to get his hands on the place and start this business. Her words had made a shutter of hurt come down in her husband's eyes, which never quite lifted.

Malcolm could be secretive too. From the start, Jean had kept the books, done the invoicing, introduced the café and organised necessary work around the place. Malcolm had bred the plants and run the polytunnels. They had both found their niches in the business. But Malcolm had never told her everything; she was sure of that. As Faye grew up, she formed a bond with Malcolm that Jean could not penetrate. If she was honest, Jean had been jealous, knowing herself to be excluded from their closeness. Faye had inherited Malcolm's green fingers too. They'd had that in common as well. Jean could kill a houseplant in five minutes. As Faye had taken over more of the work from Malcolm, he had begun going off for the day with his mate in an old van.

She would have understood if he'd wanted to retire, go fishing or hiking, or learn to paint. It hadn't been like that. In retrospect, Jean supposed that it had been a hobby of sorts. Bit by bit, the old barn had become stuffed with rubbish from car boot sales and auctions at empty country houses.

'I'll do them all up one day,' he'd promised her. 'Sell them on eBay. Make loads of money.'

The day had never come. Malcolm's heart attack had got to him first.

Jean gazed at the dead barn, aching for everything she had lost. 'Well, it's all gone now.'

The lanes between here, the river and the common were usually silent at night. The occasional lost motorist would curse their satnav and turn round in the riverside car park, their lights passing Jean twice. Sometimes she'd see the old SUV that Jake Willmott drove passing to or from the farm, no doubt checking up on his dad. Recently, Jean had noticed the odd night-time visitor until Kevin had explained about the rota, after which she hadn't worried.

The approach of police sirens, their distinctive sound echoing around the café yard, was frightening this late at night. Blue lights flashing, they roared past towards Manor Farm and the river. Jean felt a lance of cold fear charge through her body.

'Oh no,' she breathed. 'Not another fire. Not Thomas's place.'

She moved as quickly as she could to the middle of the car park, her eyes searching the sky. There was no sign of a red glow anywhere. Surely there would be one. Perhaps it was in another direction. Grabbing a key and a torch from the kitchen, Jean headed through the hedge and down the polytunnel path to the back gate. With a gasp at the weight, she managed to swing one side open and went into the back lane.

She scrambled up the bank opposite to scan the horizon. Bright white lights, underpinned by flashing blue ones, bounced above the hedge line. Belaugh Common was across Willmott's fields, and whatever was going on, it was happening over there. Unsure what to do, she watched a set of headlights wind along the lane towards her. They were in a hurry, so Jean stayed where she was until the vehicle passed. The large black SUV skidded to a halt a few yards beyond her, as if the driver had spotted her torch beam. The door slammed and footsteps approached.

'Is that you, Mrs Simpson?' called a woman. 'It's DS Hirst. Are you all right?'

'I'm fine,' replied Jean. For some reason, she was trembling. 'What are you doing out here at this time of night?'

Hirst had reached where Jean was balancing. She held out her hand to help Jean down the bank.

'Thank you. What's going on at the common?' Jean asked again.

'A young lad has gone missing,' replied the DS. 'Ryan Atkins. Do you know him?'

Jean gasped. 'Kyle's younger brother? He's missing?'

'He ran off, and we're concerned for his safety.' Hirst looked into the farmyard. 'We're hoping he's just holed up somewhere. Hiding in an outbuilding or something. Could I send a team over to check your place? They're down at the farm at the moment.'

'Of course,' said Jean with a firm nod. 'Why on earth would Ryan run away?'

Hirst looked at her closely in the light from the car. 'I can't really say.'

Jean turned panic-laden thoughts rapidly over in her mind. 'Something to do with these fires, isn't it? Do you think he started them? You think he started mine?'

'We just need to find him,' the DS deflected. 'We're really worried about him. Do you still have my number?' Jean nodded. 'I'll divert that team asap. They'll come to the front gate.'

'Of course,' called Jean as Hirst strode back to the car. 'I'll wait in the yard.'

Struggling to swing the gate back together, Jean's fingers ached by the time she got the padlock closed. Hurrying along the path in case the searchers turned up before she could get there, Jean's breath became ragged and short. She was glad to reach the café, where she could lean on the table to recover. Waiting in the dark, she made herself and the image of her dead husband a promise.

'Enough now,' she swore. 'Time to tell them everything I know. Those boys can't be held responsible for this.'

CHAPTER 58

She looked really distressed, thought Sara, as she drove away from Mrs Simpson. *Hardly surprising, I suppose.*

There were two police cars already parked at Belaugh Manor Farm, and the officers were searching the outbuildings surrounding the farmhouse. Where there were lights available, they had been turned on. Sara could see the beams of torches flickering where the building was dark. Occasional voices shouted progress as somewhere was declared clear. The noise of her car drawing up brought Thomas Willmott to the front door.

'Any news?' he asked.

'Not so far,' said Sara. 'Thank you for allowing us to search your buildings.'

'No problem. Who is this youngster?'

'Didn't the officers tell you?' Sara thought for a moment, then decided he ought to know. 'It's Ryan Atkins. Your grandson.'

Reality dawned on the old man's face. 'I didn't realise.'

'Were you aware that your daughter-in-law and grandsons lived only a couple of miles away?'

'You'd better come in,' said Willmott. He didn't meet Sara's gaze as he waved her to follow him into the messy kitchen. When he pointed to a chair, Sara shook her head. The back door was half open, and she could see the officers moving between the various buildings in the gloom beyond the pool of light in the yard. The dogs stood panting at the door, waiting obediently and watching intently.

'I'm needed elsewhere,' she said, her tone short and brisk. 'Is there something I can do for you, Mr Willmott?'

'Yes, I did know,' said the farmer. He sank into a chair, folding his arms tightly across his chest. 'They live on Low Lane.'

'You never see them or speak to them?'

Willmott shook his head in misery. 'I didn't think they'd want to see me. Not after what happened.'

An outraged squawk made one of the dogs whine and reverse into the kitchen. The punk chicken stalked into the room, attitude blazing. Dipping its head, the bird spotted the farmer, and with its claws clacking on the floor tiles, the creature marched up to the man. With a flap of wings, it launched itself on to Willmott's lap. Unsurprised, the farmer ran his hand along the chicken's back, smoothing its feathers.

'It looks like they've let the birds out by mistake,' he said. 'Easy thing to do. I'd better round them up again. Foxes might get them if they're out at night.'

He deftly tucked the half-bald bird under his arm and headed for the yard. Pausing to look back, he said, 'Please find him. Those boys are still family, despite everything.' Then he strode away, the dogs following at a discreet distance.

Sara could see two officers searching in one of the dilapidated barns. At least that one had lights on inside.

'Any luck?' she called as she joined them.

'Sorry, sarge,' said one of the officers. 'Nothing so far.'

'Have you much more to do here?' The officer told her they were nearly finished. 'I'd like you to go up to the herb farm next. The owner is expecting you. She knows the boy a little and is keen to help.'

'Good idea,' agreed the officer. He pointed to the other men, who could be seen lifting blankets in an old stable block. 'We can go now and leave the others to finish here.'

'Great. If you don't get lucky there, go back to the search coordinator at the common.'

Skirting past the farmer gathering his little flock of rescue chickens, Sara hurried back to her car and left.

* * *

A mobile office unit was already parked near to where the youngsters had their drinking den, and a roadblock had been set up at either end of the lane. Sara signed herself through the cordon and parked at the back of the queue of cars. She recognised everyone's vehicle, from DCI Hudson's down to DC Noble's. There were also several police cars and a dog unit van. It was cramped with people inside the mobile unit, all reporting in for instructions. A detailed map of the area was pinned up, with notes surrounding it showing where the search teams were active. DCI Hudson stood at a whiteboard, clearly in her administrative heaven.

'No joy at the farm,' Sara reported to Hudson. 'I asked them to go on to Wild Thyme.'

'Thank you, DS Hirst.' Hudson pencilled a huge tick over the farm on the map and pulled down a post-it note with the farm's name on it. She crumpled it up and threw it on the table next to a small pile of similar bits of yellow paper. She began allocating search objectives for the waiting teams, marking names on a notepad as the officers left to move to their new areas.

Sara felt nothing but admiration for her boss in moments like these. If she were in charge, she'd prefer to be out there doing something, anything, to help, not working out an action plan or waiting for news. The wall clock told her it was nearly half past one. Ryan had been missing for eight and a half hours.

* * *

Claudia sat at the kitchen table with Eric Beatty and Michelle Atkins. She wanted to do something to help but couldn't figure out what. Cold cups of tea sat congealing on the table in front of them. Eric was holding Michelle's hand, although the poor woman didn't seem to notice either of them.

'Ms Atkins . . .' Claudia began.

Eric looked up at her. 'You'd best call us Eric and Michelle, under the circumstances.'

'Yes, and me Claudia, please. Look, I think it would be a good idea if you accepted DS Hirst's suggestion of allowing the family liaison officer to join us. It might be difficult to hear any news quickly without that point of contact.'

Michelle didn't reply or look up.

'I think Claudia's right. Shall we do that?' Eric shook Michelle's hand gently. She continued to stare into space. 'Can you call them and sort that out?'

'Of course. And another thing —' Eric frowned at her — 'now that we know the search is happening, can you think of anywhere Ryan might have gone? Somewhere special to him? A hideout or a den? Boys like that sort of thing. Have you thought of anything you didn't remember to tell DS Hirst?'

Michelle still didn't reply.

'The boy don't say much,' offered Eric. 'Bit of a loner, really. When he does talk, it's always about the wildlife. The birds and things that he sees by the river.'

'Can I tell that to DS Hirst? It might help.'

Eric agreed, and Claudia went outside to make the call, where Michelle couldn't hear her.

* * *

'I've requested the Broads Beat patrol boat to be launched,' said DCI Hudson.

The office was almost empty now as the various teams headed out. Noble had gone with one of them, Edwards with another. Bowen hovered nearby, and Sara almost cringed when she saw him. Gone were his well-worn suit and tie, replaced by a police-issue stab vest over black jeans and a pale sweatshirt, making him look like a podgy panda.

'Have they agreed?' she asked.

'Gave me some guff about not going out in the dark,' replied Hudson. She sounded grimly angry. 'I told them to bloody well get on with it, or the ACC would be hearing from me about lack of cooperation.'

'We could search the riverbank without leaving the deep part of the river,' suggested Sara. 'If they're worried about running into debris.'

'They can see well enough,' snapped Hudson. 'The damn thing has a searchlight on the roof.'

'Where are they launching?' asked Bowen.

'From Hoveton.' Hudson pointed to the map. 'There's a slipway there that they often use. Said they'd be ready by two o'clock. I want you two out with them. I don't trust them to be thorough, and you know what the lad looks like.'

'Best take one of these,' said Bowen, handing Sara a stab vest.

'They're not life jackets, Mike,' she muttered.

'We could look for the reflective bits if you fall in.' He grinned at her as she strapped it on.

* * *

Jean Simpson gave the police officers keys to all the buildings.

'Be careful in that barn,' she said, pointing to the burned-out structure. 'I doubt he'd be in there anyway. There's nowhere left to hide.'

'You know the boy?' asked one officer.

'Slightly,' Jean answered. 'His older brother had a Saturday job with me.'

'Would he recognise you? Or be prepared to talk to you?'

'I doubt it.' *On either count*, Jean thought to herself. 'There's no point in me coming with you. I'll be in the house if you need me. Feel free to look anywhere and lock up afterwards, won't you?'

The officer agreed that they would.

Jean went back inside and took herself to her study, despite the lateness of the night. Turning on her computer, she slowly typed a long letter.

* * *

The boat and crew were waiting for them in Hoveton, and they were soon chugging upstream away from Wroxham Bridge.

'How far does this river reach?' Sara asked.

The young officer who was piloting the boat glanced sideways at her. His look told her that he had her pegged as a townie. Bowen had warned her that the river police boat was uniquely manned by people who were 'born with webbed feet'.

'Goes well up beyond Aylsham,' he said. 'Only navigable as far as Coltishall unless you're in a canoe. The place you're talking about is on a big loop in the river.'

'Could he get across to the other bank?'

The driver snorted. 'Not unless he had a boat or paddleboard. Just as marshy on the other side. No footpaths.'

'What about swimming?'

'Swimming!'

'If he's fallen or thrown himself in.'

'You think he might have been trying to top himself?'

Sara wished silently to have patience with this arrogant waterman. 'I don't know. I just don't want to miss any possibilities.'

'If he's a local lad, he would be in no doubt. You don't swim across the river there.' The man's contempt was obvious. 'It's dangerous. There are holidaymakers in boats who have no idea what they're doing. There are kayaks and paddleboarders everywhere. We spend half the summer rescuing them. Then there's the pull of the flow.'

'Meaning?'

'It's reasonably strong in this section, and it's tidal. You could get swept along until you reached Wroxham or got driven upstream. Either way, if he'd drowned, someone should have seen him by now. The water moves fast at times.'

Grateful for small mercies, Sara waited.

They had left the last of the houses behind them now. The water stretched ahead like a dark rippling ribbon. The boat slowed, and an officer standing half out of the roof began to swing the searchlight along the banks in long, methodical sweeps. Bullrushes, reed beds and alder carr competed to find a growing foothold on the marshy land. Sara watched out of one side and Bowen out of the other. Their progress was frustratingly slow.

* * *

Claudia was pleased to meet the family liaison officer, who introduced herself as Tracey Mills.

'Have they gone through what Ryan was wearing?' was her first question.

'Yes, and we've given them a recent photo of him,' Claudia assured her.

Tracey turned to Eric. 'You say he's fond of the wildlife here. Is there any special place he goes to watch the birds and animals?'

Claudia checked her mobile while Eric pondered. No wonder they were all so tired. It was getting late, almost three o'clock. Or early, if you thought about it the other way. Sunrise was only a couple of hours away. Perhaps Tracey had been lucky enough to get some sleep before she'd come out to Michelle's house. She sounded more alert, at any rate.

An hour ago, two police officers with dogs had gone past the house on the footpath. She assumed they were following Ryan's trail. They eventually returned to their van, parked with other vehicles up and down Low Lane. It had brought no news.

'I've got it.' Eric suddenly perked up. 'It's miles away, mind. He's pestered me to take him there once or twice before. It's a reserve on a fen, round by Woodbastwick. Got bird-watching huts and all that. You can only go part way in the car, and the rest you have to walk.'

'How far is it?' asked Tracey.

'By road, I'd say five, maybe six miles.' Eric pursed his lips as he concentrated on a map in his mind. 'There's a footpath that cuts the corner off. You have to go through Wroxham and past the boatyards to reach it. It's actually quicker on the river.'

'Could Ryan do it on foot?' Claudia asked excitedly.

'I suppose so. He's no slouch, though it'd take him several hours. It's called Parson's Fen.'

* * *

As far as Sara could figure it out from the river view, they had just passed the point where Ryan had reached the riverbank when he first ran away. The river was curving away on a giant loop, which would lead to the parking area beyond Belaugh Manor Farm.

'Could he have doubled back through the car park and gone home?' she asked Bowen.

'Staying closer than we think or expect?' pondered Bowen. 'It might make sense.'

'The tide is against us now,' said the boat driver. 'I'm going to have to turn round.'

The engines revving to reverse almost drowned out the sound of Sara's phone. The buzz in her trouser pocket alerted her.

'How far have you got?' asked DCI Hudson.

Sara explained their new theory. 'We're turning to go back to Wroxham.'

'Good. There's some news at this end.' DCI Hudson sounded quite excited. 'The dog boys followed a trail to the riverbank, just like you suggested. Then it cut through the marsh to a car park, then across a couple of fields until it reached Low Lane. It looks like he went home.'

Sara breathed a sigh of relief. 'Is he in the garden shed or the empty house next door?'

'Nope,' said Hudson. 'I sent a couple of officers to check that out. Tracey Mills is with the family now.'

'That's great,' said Sara with feeling. Tracey was the best in the business, in her opinion.

'Between them, they've come up with a place called Parson's Fen. A bird-watching sanctuary on the other side of Wroxham. I'm sending a team down there immediately, but getting there from the river might be quicker. Can you do it? No blues and twos from anybody.'

'Parson's Fen?' Sara asked the driver loudly. 'Do you know it?'

'Of course,' he said.

'Can we get there on the boat?'

'Certainly. Good job I was turning round, though.' He opened the throttle on the boat and it began to pick up speed. Sara could swear she saw him grin as he did it.

* * *

The boat buzzed and stuttered along the water, past the houses and boatyards of Hoveton and Wroxham. With gritted teeth, the driver guided the police boat under the old stone bridge with only inches to spare. Sitting on a bench seat with the other two crew members, Sara hung on to the rail on the side of the boat, her fingers numb. Bowen sat opposite, looking a little green at the bouncing of the boat as it ploughed on. The stars were fading, and a faint light grew on the horizon as dawn broke. They raced between Wroxham Broad and Hoveton Great Broad and around a long bend.

'It's on this side,' called the driver. He waved to his left. 'There's a mooring place a bit further on.'

A jetty with room for a couple of keen boaters, it seemed, when they found it. One of the crew jumped on to the wooden boardwalk and secured them. He reached down to help Sara climb out and, for once, she didn't disdain the assistance. She was tired now; they'd been up over twenty hours. A footpath wound away from the land end of the jetty. High reed beds cut off the view, even for someone of Sara's height.

'I know this path,' said the crewman and led the way. 'Be careful where you step. It's pure fenland on either side if you make a mistake. Suck you down in minutes.'

'This leads to the bird hides?' she asked quietly at the man's back. He nodded.

'Four of them in a semi-circle, spaced out along the path. They all face in different directions so you can see the various habitats.'

Within two minutes of leaving the riverside, Sara had lost all sense of direction. She focused her torch beam on the path in front of her and concentrated, pulling up in shock when the man in front of her cursed.

'Little bastard!'

'What?'

There was no warning or suggestion that they'd been seen. Perhaps Ryan had heard the speeding police boat coming round the bend and decided to have one last moment of blazing ecstasy. The delayed thump of a small explosion reached them. It rattled a dry wind through the reed beds, rapidly blowing past them, leaving a smell of burning in its wake. Sara looked into the sky above the man's head. Bright red and orange flames danced upwards, reaching for the retreating stars.

'Are these hides covered in thatch, by any chance?' she asked.

The crewman looked at her as if she were mad. 'Yes, we need to hurry.' He took off at a run.

Two other crewmen rushed past her as Bowen caught up. Sara knew that they must have found Ryan now. Noble had been right about the lure of the thatch. She muttered a quick prayer for the boy's safety, then ran after the others.

* * *

The boat driver arrived immediately behind them, bearing long-handled fire beaters from the jetty. The officers ignored the burning hide. It was far too heavily on fire to be saved. Instead, they began to run around the small clearing surrounding the hut, beating furiously at any debris that threatened to provide a bridge for the fire into the reed beds. Four more officers arrived by another path. Sara assumed these were the men Hudson had sent by road. They also began to beat out any gouts of fire with their jackets, or stamp on small flames with their booted feet. The burning hide roared on, spitting up fresh pieces of debris in defiance of their efforts. One side of the thatched roof collapsed with a crash, leaving the remaining walls leaning drunkenly against each other. The men redoubled their frenzied beating.

Ryan was making no attempt to run away. He stood on the far side of the hide, mesmerised by what he had done. His arms hung limply at his sides, a box of large cook's matches crushed in one hand. As he watched the flames shooting into the sky, his eyes reflected the heat and the burning colours. Sara wondered how on earth he could stand it; he never blinked once, so far as she could see.

'I think you'd better come with me,' she said quietly.

'You're that police lady who came to the house,' he replied. His gaze remained locked on the flames. 'Will you let our Kyle go if I do?'

'I suspect so.' Sara held out a hand to the lad. 'Come on. Let's go where it's safe. Do you know how to get off the fen?'

Ryan turned slowly to take in the chaos that surrounded them. The men shouted, beating and stamping to put out the grass and prevent the fire from spreading. His face suddenly crumpled and he began to cry.

'I didn't mean to hurt the birds,' he sobbed. 'I love the birds.'

'I know you do,' said Sara. She opened her arms, and the boy tumbled towards her for a hug. She let his grief subside, although she could feel the heat of the burning hide scorching her back and legs. After a few minutes, Sara pushed him gently upright. 'Now, can you show me how to get out of here?'

And he did.

CHAPTER 59

Once the police search party had left, Jean returned to her bedroom. She watched the sunrise with a deep sense of pleasure before going to the study and reading over the long letter she had written. Satisfied with the contents, she printed it out and signed it. Before opening her wardrobe, Jean ate toast for breakfast and drained a cup of her favourite tea.

'This will have to do,' she said, choosing the black trouser suit she had last worn at Malcolm's funeral. It didn't fit very well. The waistband nipped at her tummy rolls, and the jacket no longer fastened across her breasts. The dark purple blouse that once went comfortably with the outfit now stretched tightly, showing the outline of her bra. 'I've been putting on weight. Never mind.'

She had nothing more formal among her collection of faded items, and today she wanted to look as smart as possible. Today, Jean promised herself, she was going to rescue Faye from the clutches of the police. A last act of love for the daughter she'd been so stupidly jealous of for so long.

Locking the gate behind her, Jean drove sedately from Wroxham to Wymondham, much to the annoyance of the rest of the rush-hour traffic. The cars and vans crowded behind her were intimidating, which didn't help her go any faster. It was only her nine o'clock appointment with the solicitor Toby Byatt that gave her the courage to keep going. Jean wasn't going to be late and give the wrong impression.

There were a handful of visitor parking spaces outside the Norfolk Constabulary's headquarters. Jean manoeuvred into one, although it took her several goes to get her car straight. This was the longest drive she'd done in at least two years. The lack of sleep and the hassle of the drive had left her feeling weak. For a moment, Jean let her head sink on to her chest.

'Come on, woman,' she scolded herself. 'Time to sort things out.'

The letter was folded in an envelope. It peeked out of the top of her handbag as Jean locked her car. A scan of the car park failed to show the presence of Toby Byatt, although her watch told her that it was already five past nine. Squaring her shoulders, she walked with determination into the glass reception area.

She couldn't have known it, but Jean was lucky that morning. The desk was manned by the genial and patient Trevor Jones. As she walked over, he looked up and smiled. Jean's knees wobbled.

'I've come about my daughter, Faye Rushworth,' she began.

Jones nodded. 'I think they may be about to interview her again. Shall I ask if you can see her first?'

'It's not that.' Jean looked around the reception area in a panic. 'I was expecting to meet our solicitor here. I can't see him and don't know where he is.'

'Could he be with your daughter?'

'Oh, I hadn't thought of that.'

'I'll check for you,' promised Jones. He pointed to a set of upholstered chairs that surrounded a coffee table. 'Have a seat while I ring upstairs.'

Jean sat on the edge of a chair, her fingers grasping her handbag, which shook slightly with the pressure. The white envelope wavered on the edge of Jean's vision. Her heart pounded as the anxiety built up inside her. Sweat popped on her forehead, just as it used to when she was having one of those horrible menopausal hot flushes. She knew her face was turning red.

Jones put down the phone and came over to see her. 'Are you feeling all right?'

'I'm fine,' said Jean. She knew she didn't look it.

'Mr Byatt is advising your daughter at the moment. DS Hirst says he can pop down in about five minutes. Is that okay?'

Jean scrabbled in her handbag until she found a business card. 'Is that the same DS Hirst who gave me this card?'

Jones briefly took the card from Jean and read it. 'Yes, that would be the same officer.'

'Is there a private room where I could speak to her?' Jean took the card back. 'With Mr Byatt there too?'

'I'll just check on the booking system,' said Jones pleasantly. 'Won't be long.'

As he went back behind the reception area, Jean wondered just how long the man had been a copper. He might be a glorified receptionist, but she would take a substantial bet that nothing much got past him. No doubt he had seen it all before. She watched him tapping at a keyboard and then picking up the phone again.

The pressure inside Jean was reaching its limit. She could hardly bear it anymore. Tears threatened to roll down her cheeks. Her eyes flickered manically around the room and across the car park through the window. Her jaw clenched as she ground her teeth and began to pant short, shallow breaths. She would be in a pile on the floor if this wasn't over soon.

'Mrs Simpson,' said a man's voice quietly beside her. 'Are you feeling unwell?'

Toby Byatt must have come downstairs. Jean was so preoccupied she hadn't noticed him. The jolt of recognition released the tension like a valve. When Jean tried to speak, her breath hissed out without meaningful words. Another scrabble in her handbag unearthed a packet of tissues. Jean blew her nose and wiped her eyes.

'I'm just a little frightened,' she admitted.

'Do you want to tell me what this is about?' the solicitor asked kindly.

'I think I can only say it once,' admitted Jean. 'Is that policewoman coming?'

'I believe she is,' said Byatt. He looked around at Jones, who beckoned them across to a small interview room.

'Sure you don't want a cuppa?' he asked. They both refused and he shut the door behind them, leaving them alone.

'Mrs Simpson,' began Byatt. 'Whatever it is you have come to say, can I suggest that it would be better for everyone if you were to talk to me first?'

Jean just shook her head and waited.

DS Hirst soon arrived wearing a cautious smile. The detective looked tired. There were bags under her eyes, and when she sat down, it was with an exhausted thump.

'Mrs Simpson,' she acknowledged. 'How can I help you?'

'I've come here to ask you to release my daughter,' said Jean.

'I'm afraid we have some more questions for her,' said Hirst. She indicated Toby Byatt. 'Mr Byatt is here to represent her interests. There's no need to be worried.'

'You don't understand.' Jean pulled the envelope from her handbag and laid it on the table in front of her. 'Faye isn't responsible. It was me.'

'Hold on,' spluttered Byatt. He reached for the envelope, and Jean swatted his hand away.

'I set the fire at Wild Thyme,' continued Jean. 'I did it for the insurance money. I didn't know who was setting the other fires. I just thought they would get the blame for our barn too. I had no idea that Darren was in there. What I did to him and Faye is terrible. Unforgivable. When you told me last night that you were investigating Kyle and Ryan, I knew I had to come forward. I've already robbed my daughter of her happiness and taken the life of the man she loved. I couldn't also ruin the futures of two more innocent young men. I've allowed it all to go too far. It's my fault, and the details are in this letter. You can arrest me now and let Faye go, can't you?'

'That depends,' replied DS Hirst, opening the envelope.

'On what?'

'Whether we believe you or not.'

CHAPTER 60

When Trevor Jones rang from reception, Sara was annoyed at having to break off to see what Jean Simpson wanted. Last night, she had walked Ryan Atkins along the reserve track to the parking area, where an ambulance and several police cars were waiting. Although he'd appeared unharmed, she'd insisted that he went to A & E to be checked, and rang Tracey Mills, who was still with his mother.

'I'll take them to the hospital,' Tracey had assured her. 'What will happen to him after that?'

'He's already been arrested for setting fire to the hide,' explained Sara. 'He'll be interviewed once the doctors give him the all-clear, with the usual precautions.'

'I'll stick with the family, then,' said Tracey. 'Unless they tell me to leave.'

After that, Sara had got one of the officers to drive her back to Wroxham, where her car was parked. It was almost six o'clock, and she was due at work at eight-thirty. Unable to face the drive home and back again, she'd tilted back the passenger seat in her car and dozed for an hour. It had helped, though not much. Spruced up by splashing her face with cold water and a quick blast of deodorant from an emergency tin she kept in her desk drawer, she went to the canteen for a large breakfast and two mugs of coffee. There were interviews still to be done, and she was determined to be part of that.

DCI Hudson sat in her office, tapping at her computer keyboard, apparently none the worse for having been up all night. Bowen and Aggie had made it in, though she looked much brighter than he did. His face was grey with tiredness, and he needed a shave. The rest of the team hadn't arrived yet. At half past eight, Sara collected Toby Byatt from reception and Faye Rushworth from the overnight cells, leaving them in the interview room alone so they could confer. When she checked through the observation room window, Byatt was talking a lot while Faye was staring at the wall absently. Sara was pleased when DI Edwards arrived. She much preferred running interviews with him than with DCI Hudson. He looked rejuvenated by a change of clothes and a shower. Sara envied him. Living so far from headquarters meant issues for Sara that the others who lived in Norwich didn't have to contend with.

'She's written this,' said Sara, handing the letter to DCI Hudson. 'It's fairly detailed and fits our evidence so far. It's only her word, of course. She could be doing this to save her daughter.'

'There's only one way to find out,' said Hudson. 'Start the interview with DI Edwards by showing Faye this letter.'

Toby Byatt sprinted up the stairs and darted into Interview Room One ahead of them. He was still talking urgently in a low voice to Faye when they came in. Edwards set the recorder going and gave them the usual warnings.

'Mrs Rushworth,' he began, 'are you aware that your mother is downstairs?'

Faye looked at Byatt before agreeing that she knew.

'Do you know what she's claiming?'

'Yes. Silly old cow.'

Sara was taken aback by this. If her own mother had taken it upon herself to protect Sara like this, she would have loved her for it.

She lay a copy of the letter on the desk between them. 'I think you should read what she says.'

Faye stared at the printed sheets for several heartbeats before picking them up. They trembled in her hand as she read each of the three pages. Then she slowly ripped them in half several times until there was only a pile of scrap on the desk in front of her. Sara knew the original was safe on Aggie's desk and that Faye was baiting them. She pulled another copy from the folder in front of her.

'Do you agree with what your mother has claimed?'

'Who cares?' Faye looked steadily at Sara. The careful blankness she'd kept on her face until now began to crack. 'What does any of it matter?'

'Did you look at the list of dates we gave you at the previous interview?'

'No,' snorted Faye. 'You didn't give me time before you arrested me.'

'It doesn't matter now,' put in Edwards. 'We're only interested in what happened at Wild Thyme. Did you set the fire in the barn, Faye?'

Faye looked at the pile of torn paper, shuffling them under her fingers as if mixing them for a card game. She was trembling. Then she shrugged. 'No. No, I didn't burn down the barn or kill my own husband. I loved him. Why would I do that?'

'Did you know where Darren had gone after you'd had that row?' asked Sara.

'I wasn't sure. It all seems so pointless now.'

'Why did he go back to the barn that night?'

'No comment.'

'Do you believe what your mother is claiming?' Sara indicated the second copy of the letter.

Faye tried to school her face into blankness again before answering. 'What Mother said here?' Lip trembling, she pushed the pile of scraps towards Sara. 'Doing it for the insurance? I wouldn't put that past her.'

'You didn't want the insurance money yourself?' interrupted Edwards. 'To buy yourself a house, perhaps?'

'I didn't need to,' Faye snapped at him.

'We've looked into the company's finances,' Edwards continued. 'It looks unlikely that you could have afforded to buy a separate property. In fact, the place could have done with a cash injection to keep it running.'

'The business always comes round,' said Faye indignantly. 'Besides, we were leaving. It wasn't going to be our problem anymore.'

'Why didn't you need the insurance money, Faye?' Sara persisted. 'Did you have other resources?'

'We only needed to find Dad's rainy-day fund,' said Faye. The trembling came back, and her entire body was vibrating. She gripped her hands together.

'What fund?'

'Just before he died, Dad told me he had left us two items we could sell if things got bad. Said he'd hidden them in the barn where no stranger would find them.'

'That's why Darren was clearing out the barn? Looking for these things?'

'Mother didn't know about them. Dad only told me. He said they were for me in case I ever needed them.'

'That was why Darren went back that night?'

Faye nodded slowly. 'We had a fight about leaving the business, and he stormed out. I thought he'd just gone to cool off. Or on a bender, like he did once before.'

'What are these items, Faye?' asked Edwards.

Even Sara gasped at the woman's reply.

'A pair of antique Purdey shotguns. Dad said they were worth about £200,000.'

CHAPTER 61

'How on earth did he end up with a pair of antique Purdeys?' asked DCI Hudson.

She sounded as shocked as Sara had ever heard her. The team sat at their desks in the office, and everyone focused on Sara. They all knew that the shotguns were the holy grail of sporting weapons. The company was still making them, and a new, tailor-made James Purdey gun would set you back at least £150,000.

'A matching pair?'

'Made for the Maharaja Victor Duleep Singh, no less.' Sara shook her head. 'And the provenance to prove it. An invoice from the maker with the guns' serial numbers and made out to Singh at his Elveden mansion. Mr Simpson had taken to going around old house sales. The sort of thing where an elderly lady dies, leaving a Georgian rectory full of knackered furniture, and the relatives auction things off before ditching the house to a developer. Mr Simpson had bought an Edwardian gun cabinet for a song, thinking it was empty. Then he discovered the pair locked behind a second panel in the back of the thing. Faye says she only saw them once when she was a teenager. Just before he died, her father told her he'd hidden them in the barn.'

'Not exactly where?'

'No, just "in the barn",' said Sara. 'Apparently, Faye and her husband have been looking for them for months. It proved difficult and time-consuming because they didn't want Mrs Simpson to know anything. Finally, Darren came up with the idea that they should put the barn to better use in the business. That gave them the excuse to empty the place, searching as they went.'

'And that's why Darren had gone back that night?'

'Faye isn't certain,' said Sara. 'Thinks he was trying to prove a point.'

'On the same night that Mrs Simpson decided to fire the place for the insurance. Bloody unlucky. Can we trust this confession of hers?'

'I don't see why Faye would have started the fire if they were looking for this nest egg.'

'Did she set fire to her own moped?' asked Hudson.

'She's admitted to that,' confirmed Sara. 'She took it to the woods, where she knew the boys had their drinking den. Faye sometimes went there to buy weed from one of them. That's where she was the night of the first fire at Wild Thyme. Faye thought we would use the bike or the dope smoking to frame her. Doesn't have a very high opinion of the police in general.'

'And it seems likely that young Ryan is responsible for the other fires,' Hudson continued. Aggie quietly murmured a sympathetic noise, which Hudson quelled with a glance. 'Any news on him?'

'He's been declared fit to leave the hospital,' said Bowen. 'I thought Sara and I could fetch him over here for an interview. He might recognise us from our previous visit.'

'Make sure the responsible adult is in place,' warned Hudson. 'And the solicitor. I don't want it to look like we're bullying the lad.'

'That leaves Kyle,' said Edwards. 'We should talk to him before we run out of time.'

'And let's arrest Jean Simpson on suspicion of murder so we can interview her under caution,' said Hudson as she broke up the meeting.

* * *

Sara had left the owner of Wild Thyme in the small interview room near reception under Trevor Jones's kind and careful supervision. Apart from one trip to the toilet, she'd not moved, Jones told Sara.

'Jean Simpson,' said Sara formally. 'I'm arresting you on suspicion of murder.'

The older woman sat back in her chair with a sigh. 'You believe me, then?'

'We want to talk to you under caution,' replied Sara. She finished the proper form of words.

'What about Faye?'

'Being released on police bail,' said Sara. 'Mr Byatt says he'll stay with you once he's organised Faye's release. I'm sorry to say we'll have to take you to the cells for now.'

Jean Simpson stood up as tall as she could. She walked with her back straight and a sense of dignity that Sara couldn't help but admire. Not wanting to leave the woman immediately in the custody officer's care, Sara took Jean to the cell herself. If she hesitated at the door, it was so briefly that Sara had no time to send her forward. Taking a deep breath, Jean Simpson stepped into the cell, only stopping when she reached the bench bed on the far wall. As they closed the door, Sara watched through the inspection hatch as Jean turned to look at her. There was no sign of shock or shame to be seen. Just a sense of duty done, whatever the consequences.

* * *

The atmosphere was noticeably subdued in the office. Just the muted sound of people clicking at keyboards and the occasional whine of the printer. Aggie looked to be distracted as she began to organise the paperwork. None of them liked it when youngsters were involved in a case, let alone if they were likely to be charged.

Loading herself with another large mug of coffee, Sara returned to the interview room with DI Edwards. Lee Smith, the solicitor provided by Coles Construction, sat next to Kyle. Sara knew she was getting flaky, no matter how much coffee she drank. With luck, this would soon be over.

After the formalities, Edwards began, 'Kyle, are you aware that your younger brother, Ryan, has been arrested?'

Kyle looked pale under his suntan. His cheeks were sunken, and there were hollow areas under his eyes. 'Mr Smith just told me.'

'We have yet to interview him fully. Do you know why we arrested him?'

'Burned down a bird hide. At Parson's Fen.'

'That's right.' Edwards sat back in his chair, attempting to look avuncular and friendly. Sara knew it wouldn't work. Her boss had a sense of authority that would intimidate any youngster. 'Does Ryan like to burn things, Kyle?'

Kyle wouldn't look at DI Edwards. With a glance at Lee Smith for reassurance, he looked at Sara instead.

'I thought so,' he admitted. Sara nodded encouragingly. 'Sometimes, when I got back from seeing my mates at the common, he wouldn't be in bed. He'd come back later 'an me.'

'You share a room?' asked Sara.

'Yeah.'

'And a bike?'

Kyle didn't reply.

'Do you use your bike when you meet your friends?'

'Not always.' Kyle dropped his gaze to the table and wriggled uncomfortably.

'We found your den,' said Sara. She was trying to make it easier for the lad to say what he wanted without losing face. 'We already know that you are experimenting with alcohol and smoking joints. Does that help you?'

Kyle looked at her, his mouth twisted in a rueful pout. 'Yeah. So, I didn't want to use my bike when I was doing that. I walked. Only takes a few minutes.'

'Your bike would be left at home? You told us that Ryan had tried to ride it and didn't get the hang of it?'

'I thought he might have been having another go on it,' admitted Kyle.

'Ryan sometimes had access to your bike and stayed out late?' Sara confirmed. Kyle nodded. 'We'll ask him about that, of course. Was the bike there when you came in, and Ryan was missing?'

'Can't remember.'

'Why didn't you hide the keys so he couldn't use them?'

'I wasn't sure he was getting up to anything bad.'

'What about the fire at Wild Thyme?' interrupted Edwards. 'Did Ryan start that?'

Kyle looked angrily at the DI. 'No, he didn't.'

'Your fingerprints were found on a fire extinguisher at the scene. How do you account for that? Did you start the fire?'

'No chance.'

'If you didn't start it, how can you be sure Ryan didn't?'

'Because I know who did. I saw them do it.'

* * *

Kyle's solicitor asked for a break, which DI Edwards agreed to. Sara and Bowen used the time to escort a very subdued Ryan Atkins to the headquarters. They left him in the family room with his support team of a responsible adult, a solicitor and his mother. Sara almost felt sorry for him, he was so surrounded. He looked shell-shocked and shuffled his feet as if lifting them up was too much effort.

He's probably as tired as I am, thought Sara.

* * *

'Tell us what you saw at Wild Thyme, Kyle,' said DI Edwards when they returned to the interview room. 'In your own time.'

'I'd been at the den,' said Kyle. He looked embarrassed having to talk about what they got up to as if he had suddenly moved beyond such teenage antics. The shock of his younger brother's arrest had made him grow up very fast. 'I knew . . . one of them . . . said they'd bring some weed. So I'd left the bike at home. We never see anybody out there at night. Not even hikers or dog walkers.'

'Did you that night?' asked Sara.

'Yeah. This car came down the lane and parked in the passing place. We thought it was funny.'

'Odd or hilarious?'

'Laughing funny,' shrugged Kyle. 'Maybe a hooker with a client or something. I crept over for a look, and there was this bloke on his own. It was Darren from the herb farm. I couldn't figure out why he was parking there when he should have been at home.'

'You know the family at the farm, don't you?'

'I had a weekend job there for a few summers before leaving school. They were nice to me. To be honest, I was a bit off my face, and it just seemed silly, a bit of a laugh. So I followed him.'

'Did any of your friends go with you?'

Kyle shook his head. 'Darren went across the fields to the back gate. I watched him climb over the fence near those old containers they've got. Easy really. I'm surprised no one else ever did them over by going that way.'

'You kept Darren in sight?'

'I lost him for a bit after I climbed over. Then I heard the little gate in the hedge close, so I figured he was going to the house. I either had to climb back the way I'd got in or go through the car park.'

'Which did you choose?'

'Car park. It was easier. That's when it all went mental.'

Kyle paused to speak quietly to Lee Smith before he continued.

'In what way did it seem mad?' asked Edwards. Kyle refused to look at him and kept talking to Sara.

288

'Darren had vanished when I reached the yard. I was sneaking behind the tables where the herbs are put out for sale, pretending to be Bear Grylls tracking an animal. Because I was high, I guess.'

Kyle looked even more embarrassed to admit that he'd been playing a game.

'And?' Sara prompted.

'The back door of the house slammed, and Mrs Simpson came out. She had a torch and was carrying something in her arms.'

'Could you see what?'

'Not really. Old clothes, maybe? She put them in front of the barn door, piled some dead weeds and twigs on top, and went back into the house.'

'You didn't try to escape at this point?'

'She was only gone about half a minute. She brought a canister of petrol, like I've got in my bike, and spread the stuff everywhere. Up the front of the door as high as she could throw it. It only took one match, and the stuff went up — *whump!*'

'Didn't you try to stop her?'

Kyle shook his head. 'I was shocked and, like, must have cried out because she looked behind her to where I was crouching behind the table. Then the place went up like a rocket. She realised she'd left her car between the barn and the house. And there was a moped there as well. She ran off and started to move them. I was in a real panic by this time.'

'What did you do next, Kyle?' asked Sara quietly.

'Like I said, I was stoned, and I got frozen to the spot. There was this surge of fire in the thatch, like something out of a bible story we was told at school. The whole yard was lit up. I saw the fire extinguisher by the paying shed, so I ran over and grabbed it. They taught us how to use it once when I worked there. Pull out the pin and point it. Press the handle.'

'And it worked?'

'For a minute or two. Then Mrs Simpson was coming back, and I didn't want her to use me to blame. I dropped it and ran off to the back gate. I thought she'd follow me, but she didn't. By the time I'd climbed into the back lane, I could hear a fire engine in the distance, so I legged it as fast as I could.'

'Did you know where Darren was?'

'I'd no idea. I only heard afterwards that he'd been inside.' Kyle put a hand to his mouth to stifle a sob. 'Then I wished I'd tried harder to put the fire out.'

CHAPTER 62

Michelle Atkins looked bleakly at Sara when she spoke to them in the family room. She outlined the procedure that would be followed and suggested that everyone might benefit from some rest.

'I'm afraid Ryan will have to stay here with us,' she told Lee Smith when he opened his mouth to ask for police bail. 'At least until we've interviewed him. Let's all get some rest and come fresh to this tomorrow. Shall we say nine o'clock?'

Ryan settled the matter with a jaw-splitting yawn.

'I think Kyle would have taken the fall for his brother,' she told Trevor Jones as they watched the beleaguered family trudge across the car park. Lee Smith was taking them home. 'You have to admire that.'

'Any idea why you think he was doing it?' asked Jones. Sara glanced around reception to make sure no one could hear her.

'I expect it will be something to do with this family break-up.'

'Then he just got obsessed, I suppose,' said Jones wisely.

'I imagine that will be it.'

Having double-checked the two prisoners in the holding cells, Sara gratefully went home.

* * *

'I've agreed to bail for Ryan,' confirmed DCI Hudson the next day. 'Tracey Mills will keep in contact with the family for now. The court is bound to ask for psychiatric reports for him to assess his mental state while setting these fires. That will all take time.'

'Will he miss school?' asked Aggie.

'It's still the holidays,' replied Hudson. 'We might have to review that in September. Or if he breaks bail conditions.'

'He won't want to go and face his peers,' said Bowen. He pulled a grim face. 'At least, I wouldn't.'

'The alternative is the young offenders' wing in Norwich prison,' said Hudson. She looked equally grim.

The team were gathered in the office. There was an atmosphere of anti-climax in the room. Sara and DI Edwards had interviewed Ryan that morning. The youngster had been almost zombified and unwilling to say much. Lee Smith had read them an agreed statement in which Ryan admitted to setting all the known fires at Belaugh Manor Farm, behind Howards food growers and at the West Ruston building site.

'Can you tell us why?' Sara had asked. Ryan shook his head. 'Was it the thatch? Did it burn better than the rest?'

It was the only moment that Ryan had looked her in the eye. He seemed on the verge of saying something until the solicitor had deliberately rustled the sheet of paper with the statement. Ryan had dropped his head and returned to gazing at his hands on his lap.

'Will he be charged with all of these?' asked Noble. He'd read the statement and was in charge of collating evidence about the fires.

'That's up to the CPS,' sighed Hudson. 'Howards never reported their fire, so I can't see them being worried. Who knows if his grandfather will be feeling vindictive — or the wildlife trust who owned the hide. But the Crown solicitors have the final say.'

'It all comes down to the building site, then?' asked Noble.

'It might.'

'I doubt Coles will be keen to pursue it,' said Sara. 'Given that they paid for Lee Smith to represent Kyle in the first place. Georgian Housing Association might.'

'Will he keep going for Ryan?' asked Aggie. 'Or shall I arrange a duty solicitor for him?'

'Lee Smith is a decent chap,' DI Edwards put in. 'Told me after the interview that he would represent Ryan pro bono if there's no legal aid available.'

'What about Jean Simpson?' asked Sara.

Hudson frowned. 'No bail for her, I'm afraid. Her charge is involuntary manslaughter. Far too serious to be let out at this point. She's due in court on Friday, after which I imagine they'll send her to Peterborough.'

It was the nearest women's prison. Sara shuddered at the thought of how the sixty-nine-year-old would cope with being inside such a place. She'd never had so much as points on her driving licence in her life.

'Don't forget she's diabetic,' she said. 'They'll need to keep a close eye on her health.'

'Hospital wing, for sure,' murmured Bowen. Aggie gave him a grateful smile.

'I've spoken to the ACC to confirm this,' said Hudson. 'We're not going to charge Kyle with anything to do with underage drinking or smoking pot. He'll get an official warning and be sent on his way.'

'What now then, ma'am?' asked Bowen.

'We collate the evidence we have in all the cases,' said Hudson. She started a new column on the whiteboard to allocate their tasks. 'It isn't often we have two confessions like this, but let's ensure we have everything in place to prove things as required.'

The team began the process with little enthusiasm. It had been a wearing and unsatisfactory case. The victims and their families had been caught up in adverse events that would affect them for the rest of their lives. Perhaps it was the excess heat of the summer, or the knowledge that although they had solved the crimes, there were no winners to be found.

The air conditioning struggled over their heads, and the room grew ever warmer. Sara toyed with the idea of opening the window.

CHAPTER 63

Jamie had turned up on Claudia's doorstep for their first official date bearing a bunch of flowers. He'd seemed nervous, which Claudia thought was rather sweet. The visit to the pub had gone well enough and now he was taking her out to the cinema at the end of the week. She was grateful that the handsome site manager was prepared to go the traditional route when it came to dating.

It took Claudia a whole week to persuade Eric Beatty to explain the full story about his nephews and their lack of a relationship with their grandparents. She had a reason for asking, which Claudia wasn't sure she should share with anyone. After all, it might not work out.

Having tracked down Thomas Willmott at Belaugh Manor Farm through the electoral register, it took her three more days to summon up the courage to go there one sunny evening and knock on the door.

Any conversation that had to start with 'You don't know me, but . . .' was destined to be difficult.

Claudia had no business cards, as she hardly ever left the office. Instead, she had taken a sheet of headed notepaper and a blank order form from the warehouse pad to prove who she was. At first, Mr Willmott had seemed inclined to slam the door in her face.

'I know how this must seem,' she had rattled on. The man looked at her angrily. He kept one hand on the door, and the other held back a barking dog that worried Claudia. She explained who she was. 'I just wanted to see if I could help in some way. Your grandsons are having a very hard time. I think they need some support.'

'Ain't that mother of theirs coping?' he'd snapped.

'Only just.' Claudia used her best 'reasonable' tone. 'Don't you think you could talk to them at least?'

'Little bugger set fire to my barns and crops.' Willmott had sounded like a sulking teenager. Claudia couldn't help but wonder if she was doing the right thing. Her heart was pounding and her mouth was dry.

'That's true,' she said shakily. 'Kyle also tried to put out a fire at the herb farm. Now he's trying to help his mother and Ryan through all this. You might be proud of him.'

'Did he?' The man suddenly sounded unsure of himself. 'The police told me they be gonna prosecute little 'un, and he'll end up in prison.'

'That's possible,' agreed Claudia. 'Can you imagine how he feels right now?'

When Willmott failed to reply, she handed him the headed notepaper with her mobile number written on it. She was grateful that he actually took it.

'I know you think this is nothing to do with me,' she said. 'Kyle and Eric Beatty are only workmates. The truth is that I feel sorry for those youngsters growing up without their dad or grandad, so I guess that's making me feel protective. Here's my number. Please call me if you change your mind or want me to help somehow.'

Claudia beat a hasty retreat before the dog could get out of the door. She had barely got home before Willmott rang her mobile.

'Seeing that you're busybodying . . .' he began. She slumped on to her sofa with a sigh. 'You'll know the answer to this. Do he got a lawyer person helping him?'

'Yes, Mr Willmott. My company has agreed to help if legal aid doesn't cover it.'

'That's right kind,' he conceded. 'You arranged that?'

'Yes, and the boss sanctioned it. He's also offered Kyle a permanent job so he doesn't have to stay on the apprenticeship rates. We're doing what we can, in our own small way.'

'Can you do one more thing?'

'Such as?'

She waited as Willmott drew a couple of noisy breaths. When he'd summoned up the courage, he continued, 'Will you tell 'em I'd really like to see 'em? If they'll have me.'

So here they were, two weeks after the fire at Parson's Fen. Claudia and Thomas Willmott, standing at the Atkins' cottage doorstep. Claudia knew they were expected, so she hung back. She'd acted as a go-between to arrange the meeting and had no idea how it would go.

Michelle's reception of the older man was frosty. Kyle and Ryan sat side by side on a sagging sofa, watching their mother to gauge their own reaction. Ryan looked especially withdrawn, which was hardly surprising. The conversation stuttered for a while. Willmott asked Kyle about the fire at Wild Thyme and Ryan about school. No one dared touch on the fires the younger one had started. Not yet. Things ground to silence. It wasn't the scene Claudia had imagined.

'Would you like a cup of tea?' Michelle asked in a rather formal tone.

Willmott nodded. 'I can help you make it.'

'If you like.' Michelle looked at Claudia. 'You can come too.'

The three adults crowded into the kitchen, leaving the boys behind. Michelle clattered around with mugs. Claudia stopped by the door between the living room and kitchen, trying to be unobtrusive. Willmott hovered uselessly by the table, his hands shoved into his trouser pockets. He surveyed the kitchen with its dilapidated cupboards and grubby walls.

'You should get this seen to,' he said suddenly.

Michelle turned on him. 'Wouldn't that be nice? The rent here is cheap, and I can't afford to move. So I daren't make a fuss. You shouldn't come in here saying things like that.'

'You don't have to stay here.'

'Under no circumstances are we moving in with you,' snapped Michelle.

Willmott chewed his lip for a moment. 'The landlord should be sorting that out for you,' he persisted. 'Would you like a new kitchen?'

'Oh, don't start,' replied Michelle. She threw tea-bags into the mugs aggressively, something Claudia hadn't thought possible. 'I do my bloody best.'

'See, the thing is . . .' Willmott scuffed his feet on the old floor lino like a schoolboy facing a headmaster. 'Well, I'm your landlord.'

Michelle dropped the teaspoon she was holding with a clatter. 'What?'

'I own all three of these.' Willmott waved vaguely out of the window. 'When the man at the letting place told me you was looking at it, I made sure it was a low rent.'

'You own our home?' Michelle's voice was low and aggressive. 'You've left us to live in these conditions all this time?'

'Don't go on at me. I'll arrange for a new kitchen for you.' Words tumbled anxiously from Willmott. 'I thought if you knew I was the landlord, you'd leave. I didn't know what to do for the best. I want to make sure my grandkids are all right.'

'Bit late for that,' snapped Michelle.

'Maybe. Maybe not.' Willmott held up his hands in a gesture of defeat. 'Either way, I would like to see you all again. Will you think about it?'

Michelle looked at Claudia, who nodded encouragingly.

'All right. We'll see how it goes.'

CHAPTER 64

The culture shock had been enormous. Jean simply wasn't used to living with so many people this close to her. The journey to Peterborough from Norwich in the confined prison van had been a nightmare. Her travelling companion shouted and screamed about her innocence for eighty miles. Jean wondered how she hadn't lost her voice. No such luck.

Jean soon discovered that she was the oldest woman in the place by some margin. Initially, her diabetes had earned her two weeks in the quieter hospital ward before she was moved into the main prison. The guards took pity on her and gave her a cell alone. Even so, she couldn't bring herself to leave the room when she was allowed to. Mercifully, someone was allocated to bring her trays of food. Otherwise, she might have starved.

Eventually, clearly bored and with nothing better to do, a young woman had waltzed into Jean's cell one morning and sat on the chair. Jean was, as usual, curled up on her bed. She rolled over to turn her back to her unwelcome visitor.

Undeterred, the woman spoke. 'All right, Granny,' she said with a laugh. 'What you in for? We've all been laying bets, and I got the short straw, so I've been sent to ask you.'

'Go away,' said Jean.

'Shan't, not until I got an answer,' said the visitor. 'I've got three lunches riding on this. What did you do? Steal something?'

'No.'

'Come on,' roared the girl. 'Why'd you end up in here?'

Suddenly Jean rolled over and sat up face to face with the newcomer. The woman was slight. She couldn't have been more than twenty-one or so. Her skin was sallow, her hair a dull mousy colour. It needed a wash. 'I killed someone, all right? Now leave me alone.'

'You never.' The visitor's disbelief was obvious. 'Posh bint like you? You never did.'

'My son-in-law!' screamed Jean. Then she began to sob. 'I didn't mean to. It was an accident. I was only trying to get some insurance money. And I killed him.'

'Fuckin' hell,' breathed the woman. 'That's awesome! Oh, hey. Come here.' She dragged Jean into her arms. 'Go on, get it all out. You'll feel better after that. My name's Jelly, by the way.'

When Jean had sobbed her heart out and was calm enough to remember what the girl had said, she asked, 'Jelly? Who gave you a name like that?'

'The screws. On account of it being my favourite food. Any flavour, I don't care. And you cost me three lunches, by the way. My bet was on you cheating the tax man.'

It was Jelly who took Jean out of the cell and introduced her around, Jelly who showed Jean how to make phone calls, and Jelly who told her about visiting arrangements. Jean didn't hold out much hope, but she sent a form to Faye all the same. When the officers told her she had a visitor booked for the next visiting day, Jean assumed it would be her solicitor.

'I didn't think you'd come,' she told Faye when she sat on the opposite side of the table in the visiting room. Faye looked around the place in horror.

'How are you getting on?' she finally asked.

'I'm learning to live with it,' said Jean. She shrugged. 'I don't have any choice. My case doesn't come up until

November. My brief says he hopes to get me a reduced sentence. Maybe even a suspended one because of my age and health. I'm not holding my breath. I deserve to be punished. Did you ever go to see Darren?'

'In the mortuary?' Faye looked into the distance, choosing her words carefully. 'Yes. It was . . . difficult. I told him I loved him because we parted on an argument. I needed him to know.'

'How are you coping?'

'I'm managing,' said Faye. 'People are being very kind. Mavis and Rachel have got the café up and running again. Kevin helped me find a couple of part-time people to help with the polytunnels and herb sales. Actually, we were rather busy for the first couple of weeks.'

Jean thought about the fire officer's warning about the ghouls who would gather when they reopened. She just hoped they had spent some money while they were there.

'Are you still in the house?'

Faye nodded. 'It feels odd without Darren and you there. I was worried about being on my own until I got a dog. A rescue. He keeps me company, and he barks at night. Usually at the barn owl.'

'I'm glad you haven't moved out. What about the barn? The insurance won't pay out now they know I started it on purpose.'

'No, they won't,' agreed Faye. 'It doesn't matter anyway.'

'Why? What will you do?'

'You remember that builder who came to make the place safe?'

'Of course,' Jean nodded.

'He's buying the thing. We've worked out an access route and a patch of land for a garden. He's going to turn it into one of those barn conversions that the townies love so much.'

Jean opened her mouth to speak. Faye continued before she could ask anything else.

'And there's Dad's rainy-day fund.'

'What do you mean?'

Slowly Faye explained about the shotguns.

'You mean Malcolm hid them, so I couldn't find them?' The idea hurt Jean more than she thought possible. 'That we could have sold them years ago and bailed out the business then?'

'That was his point, I think,' said Faye. 'He didn't want them to bail out the business. He wanted me to have it when I needed it. My nest egg, not for use in the business.'

'Weren't they burned in the fire?'

'Nope. For a few weeks, I assumed they must have been. After the builder cleared the debris, I carried on searching in the evenings. My God, the place stank. It was horrible. Found them in the end.'

'How on earth had they survived?'

'He'd wrapped them in oilcloth and stored them in an old tin ammo box from World War Two. Then he'd buried them and put the gun cabinet on top of the spot. Obvious really. The cabinet was right at the back, and Darren hadn't got that far. It was destroyed in the fire, so all I had to do was test the theory with a shovel.'

'How did you know that you had to dig?'

'Something Dad had said to me once. About pirate treasure and guns. Told me to remember that pirates didn't only bury gold; they also buried weapons. It was the only thing that made sense. Anyway, I've sent them to James Purdey to be sold. The price tag is enormous.'

'You're set up for life, then?' Jean sat back in relief.

'It won't be the life I wanted, not without Darren.'

'I'm so sorry, my love,' said Jean. Her lip trembled. 'I only meant to raise some money. I just wasn't thinking straight.'

'To buy us a place of our own? It's going to take me a long time to forgive you, Mum.'

'Will you visit me again?'

Faye looked her mother in the eye. 'I might.'

Jean felt a sense of relief. It was enough for now.

CHAPTER 65

It had been an exceptionally hot summer. Sara's garden looked naked without all the weeds and junk Adie had removed. The ground was too hard for her to plant anything new, and she was too exhausted when she got home from work to tackle it. The herb plants she had bought at Wild Thyme stood in a row on her kitchen windowsill. Despite looking at them every day, she still forgot to water them regularly and they looked thirsty.

When the rain finally came at the beginning of September, it was like a monsoon. It bounced off the earth and collected rapidly, forming streams from the higher points, which ran swiftly towards her back door. Tilly watched her human trying to sweep the giant puddle away with a broom before it got into the cottage. It was an unequal struggle. Sara gave up and packed a wodge of bath towels against the bottom of the door. It just about held the flood back.

The team had spent the last few weeks collecting information for the CPS. It was a necessary, if dull, part of the job. At least it gave them all a chance to recover.

Aggie and Bowen swanned off on another cruise. A last-minute booking that took them around the east of the Mediterranean. Sara wondered how long it would be before the pair decided to retire. Bowen must be due his pension by now, and they had found a buyer for Bowen's old house. It couldn't be a lack of money that kept them at work, she suspected.

DCI Hudson had spoken to Sara again about her inspector's exams.

'I know I've been a bit rough on you,' the DCI admitted. 'My mind has been elsewhere. I'm being pressured to make some cuts to the department.'

That explains the bad temper and the outbursts, thought Sara. 'Have you agreed to any?'

'No.' Hudson smiled briefly. 'I've managed to prevent them. For this year. If you pass your exams, I thought you could take a promotion elsewhere if they get pushy in the next budget year.'

Hudson was right, Sara realised. The DCI was actually trying to protect her. 'I see. Okay, yes, put me up for them. I don't want to do the autumn ones, though. It's too close.'

'The next opportunity is May,' said Hudson. 'I'll put your name forward for then.'

As the weeks passed, seeing Dante around the place didn't get any easier. Sara wished he would stop blanking her in the corridor. It made things so obvious. Even so, she didn't regret her decision and could only hope things would get easier with time. It wouldn't do her any good to get a reputation for being single and available among the more macho element of her colleagues.

Sara hadn't heard from Adie since he'd finished his work in the garden. At first, she'd been disappointed. Now she was learning to be content with her status as a single, mad cat lady. Her mobile ringing disturbed her as she wrung out the bath towels before lobbing them into her washing machine. The number was his.

'How are you?' he asked. Sara told him about the rain. 'Bound to be a bit hard. And no plants to soak it up.'

'I'm managing. When do you go back to college?'

'End of the month. I just wondered if you were free one evening this week?'

'I could be.' Sara glowed in anticipation, then smiled at herself for being ridiculous.

'I have something I'd like to talk to you about.'

THE END

ACKNOWLEDGEMENTS

I would like to thank Antony Dunford and Wendy Turbin for their beta readings and notes. I am so grateful for your time and energy on my manuscripts. I am also thankful to Clive Forbes, a former DI, for his police procedural advice and thoughts on whodunnit. Any incorrect procedures remain because I made an executive author's decision (or mistake!).

My gratitude goes to Jasper Joffe for welcoming me to Joffe Books. It means more than I can say to belong to this fantastic publishing house. I am grateful to all the other authors and the staff who are so supportive and generous with their time. My special thanks to Emma Grundy Haigh, Matthew Grundy Haigh and Rachel Malig, who helped me improve the novel with their suggestions, edits and weeding out random punctuation. My grateful thanks to the rest of the Joffe Books team for all your work, from organising blog tours to spending time on reviews. I am proud to be a member of this wonderful band.

Last but not least, my husband, Rhett, and my daughters, Gwyn and Ellie. This novel was created in a storm of health issues, which nearly derailed the enterprise entirely. Your support and understanding are crucial to me.

THE JOFFE BOOKS STORY

We began in 2014 when Jasper agreed to publish his mum's much-rejected romance novel and it became a bestseller.

Since then we've grown into the largest independent publisher in the UK. We're extremely proud to publish some of the very best writers in the world, including Joy Ellis, Faith Martin, Caro Ramsay, Helen Forrester, Simon Brett and Robert Goddard. Everyone at Joffe Books loves reading and we never forget that it all begins with the magic of an author telling a story.

We are proud to publish talented first-time authors, as well as established writers whose books we love introducing to a new generation of readers.

We won Trade Publisher of the Year at the Independent Publishing Awards in 2023. We have been shortlisted for Independent Publisher of the Year at the British Book Awards for the last four years, and were shortlisted for the Diversity and Inclusivity Award at the 2022 Independent Publishing Awards. In 2023 we were shortlisted for Publisher of the Year at the RNA Industry Awards.

We built this company with your help, and we love to hear from you, so please email us about absolutely anything bookish at feedback@joffebooks.com

If you want to receive free books every Friday and hear about all our new releases, join our mailing list: www.joffebooks.com/contact

And when you tell your friends about us, just remember: it's pronounced Joffe as in coffee or toffee!